Quest
for
Freedom

The Saga of the Men and Women Impacted by the Murderous 1871 Nevada State Prison Escape

Who were these men? Why were they in prison? When did they plan the escape? Where did they go? What happened to them? How did a beautiful Sierra Nevada lake receive the moniker "Convict".

Written by Richard Delaney
Illustrated by Debora Delaney

Quest for Freedom

Written by Richard Delaney
Illustrated by Debora Delaney
Cover Design and Graphics by Talahi Media Arts
Printed and Distributed by Talahi Publishing
Publishing.Talahi.com
P.O. Box 360, Prather, CA 93651
ISBN 978-0-9706798-2-6

Foreword

The Quest for Freedom is the historically fictional account surrounding the escape of nearly 30 hardened criminals from the Nevada State Prison in 1871.

Based on actual newspaper accounts, it spans a period of nearly four years. The story chronicles the outlaws' journey as they punched their tickets, earning them a cell at the Carson City facility. It details the planned escape, vividly describes the actual event and follows the escapees as they fled into the high Nevada desert and beyond. Learn their fate and the impact of their interaction with lawmen and regular citizens of Nevada and California at the time.

Few actual pictures of those involved exist. Thus, the book's personal photographs are based on "Pen Portrait" descriptions written by journalists of the era. Other pictures were created to highlight the story and help depict the actions described therein and are based on accounts given by the participants as noted in the periodicals of the time.

To develop the story, a thorough search was made of Nevada State Prison records, documented newspaper reports of the time, Nevada State Library Historical Archives, Nevada State Museum and the Nevada Historical Society at the University of Nevada, Reno, Mono County Museum and Historical Society, Eastern Sierra Museum in Independence, CA, and the Laws Railroad Museum in Bishop, CA.

The following helped make this book as factual as possible: Kent Stoddard, Mono County Historical Society; Terri Gessinger, Bodie State Historic Park Historian; Kathy Edwards, Research Librarian, Nevada State Library Archives; Jeff Kintop, State Archives Manager, Department of Cultural Affairs, Nevada State Library and Archives and Robert Nylen, Curator of History, Nevada State Museum.

Table of Contents

Nevada Map

Chatper One
In the Beginning

The day started pleasant enough. A light, cool breeze played on the late summer flowers. Birds vied for early morning worms. It was Sunday. Soon church bells would be ringing. The year was 1871. The month September, the 17th to be exact. It was shaping up to be an ordinary morning in western Nevada.

No one expected this pleasantness to last. Sure enough, before long it became just another hot, dry afternoon. This particular one though, was punctuated by additional weather miseries. Gale force winds swept off the majestic Sierra Nevada. Tumble weeds cart wheeled over the yellow tops. The winds drove dust along the streets of Carson City. Those foolhardy enough to venture outside could hardly see. Winds swirled through the Carson Valley and over the Carson River. Who knows where they headed after passing up and over the Pine Nut Mountains on their way to Utah? But as unsettling as this late summer wind storm was, it was nothing compared to the storm that was about to break at the Nevada State Prison.

From the time prisons were first introduced, prisoners have been figuring out how to escape from them. It was certainly no different at the Nevada State Prison. This facility was located about a mile and a half east of Carson City. Originally, it was the Warm Springs Hotel, built in 1860 by Abraham Curry. This crude structure was made of hand-hewn sandstone taken from the nearby quarry. For the 1860s, it was a fairly impressive edifice.

Carson City, originally known as Eagle Station, was settled in late 1851 by Frank Hall. Hall had lost his interest in the California Rush, so he packed up to head back east over the Sierra to Utah territory. A few miles north of Mormon Station, Nevada, established early that same year, he found a perfect place for another trading post.

Along with five associates, he erected a crude log station

that November. In a moment of inspiration, the skin and feathers of an eagle, Hall shot that morning, was tacked up over the door. Eagle Station was open for business. It was an excellent location, but fell on hard times. Soon it became known as Eagle Ranch. It had exchanged hands several times by 1858.

Then Abe Curry came on the scene. He was a serious businessman with a vision. Thwarted in an attempt to buy land nearby, he learned the Eagle Ranch owners were in financial trouble.

He found them eager to sell. For a measly $500, he bought the trading post and the ranch, which included a select herd of Mustangs.

Abe Curry

Curry was optimistic. He had a town site laid out. He named it Carson City, after the famous frontier scout Kit Carson. Ten acres were set aside for a Capitol building. Curry just knew that Nevada would become a state. At first he had to give plots of land away. Anyone who promised to build was given one.

Early Carson City

The early Warm Springs Hotel

One day, Curry discovered a hot spring on the outskirts of the ranch. He decided this would be an excellent place for a hotel. Thus was born the Warm Springs Hotel.

His faith in Carson City paid off when silver was discovered in nearby Virginia City. Carson City became a thriving center of commerce as folks from all walks of life came through in hopes of striking it rich. Carson City found itself a lively freight and transportation center. The Virginia and Truckee Railroad was completed between Carson City and Virginia City in 1869, with the shops and main offices in Carson City. Long shallow flumes carried huge pine logs in a flow of fast water down the steep eastern slope of the Sierra from Spooner Summit to Carson City. The timber was fed into the sawmills. Here the wood for the underground mines was cut, and building materials were milled. The finished products were loaded onto the railroad cars for delivery to the nearby towns by way of the Virginia & Truckee Railroad.

When Carson City was selected as the territorial capital in 1861, Curry leased his Warm Springs Hotel to the Nevada Legislature as a meeting hall. The First Territorial Legislature was held at the Warm Springs Hotel in 1861. Curry provided the facilities rent free. They were certainly not deluxe.

The delegates met in a room divided by a canvas partition. The sawdust on the floor served as both carpet and spittoon for the tobacco chewing attendees. Transportation to and from Warm

Springs for the officials was provided by a horse-drawn streetcar moving along on wooden rails.

Mark Twain said of Curry's generosity, "But for him the legislature would have been obliged to sit in the desert."

Curry was not the only generous contributor. Two leading women of the era, Hannah Clapp and Margaret Ormsby collected chairs for the participants so they would have a comfortable place to sit. Margaret Ormsby was the wealthy widow of

Mark Twain

Major William Ormsby, a business owner and military man. He had been killed in action against Chief Winnemucca in 1860 near Pyramid Lake, north of Reno. In his honor, the legislature established Carson City as the seat of Ormsby County.

Hannah Clapp was known for her activism in the movement for women's rights. She was an astute business woman with an indomitable will. When she was 35, back in 1859, she decided

Hanna Clapp

to move west with her brother and his family. In an early letter written to other family members back home in Michigan, she had this to say:

"This Sunday is very much like other days with us here; although now we have the privilege of attending a Mormon meeting. I embraced the opportunity on Sunday and went with my bloomer dress and hat, along with my revolver by my side."

Curry, ever the entrepreneur, leased the Warm Springs Hotel to the Nevada Territory in 1862, so it could be used for holding prisoners. He was appointed the prison's first warden. Using convict labor and the ready supply of rock at the quarry, the facility was enlarged to help accommodate the ever-increasing number of prisoners. Curry sold the property to the state in 1864,

The early Nevada State Prison

although title to the property remained a topic of discussion for many years. The original hotel was destroyed by fire in 1867, but was soon rebuilt. The prison survived and unfortunately thrived.

It was not a pleasant existence at the Nevada State Prison. Most of the men had to toil in the rock quarry. The local town was expanding. The rocks were used to construct buildings in Carson City. It was hard, gruelling work.

In his report of January 1871, outgoing Warden James Slingerland pointed out that the quarters for the prisoners was far too crowded for the comfort and health of the inmates. Each man was supplied with clean clothes when he arrived, complete with black and white stripes. They were well fed. Breakfast consisted of a beefsteak, potatoes and bread. The mid-day meal would feature cold meat, hash, potatoes and bread. Stewed peaches or apples were provided every other day. Vegetables were served when available. For dinner they had roast beef or stew.

On Monday, Wednesday and Saturday, they got baked beans. On Tuesday, Thursday and Friday, mush and molasses or pudding was on the menu. Tuesday was soup day. Bread and potatoes were served daily. By 1870, it had become a very unpopular place for those forced to take up residence.

On December 1, several convicts decided it was time to break out. As night guard Theodore Hawkins unlocked the iron door to let the kitchen hands out, prisoner Charles McCluer viciously hit him in the neck, knocking him away from the door.

McCluer ran through the doorway, followed by William Shea, Thomas Heffron and Michael Loon. The four made a rush at Captain of the Guard, Jake Whipple. McCluer swung at Whipple with a butcher knife, slicing the palm of Whipple's hand. He swung again and harmlessly drove the knife through the rim of Whipple's hat.

Hearing the noise of the scuffle, two guards, A.L. Biggs and Wellington Bowen, quickly came to help their fellow officer. Seeing Biggs raise his revolver to fire, Heffron grabbed his arm and prevented him from firing the weapon. Bowen saw McCluer attacking Whipple and fired two quick shots, hitting McCluer in the head and the chest, killing him instantly.

Bowen turned and shot Heffron just below the right shoulder-blade. Coming from behind, Shea dealt Bowen a terrible blow with a slung-shot. The convicts made these weapons out of a lead pipe sewn into a woolen stocking. Stunned, but not out, Bowen turned and shot Shea in the stomach. During the melee, Loon ran out the front door and hid in the cellar. Shea, bleeding profusely, was slowly dying from his wound.

Thomas Heffron

Meanwhile, night guard O.A. Dingman was inside having a perilous time. Prisoner James Garnett thought Dingman was unarmed and seized the guard, attempting to drag him away. As he did so Dingman drew a Derringer and shot him in the abdomen. The man died several days later. Freed from his adversary, Dingman ran outside. He rushed to the armory and grabbed a Henry rifle. He mounted the roof. He saw Pat Hurley and other prisoners trying to escape through a skylight. He turned his rifle toward them and fired a warning shot over their heads. They quickly saw any further attempt to flee would probably end in their deaths. The 45 year-old Biggs rushed up to Dingman.

"You all right Captain?"

"Yeah, I'm fine."

"Hell, I'm getting too old for this," concluded Biggs.

The melee was over in a very few minutes. None of the convicts escaped. Shea, Garnett and McCluer left the prison in pine boxes. This left a bad taste in the mouth of the remaining convicts. Several were especially upset with Captain Dingman. They mistakenly thought he had killed all three convicts, when in fact, he only killed one. Bowman got two. Dingman knew of the hatred toward him and decided soon afterward that another profession would be to his benefit. He headed toward Aurora, Nevada and a job as a mail rider.

The bloody unsuccessful escape attempt was naturally a topic of much discussion by the guards and prisoners alike. The guards laughed about what they considered a dumb move by the prisoners. They were very vocal in taking pride that they thwarted the attempt. They bragged about how they took out three prisoners in the process.

On the other side of the iron bars, the talk was very different. Most of the convicts realized the escape attempt had been a hasty, spur of the moment decision. It wasn't thought out at all. The deadly consequences of that entire episode was not lost on them either. They naturally wanted out, but didn't want to die in the process. It was obvious to the more intelligent convicts that any successful prison break would have to involve some careful planning and skillful execution. Several such plans were discussed and rejected.

Chapter Two
Charlie Jones - The Boy From Ohio

One such plan was developed by Charlie Jones and Leandor Morton. It was taken much more seriously by their peers than those put forth by others.

Morton was a vicious, hardened criminal. He was currently doing time for his part in robbing a train in the latter part of 1870. At the time of his arrest, he was wearing the gloves of a U.S. Calvary soldier named Carr. Carr and another man had deserted.

The two men were never found. It was widely rumored that Morton knew exactly where the men were. Many of the other prisoners were afraid of him.

Leandor Morton

Jones was a native of Ohio. Charlie was a good boy from a fine upstanding family. He was athletic. He could ride well and shoot straight. Like many young naïve fellas of the era, when the War Between the States broke out, he lied about his age and joined the army. He served several years as a Union soldier. His experiences in the war left a lasting impression on him. Jones was no longer the innocent young man that left Ohio in the early 1860s.

After his stint in the military, Jones longed for a change of scenery. Like a lot of former soldiers, southern and northern, he heard about the riches to be had in California. By this time he was in great physical shape. He was strong and extremely well built. He

Charles Jones

stood 5'10", a rather tall man for the times. He was wiry and timid. When cornered, he could be a most dangerous man.

Charlie was always good with horses. He got along with people and was likeable. This trait helped him to find regular work no matter where he was. He spent several months as a teamster in Esmeralda, Nevada as well as in Mono and Inyo Counties in California. He managed to save some of his precious earnings. His most prized possession was his rifle. This was not just any rifle. It was a famous Henry, a .44 caliber, lever action, repeater.

Henry Rifle

Designed by Benjamin Tyler Henry in the late 1850s, it held 15 cartridges. You could put one in the breech, thus having 16 shots ready to go. Therefore, once it was loaded, it had great firepower. The Henry was said to be certain death at 800 yards. Jones found that an exaggeration. But he could hit targets at 200 yards with great accuracy.

Jones paid $51 for his Henry. He felt it was money well spent. With it, Charlie was much more comfortable on the trail. Historians consider the Henry, along with the Winchester, as one of the three inventions allowing for the settling of the American West. The other two were Daniel Halladay's windmill in 1854 and Joseph Glidden's barbed wire fence in 1873.

Early in 1869, Jones and Lucas Mathews were working as teamsters for Ben Clark. They had traveled from Bishop Creek to Hamilton in White Pine County with a load of mining implements. Mathews and Jones unloaded the freight wagons as the boss spoke with Arthur Pease, the freight agent.

"Howdy Art," Clark said to the man. "How's Laura and Thaddeus. He must be nearly as big you?"

"Thanks for asking Ben, everyone's doing just fine."

Clark planned to rest for a day or two before taking a load that Pease had consigned to him over to Carson City. He would

Freight wagon with four up horse configuration

find a load to carry back toward Bishop Creek from Carson City. They had three freight wagons with teams and saddle horses as well. They had camped near the eastern portion of Hamilton.

"Hamilton", laughed Charlie.

He knew how the town got its start and its name. It was kind of interesting. Back in July 1867, prospector Bill Leathers was sleeping in his cabin high upon White Pine Mountain. He awoke to strange noises. Arising from his bunk he spotted an Indian eating leftover beans that remained from supper.

"Get the Hell outta here," Leathers yelled at the savage.

The half clad man scampered out the cabin door and disappeared into the dark. Leathers didn't think much more about the incident. But a few days later, much to his surprise, the Indian returned. He extended his hand to show Leathers a piece of silver ore. The Indian was offering the ore as payment for the beans.

"Well I'll be damned," thought Leathers as he motioned to the Indian to enter the cabin.

Leathers fed his new 'best' friend a hearty meal while persuading his guest to show him where he had found the ore. The Indian's knowledge helped start the White Pine Mining District.

The place was first called Cave City. The miners had to carve out dwellings in the surrounding hillside. In May, a man named Hamilton came along, took an interest in Cave City and plotted out a town site nearby. The town was aptly named Hamilton. It became the First County Seat of White Pine County.

Hamilton now boosted nearly 30,000 people. It had everything that Charlie liked to avoid, except on special occasions. Things like saloons, general stores, churches, banks, a soda factory, breweries, stage station and a morning newspaper. A water works was built by a man named Von Schmidt who predicted Hamilton would be twice the size of San Francisco.

Hamilton - Once known as Cave City

Charlie Jones looked over at Ben Clark. He knew the boss was pleased with their successful trip. Clark had taken his men to town for some relaxation. The three ate a hearty meal at the best restaurant in Hamilton. Then they moved on to a local saloon for a couple drinks. Whiskey flowed freely. Every mining camp and town sported a poker table and Hamilton was no exception. Mathews saw such a set up in the back of the room. He sat down to a card game with two trail hands and a dude.

Charlie was busy exchanging glances with several of the "sporting women" crowded in the saloon. He was no fool. These ladies were around to make men stay longer and spend more money. Well today he had money and didn't mind spending some. A sweet looking, green eyed, Irish lass sauntered over.

"Hey there good lookin," she cooed, nestling up to Charlie's shoulder. "What's your name."

"Jones, Charlie Jones," he replied."

"What's yours?"

"Well Charles Jones, I'm Jessica to most of these ruffians, but friends call me Jesse, You look real friendly, so you can call me Jesse."

"Pleasure meetin ya Jesse."

12

"You have no idea. I've got a lovely room just up those stairs. It's got a big old bathtub right in the corner. How bout I take you up there and wash all that dusty old dirt right off."

"What's gonna happen when all that nasty old dust comes off me," questioned Charlie.

"Well, you look a might tired, so after your bath, we might just as soon take a nap!"

Charlie didn't need any more encouragement, he just stood up and followed Jesse as she lead him up the stairs.

Meanwhile Clark watched Mathews loose most of his money to the dude at the card table. When he suggested to Mathews that they return to camp, the idea was met with no enthusiasm by Mathews. Instead the man pushed back his chair, stood up with his hand on his pistol.

"You've been dealing from the bottom of the deck all afternoon," he bellowed, glaring at the dude. "I worked hard for that money and nobody's going to cheat me like this!"

With fear in his eyes, the dude slowly placed both hands on the table, palms up.

"Please, I don't want any trouble," pleaded the dude. "Take what you want from my stack. I don't want any hard feelings."

"You're nothing but a cheat," yelled Mathews. " Step outside and we'll settle this!"

"Hey Lucas," Clark said calmly. "Relax. The man said to take what you want."

"By all means please take the money," the frightened dude said. "I'm not going outside."

Having heard the commotion, Jones was now standing at the top of the stairs, watching the action unfold down below.

"Lucas, take the money and lets go back to camp. We have work to do," commanded Clark, walking towards his drover.

In a dialect only known to fellow whiskey drinkers, Lucas slurred an explanation of Clark's parentage. Knowing he was not a "bastard," Clark took exception.

"Mathews, calm down and leave with me right now or you're fired," he yelled.

"Damn it Mathews, pick up your money and get outta

here," Charlie barked from the balcony, pistol in hand. "I'll watch your back as you and the boss man leave."

Mathews reluctantly agreed. He and Clark walked out. Jones caught up with them shortly.

When the three got back to their camp, Clark and Mathews exchanged some heated words. This quickly escalated into an ugly brawl. Jones could see it was not going well for Clark. Mathews was a big man and Jones was concerned for Ben's welfare. His job might well depend on the outcome.

"Quit this," yelled Charlie moving in to intervene. "Move back," he said as he pushed Mathews away from Clark.

To his surprise he received a jolting fist to the face from Mathews for his efforts. Momentarily, it stunned him. Mathews went after Clark again. Jones shook off the blow. He stepped in front of Mathews to protect his boss. Charlie pushed Clark to the ground and stood guard over him.

"Come on Mathews, quit this. This is senseless."

"Get out of my way," Mathews scoffed at Jones. "Keep out of things that don't concern you. If you don't, I'll just stomp you first, Charlie, and then I'll get back to him."

Clark was still on the floor slowing recovering his senses. Mathews punctuated his threat by advancing on Charlie. Jones took a step back, reached into his boot and grabbed a knife. Seeing the blade in Jones' hand, Mathews stopped and moved back.

Jones should have known the show was over. But instead, he rushed Mathews and stabbed him in the chest. The big man

clutched at the wound. He staggered and fell. Charlie first thought the man was going to recover. But soon Mathews quit groaning and lay still. He eyes glassed over as his life's blood pooled on the ground. Realizing what he had done, Charlie instinctively knew he had to flee as quickly as possible.

"Boss are you all right," gasped Jones?

Charles stabs Mathews

14

"Yeah, I'm coming around."

"I gotta get outta here, I think I killed him."

"Charlie, you had no choice. You were only trying to save my life. I don't know what got into him. What you did was in self defense. You saved my life. How can I ever thank you?"

He reached into his pants and pulled out a handful of gold coins. Ben handed them to him.

"Here, take these. Where will you go?

"Thanks. I don't know where I'll go."

With a terrible, sickening feeling in the pit of his stomach, Charlie ran around the wagon to his horse. He quickly saddled up. He shoved his precious Henry rifle into the scabbard. He tied on his bedroll. Stepping into his stirrup, he easily swung onto his mount. He looked back at Clark.

"I'm sorry boss, to leave you this way. But I'm afraid of what might happen if I stay. I'm so sorry."

With that he rode off into the afternoon wind. When Jones left Hamilton his mind swirled with confusion. He knew he lost control of his emotions and it cost Mathews his life. At first he guided his horse hell bent through Dry Canyon, crossed over Stoneberger Creek and entered Monitor Valley. He dismounted so he and the animal could rest for a few hours. The horse nibbled at the late Fall grass as Charlie planned his escape.

In the early morning he'd mount up again and continue on. Jones knew he could reach Belmont late in the afternoon. From

Rainbow Falls on the San Joaquin River

15

there Charlie figured to work his way towards Indian Springs in the Ralston Valley, continue toward the Summit Mine and finally end up in Benton in a couple days. Not too long ago a sheep herder that he, Mathews and Clark met on the road told them of a trail that lead from the Long Valley region to the Sierra and finally meandered along the San Joaquin River to Madera. Jones decided to try and find that trail. He was successful in following the route depicted by the sheep man and ended up in the little town of Millerton along the river in just over two weeks.

The town grew up in the 1860s around the Army camp of Fort Miller. The fort had been established to deal with the hostile Yokut Indians that fought the influx of ranchers, farmers and miners streaming into their lands. The stage line from Stockton to Millerton and Visalia crossed the Fresno River not far below what seemed to be a pleasant little town. Jones felt this would be a good place to get "lost" in for awhile.

Charlie found the livery stable and arranged for the care of his horse. Then he checked into the local hotel. It had a little dining room off the lobby. He enjoyed a delicious meal. He headed for his room. He remembered that the last time he went upstairs it was with Jesse. The two of them had a wonderful time together. He'd hoped to see her again. But now figured that would never happen. Jones unlocked his door and entered the room. After a good night's sleep, he would look for work in the morning.

Nearly a year later, Esmeralda County Sheriff Francis

Millerton School House

16

heard Jones was working in a blacksmith shop in Millerton. He obtained a warrant. Charlie was caught off guard by the lawman and was arrested. He still thought he had simply defended himself. He figured he would have a good chance to plead his case in court. Unfortunately, he was tried before White Pine County Judge Beatty. The judge had actually witnessed the altercation and stabbing of Mathews from his courthouse window during a afternoon break. Jones was found guilty of murder and sentenced to 10 years at the Nevada State Prison. Fearing he would be hung, he felt he had made a fortunate and narrow escape from death.

At the prison, Jones was considered the best worker and most cheerful man in the place. Almost everyone liked him. He spoke affectionately of his parents back home in Ohio. Thinking back on his short life, he decided that running away to fight in the Civil War was pretty stupid. He believed Army life had demoralized him. His continued association with the crude civilization of the frontier worked to complete his moral downfall.

Now together with Morton, Jones devised a seemingly fool proof escape plan. But to be successful they would need some inside help. Outside assistance wouldn't hurt either. Prison guard Alexander Fleming was approached. He was considered by everyone to be a trustworthy person and loyal guard. Using the promise of gold for his part in the escape, Fleming agreed to their terms. He would find a time to be on duty that was favorable to them. He would wander into their cell where they would get the jump on him. After tying Fleming up and gagging him, Morton and Jones would "accidentally" find his pistol within easy reach.

Armed with this weapon, they would scramble about a mile from the prison, where friends would be waiting with horses and provisions. Morton wasn't sure who the friends might be. Maybe Charlie's former boss Ben Clark would help. Morton knew Jones was visited on more than one occasion by a Mrs. Luna Hutchinson and spoke of a Captain Smith, both from Bishop Creek. She was involved in the National Prison Reform Association, formed in 1870, and seemed to take a special interest in Charlie.

Once free they would rob a train at nearby Toano, to outfit themselves, get a good stake and pay Fleming, They knew that thousands of dollars in coin, gold and silver bars and the U.S. Mail came through this railroad junction on a regular basis.

What could be easier? They would find another man or two so they could be assured of success in stopping the train. Six thousand dollars from this robbery would be left for Fleming at a predetermined location. The three participants went over their plot several times. Each felt the plan would work well. They had nearly settled on an actual date. Unfortunately for Morton and Jones, the bottom fell out of their scheme. Fleming was summarily discharged. The entire plan had to be discarded. Fortunately, he never uttered a word to the prison authorities about the plot.

After a few weeks with a bout of severe depression, Jones knew he needed out more than ever. His spirits were elevated when Hutchinson visited. They had corresponded regularly. The glimpse she give him of the outside also played upon his absolute desire to get out the Nevada State Prison as soon as possible.

Jones wrote letters to Nevada Senator Cleveland requesting a parole. He felt when the man knew the circumstances of his crime he would consider the whole thing as self defense. Hopefully, the Senator would be helpful in gaining him an early release. Cleve, as most called him, had a fine reputation for being fair and his ability to find truth in all cases he handled. Unfor-

Senator Cleveland

tunately for Jones, the man was away on extended business, helping to drive cattle from California over to the Carson Valley. Not knowing this, Jones felt Cleveland was simply ignoring him. Since the man evidently was not going to help him, why should he wait around any longer?

Jones approached Morton again. He suggested they seriously discuss escaping with a few others they felt they could trust. He knew they had been very lucky that word of their previous attempt had never been discovered by either prison officials or even worse, some snitch. Naturally, they didn't need to look very far to find others wanting out as desperately as they did.

18

Chapter Three

First Pacific Coast Train Robbery

After much discussion during the summer months, a number of plots and proposals were chewed over and dismissed. However, a very workable plan started to evolve amongst several hardened prisoners during their typical Sunday routine.

This ritual consisted of gathering in the dining hall around 7 am. They were served their usual breakfast meal. Afterward, everyone was left to hang around the dining area for lunch and dinner. Some men played cards, others tried checkers. For the most part, the inmates were bored. The more astute noticed that on Sundays they were hardly guarded at all. Usually the Captain of Guard hung around outside the dining hall during the day. This observation was pointed out by old time highway man John Squires. He shared this information with some of his old time stagecoach robbing buddies, John Chapman and Jack Davis. They were all ready to escape as soon as possible. They ended up here after participating the year before in an infamous train robbery.

As it turned out, this was the first train robbery in the west. It occurred at Hunter's Crossing, just outside the little town of Verdi, not far from Reno. It was originally cited as the first train robbery in the world. While one of the earliest, it was not the first of its kind. The first U.S. train robbery occurred near Seymour, Indiana, shortly after the end of the Civil War. Frank Slim, Billy Reno, Miles Ogle and Charles Anderson held up the train, threw the express messenger into a ditch nearby and stole $90,000 from the Adams Express safe. The hold-up between Reno and Verdi Nevada in 1870 was the first train robbery on the Pacific Coast.

It was planned by several successful old time highwaymen. Lawmen in both Washoe and Storey Counties were convinced that "Smiling Jack" Davis and John Squires had been in every stage hold-up over the past couple of years. However, their skills were so smooth that whenever they were arrested and brought to

19

Passengers being held up in stage robbery

trial, they always succeeded in establishing a "reasonable doubt." Because of these men, Wells Fargo started putting more guards on the payroll to provide added protection. Thus armed guards were assigned to ride behind their stagecoaches and wagons.

As they planned their next heist, Davis and Squires cased two or three stage routes. The old outlaws saw all the coaches were being accompanied by heavily armed men. These accomplished robbers were no fools.

They could see there would be no more easy money being delivered to them by the stage companies. So they retired for the time being. During this period they hung out at the Antelope Ranch Station run by Chat Roberts. He ran this popular stage station with his sons Dick and Bedford.

The *Reno Crescent* said: ". . . the amiable landlord who runs the Antelope Ranch Hotel on the Susanville and Beckwourth Pass road in Long Valley has been in town for a day or two sloshing around generally among his friends. In town he is a bully boy and at home he keeps the nicest hotel in the country. Men who know him will ride an hour later to strike Roberts' hotel."

Davis and Squires liked Robert's place. Here they played cards and drank whiskey with their friends. But generally they were all bored to death. These men thrived on excitement and needed something to do.

Most of them could rope and ride. They had a variety of skills. Being outlaws, however, they weren't very good at regular

20

jobs. They were forced to find a new way for a big payoff and it couldn't require much effort. So they decided to rob a train. John Chapman was the ringleader of the gang. He and Squires conceived the idea of holding up a railroad train. It was a remarkably well-concocted plan. Chapman would travel to San Francisco. There he would gather information on valuable shipments being made along the tracks. He would telegraph Sol Jones in Reno with the details of a pending shipment. All the details were worked out to perfection.

The old stage robbers hang around waiting

Chapman went to San Francisco to locate a target for them. The rest of the gang hung around Roberts' place awaiting word. This included Squires, Jones, Davis, James Gilchrist, Chat Roberts, E.B. Parsons and Tilden Cockerell. They only made one mistake, but more on that later.

In San Francisco, Chapman finally found out about a Wells Fargo shipment in which he was interested. He sent a telegram to Jones that read: "Send me 60 dollars tonight without fail". It was signed J. Enrique.

This was what Sol had been waiting for. Now he knew a valuable cargo would be on the Central Pacific heading that evening for Ogden, Utah. Sol rode to Roberts' place with the news.

That very morning, the Overland Express left Oakland in

a billow of smoke. This was the No. 1 heading for Ogden. It was to stop in Reno. The express car was filled with $41,800 in gold coins, $8,800 in silver bars and lots of greenbacks. The shipment was the payroll for the Yellow Jacket Mine, near Virginia City.

The Central Pacific Railroad's No. 1

The gang gathered their provisions and rounded up their horses. Each man had two saddled mounts. They rode out to a spot on the tracks about a mile northwest of Hunter's Crossing on the Truckee River. Arriving a little after sunset, the men spent the next hour building a rock and railroad tie barrier across the tracks. They hobbled the horses they would need later. Next they rode up the trail toward Verdi, west of Reno. The men decided to wait for the train by hiding in an abandoned mine shaft just outside the town. As they waited it began to snow. It got very cold. The hours went by. The train didn't arrive. Several of those waiting were getting agitated. Naturally they had no idea that a freight train wreck near Truckee had caused a lengthy delay of the Central Pacific's No. 1. Just about the time they had decided to abandon their plan, they saw a light. The cycloptic lantern of Central Pacific's No. 1 began to shine through the bitter cold of the swirling snow.

The train was made up of a locomotive, express car, mail car, sleeper car and rear car. As it neared the small lumber town of Verdi, it slowed to a crawl. Davis and another masked man climbed into the cab of the locomotive and covered the engine crew with six-shooters. David Small, the engineer, surrendered at once. Another outlaw boarded the front platform of the express car, while two others took possession of the rear platform. The

22

rest climbed on the sleeper car platform. Two brakemen saw the masked robbers and tried to intercede, but they retreated into the sleeper car when they realized they were out matched. The conductor soon saw something was amiss. As he came out the door of the sleeper he was forced back in by the masked men. He immediately went to the rear car to get a weapon.

Up in the cab, Davis figured the train had proceeded about half a mile east of Verdi during the past few minutes.

"Give a whistle down brakes signal," he told Small, sticking his shooter in the man's ribs.

His request was complied with almost immediately. The whistle down signal was one short blast of the whistle. It was used in the railroad business to tell brakemen to go to the platforms and begin the work of setting the brakes. But on this night, it was a signal to the robbers on the express car to cut the bell-rope and pull the coupling-pin at the rear of the car.

"Give her steam," said Davis to the engineer as soon as he knew the pin was pulled.

Realizing what was being done, the engineer refused to pull out. But feeling a cold muzzle resting against his temple and hearing a hammer cocked, prompted him to obey the orders.

"Stoke that fire," Davis yelled to the fireman.

The man was nearly frightened out of his senses. He didn't have to be told more than once to do anything. As Conductor Marshall returned to confront the men, he saw his train heading round the bend. The car he was on, was slowing to a stop.

"Frank," he yelled at a brakeman, "run back to Verdi and telegraph the sheriff."

"Okay boss," replied the brakeman. He started up the tracks back toward Verdi. When he arrived, it was discovered the lines had been cut in both directions.

Davis stood with the engineer as the train traveled down the tracks about eight miles. It now consisted of the locomotive, mail and express cars. It was around midnight. They were nearing Hunter's Station.

"Stop the train," commanded Davis.

The engineer heard the order as he saw the barrier the out-

23

laws placed across the track. Small realized he had no choice and eased back on the throttle. The engine slowed to a halt about six feet shy of the pile on the tracks. After the train stopped, the other outlaws took positions on both sides of the Express Car. Davis and his companion kept the engine crew covered. The clerk in the express car was completely ignorant as to what was about to happen. He was busy with paperwork. Suddenly, he realized the train had come to a stop and wondered what was up. He heard voices from outside the car and then a loud knock on the cargo door.

"Who's there," questioned the clerk?

"Marshall," lied the outlaw at the door.

Figuring the conductor was outside, the clerk unhooked the lock and pulled the door open. To his surprise, instead of Marshall, he saw the muzzle of a double-barreled shotgun.

"Throw up your hands," yelled the voice behind the gun.

He reached for the heavens. Fearing for his life, he backed up as well. He watched several masked men enter the car. The outlaws were surprised to see the Wells Fargo safe wide open.

"Sit down in the corner, shut up and you won't get hurt."

He quickly complied and watched the men throw the sacks of gold out the door. While so doing, gold coins were scattered on the floor. The robbers completely ignored the sacks of silver also in the safe. This entire process took but a few minutes.

"Thanks for keeping your mouth shut," laughed Squires.

"Yeah, we didn't really want to kill ya," teased Jones.

The outlaws stuffed the $20 gold pieces into their saddlebags, loaded their booty on their horses and disappeared into the darkness. Before going their separate ways, the gang members hid most of the booty at a quarry near Granite Hot Springs.

After the robbers left the express car, the clerk heaved a huge sigh of relief. He began to gather up coins that were left behind. He wondered why they didn't take the silver bars.

Small and the fireman ran back to see if the Express Clerk was okay. They knocked on the mail car to see if the Postal Clerk inside was unharmed as well. Seeing that both men were safe, the two began clearing the tracks.

Meanwhile, back up the line, Conductor Marshall and his

lone brakeman used the manual brakes to allow the passenger cars to slowly drop down the grade. He had no idea what to expect, but went ahead anyway. Arriving at the scene of the robbery, he saw Small and the fireman clearing off the track. Marshal ordered his crew to reconnect the cars. Small slowly opened the throttle and they rolled on, reaching Reno at 12:30 am. Conductor Marshal checked his watch. He noted they were only 30 minutes late.

According to newspaper accounts the next day, the Express Car clerk was quoted as saying, "When the door opened I looked into something which resembled two stove-pipes"

Later that day the *Gold Hills News* reported: "The most high handed god fearing robbery ever perpetuated on the Pacific Coast occurred on the Central Pacific Railroad."

Another newspaper account noted that: "Every enemy of law and order was vociferous in praise of the boldness and nerve of the perpetrators of the robbery, and Nevada acquired the dubious credit of being the first State in the Union that could produce a set of outlaws daring enough to stop and rob an express train."

Almost immediately that morning, a reward of more than $40,000 was offered. Naturally, numerous lawmen, as well as ordinary citizens and groups of shady characters began to make plans to outwit and catch the bold train robbers.

Ironically, several hours later, a few hundred miles up the track, Central Pacific's No. 1 was about to be victimized again by other bandits. The small brisk locomotive with red trim and balloon stack was now pulling a Silver Palace car, a little yellow day coach as well as a combined baggage and express car. The latter was loaded with the U.S. mail, packages and currency. So just 20 hours after the first west coast train robbery comes the second such event. This time it occurs in Pequops, a few miles west of Toana, near the Utah line, 320 miles east of the original crime scene. The highwaymen included Daniel Taylor, Leandor Morton, Daniel Boone Baker and another man. They boarded the train and took over just as was done hours earlier. Taylor and his companion kept the engine crew covered. Morton and Baker hit the express side of the special railroad car.

While the outlaws were going through the registered mail

in the express compartment, the Wells Fargo agent was equally busy in the baggage compartment. He had taken in several thousand dollars at Elko, Nevada which was not yet in the safe. Hearing the commotion nearby, he quickly hid the cash under a pile of freight. He blew out his lamp and kept very quiet, hoping to go unnoticed. Suddenly the door opened. First the barrel of a pistol entered the hiding place. Morton covered the room as Baker entered with an oil lamp. They saw a man cowering in the corner.

"Get over there and open that safe," commanded Morton.

"Okay, okay," said the agent as he moved to the safe and placed his fingers on the knob. He turned it first left, then right and then left again until he heard a final click. He reached for the handle and opened the door.

"Get outta my way," yelled Morton.

The clerk scrambled back to the corner while Morton took $3,100 out of the safe. All the while the clerk was chuckling inside because this scary outlaw was getting such a measly sum. If that bastard only knew about what he had just hidden away.

Sticking the clerk's revolver in his belt, Morton said "Keep your head inside this car and you won't get hurt."

Baker followed Morton out the car door. The bandits mounted up and disappeared in a cloud of dust. When he knew the robbers had ridden away the clerk surveyed the scene. The engineer and train crew came back to see if the clerk had been harmed. What they saw was the man doubled over laughing.

"Those dumb bastards just rode out of here with a paltry $3,100," bellowed the clerk, holding his sides. "I hid all the cash from Elko under some freight and they didn't even find it,"

"Well I'll be damned," chuckled the engineer.

They all had a good laugh at the robbers' expense. As the engineer got the train underway, the agent jumped back into his car. Taking stock of the situation, he found a glove bearing the name of Edward Carr. He also found a brass compass engraved with the name William Harvey. He set them aside to turn over to Elko County Sheriff Fitch.

When word of this second stick up hit the streets the next morning, it was assumed by most folks that the crimes were committed by the same party. Until the culprits were apprehended, no one knew for sure. And apprehended they were.

When Sheriff Fitch looked over the evidence given to him by the Wells Fargo agent he was intrigued. He wanted to know more about Carr and Harvey of the Third United States Cavalry. Naturally, they were his prime suspects. He rode out to Camp Halleck. He discovered Carr and Harvey were two of six deserters missing from the post. He was told that on October 13, Carr had been at Sallie Whitmore's sporting house on the Day Ranch some two miles south of the military post. Carr got in a fight with his sergeant and got his "ass kicked."

Leaving the house of ill repute, he quickly rode back to camp to retrieve his carbine. He returned to Sallie's place, plan-

ning to kill the man that beat him up. He entered the premises, spotted the sergeant and took a shot at him. The sergeant saw him raise the rifle and dove for the floor. Unfortunately for poor old Sallie, Carr missed his target and hit her in the groin. The wound proved fatal.

Carr was arrested and taken to the post. Local law enforcement was contacted at Elko. When Constable William Baugh went to get Carr for trial, other soldiers prevented the lawman from taking him. Baugh quickly retreated to Elko to gather a posse. Returning the next morning with several heavily armed men, he learned that Carr was missing. The post

Unfortunate "soiled dove" commander called a muster which revealed that six soldiers had deserted. Now the plot thickens.

A report came in almost immediately that four well mounted and heavily armed men passed by the Deep Creek station on the old Overland Telegraph road. They turned east. Fitch formed a posse and went to talk with the men. They caught up with two riders on the road between Deep Creek and Salt Lake City. They turned out to be Leandor Morton and Daniel Baker.

"Hold up there a minute boys," the sheriff called out, "we have a question or two we'd like to ask."

"What's the problem," replied Baker.

"We are looking for some men that robbed a train not far from here," Fitch said. "Who are you boys?"

"I'm Daniel Boone Baker and that's Lea Morton."

"What do you boys do?"

"We've been prospecting hereabouts," said Morton.

The lawmen looked the men over. They didn't appear to be prospectors. He noted Morton's buckskin gloves and the "W.H. Harvey" ink markings. The clue possibly linked Morton to the train robbery and perhaps to the whereabouts of the deserters.

"Where'd you get those gloves?"

"I won them in a card game awhile back, why?"

"They belonged to a cavalry man named Harvey. He and another soldier, Carr, are missing from their post. Do you recall a card game with Harvey? Were there other soldiers there too?"

"I don't recall a man by either of those names. What's this all about anyway?"

"Well four men robbed a train not far from here. Evidence left at the scene points to Harvey and Carr. We haven't been able to locate them. The gloves you have on belonged to Harvey."

"Sorry I can't help ya, sheriff. I don't have any description of the man I won the gloves from. I don't recall playing cards with any soldiers. I can't believe a train was robbed. Hell, who would try to rob a train anyway?"

"What's truly amazing," said the sheriff, "is not that a train was robbed, but it was robbed twice on the same day."

"No shit," quipped Morton.

Fitch arrested Morton and Baker on suspicion of train robbery. He figured that desertion from the army was the only crime committed by Carr and Harvey. He figured these men knew exactly where the two soldiers were, but couldn't prove it. Daniel Taylor was caught a short while later. The three were indicted for robbing the express car and the U.S. Mail. The fourth member of the gang was never found. On January 17, 1871, they were convicted and sentenced to 30 years in the Nevada State Prison.

Chapter Four

Kinkead Hits the Robber's Trail

It was noted earlier that the highwaymen who planned the train robbery near Verdi made only one mistake. The mistake was taking James Gilchrist and Sol Jones along with them. They certainly didn't need the extra help and the subsequent actions of these two men led directly to the gangs arrest and imprisonment.

Telegraphic news of the train robbery reached the Washoe City Sheriff's office at 8 o'clock the next morning, it read: "Train robbed between Truckee and Verdi; robbers gone South."

Washoe County Sheriff Charley Pegg and Under Sheriff James Kinkead read the telegram, looked at each other and shook their heads.

"Well now I've heard just about everything," chuckled Sheriff Pegg as he scratched his balding head. "I've got a hunch where this bunch might be headed. Let's you and me go find em."

"Nature's calling," replied Kinkead, "I'll grab my rifle and join you in a minute or two at the stable. Please ask Gus to saddle my horse."

The lawmen mounted up and rode out just after 8:30 that morning. Sheriff Pegg assumed the robbers would take the Truckee route between Truckee, Carson City and Virginia City.

"Let's head for the mountains by that short cut we used chasing Rufus Anderson back in '68. Maybe we can cut them off," he shouted over the noise of the pounding hoof beats.

They followed the trail northerly for a few miles and soon realized that no one had passed over it since a light snow fall the week before. They returned to Washoe City. Upon further investigation, Sheriff Pegg found the telegraphic message proved misleading. The robbery had occurred below Verdi, not above. The lawmen realized they wasted their time that first day.

Early the next morning Under Sheriff Kinkead mounted a

29

fresh horse and rode out to survey the robbery scene. He stepped off his mount to examine the grounds. He observed lots of fresh tracks. After some time studying the scene, he found valuable evidence. It was simply a footprint. But this one footprint was vastly different from any other. The imprint was made by a small heel. This was not the type of heel worn by most men of the era. This heel was on footwear worn by dudes and gamblers. Kinkead knew that it was too soon after the robbery for curious onlookers to come by for a look see. He knew he must track that heel print. He planned to follow it from this point. Once he found another he would surely be on the trail of at least one of the robbers.

Kinkead rode painstakingly up and down the railroad tracks for hours. Carefully he scoured the ground for another such imprint. Finally he thought, a smile crossing his lips. Here was another footprint about a mile west of the heist. He could plainly see a small heel print and two larger ones left the track, heading north. The bad guys had walked the railroad ties to this point in hopes of eluding anyone that might try to follow them. These men were pretty smart, but obviously not smart enough.

Kinkead was pleased with

James Kinkead

the light snow fall that held the imprints. They were easy for him to follow. They went up Dog Valley Creek and over Dog Valley Hill into Sardine Valley California. He gained valuable knowledge at the Sardine Valley House. Three strangers had lodged there the night before. He suspected them to be the men he was after. They were in fact, Squires, Parsons and Gilchrist. He found two of these men had left early the previous morning. Before they left, they had a long conversation together in very hushed tones. Gilchrist was the one staying behind. Evidentially, he was in no shape to travel for a day or two. His feet were too sore from walking that far. He planned to continue in a day or so. Before the train robbery, he had worked as a miner. Up until now he had a good reputation and was an honest man. Now he was scared to death. What the hell had he gotten himself into?

Kinkead learned that this very morning that a deer hunting party lead by James Burke, from Truckee, arrived at the house. Naturally they were well armed. The men sat down, looked over a menu and ordered breakfast.

Gilchrist thought they were lawmen looking for him. He became very apprehensive. While waiting for their food, the hunters sipped coffee and talked casually. Momentarily, an excited man rushed in and yelled the news of the recent train robbery.

Overhearing this commotion, Gilchrist had a hard time suppressing his fear. He had turned a bright red and was acting strangely. Soon he stood up and quickly left the dining room.

Upon hearing the train robbery news, the landlady became suspicious of the men that arrived the previous evening. While Gilchrist was out of the room, she told her concerns to Burke and the rest of the hunting party. Burke inquired if she had seen any of them this morning.

"One of the men is still here. He seems nervous and all worn out. He was just sitting over there."

Once outside Gilchrist ran to the privy, stepped inside, closed the door and latched it. He emptied his pockets of the gold pieces he had and hid them there. He returned to the dining room, sat down and tried to calmly finish his breakfast.

After hearing her account, Burke recalled that the man had appeared a little out of sorts. Although not lawmen, Burke told his friends they needed to the find

31

the man and take him back to Truckee for questioning. Burke and a friend stood up and went out the same door as Gilchrist had. They actually passed him as they walked toward the privy. A quick inspection of the outhouse turned up six $20 gold pieces hidden for later retrieval. Burke figured these had to be coins from the robbery. Returning to the dining room, they took Gilchrist into custody. The hunting party and their quarry were on their way to Truckee as the landlady was explaining all this to Kinkead.

She also gave Sheriff Kinkead a very good description of the other two men she saw. She went into great detail.

"One of them," she remarked, "must a been a professional card player. He had those girly gambler's boots on."

Kinkead smiled and nodded his head. He was on the right trail. Based on her description of the second man, Kinkead knew him to be the old stage robber John Squires. He and other officers had been trying to jail him for years. Kinkead rightly assumed Squires was headed for Sierraville to hole up with his brother Joe. Unlike John, Joe was an honest man. He was a well established and well-liked blacksmith. Obviously, John thought he could stay there safely until things died down.

John Squires

It was now late in the day. Kinkead and his horse had been going since daylight. He ate a good meal and downed several cups of coffee. He made sure his horse enjoyed a big bag of oats. By 10 o'clock that night the snow was steadily falling. Not being familiar with the territory, Kinkead knew he needed to hire a guide to make sure he did not end up at Downieville instead of Sierraville. He requested assistance from the men in the inn. Their consensus was "they hadn't lost any prisoners lately, so they didn't see a need to help find any."

Just when he thought he would have to go it alone, a young

man spoke up.

"I can help ya, mister. For $10 I can take you as far as the Webber Lake Junction. From there I'll show you the trail to Loyalton which leads to Sierraville."

"That sounds fair."

"But, if we encounter the highwaymen, I'm leaving. You're on your own."

"That agreeable to me. When can you leave?"

"I'll be ready in a couple of minutes. I need to tell my mom where I'm going."

They climbed aboard their mounts and headed down the trail for Sierraville. Kinkead was very pleased. The boy did a good job of getting him pointed in the right direction. Kinkead arrived in the little town of Loyalton without incident. He woke up the clerk of the only lodging facility in the town. He told the man who he was and what he was after. He asked if there were any recent guests in the house. The clerk described one, but the description didn't fit either man he was seeking. Kinkead decided to check him out anyway. The clerk declined to accompany him, but told the sheriff the man was in Room 14. He gave Kinkead the room key and his candle holder.

Reaching the second story, Kinkead readily found Room

14. He noticed the door was partly ajar. He gently pushed it until it was open far enough to enter. He accomplished this without waking the occupant. Then, bingo, there was the boot with the little heel he sought. This evidence would be very important at the trial of the robbers. Parsons was in a deep slumber. Kinkead removed a six-shooter from under his pillow. He went through the man's clothes in search of further evidence to connect him with the robbery. Enough was found to assist in the

Edward Parsons

33

later conviction of the man. When Kinkead aroused Parsons, he bounded from his bed and landed in the center of the room like a wild animal. He rushed back to the bed and reached under the pillow for his gun. Naturally, it was missing. He looked around to see the barrel of Kinkead's pistol. He was told to get dressed. He was then marched down to the saloon. Here he was put under guard while Kinkead went after John Squires.

The sheriff rode on to Sierraville. He easily found Joe Squires' house. It was now just before daylight. Knowing he might have trouble with John, Kinkead hid around the back of the house, in some willows. There he waited. Soon someone came out of the kitchen and left the door open. They headed to the barn with a pail. It was time for the morning milking. Kinkead quietly crept into the house through the kitchen and searched through four rooms where people were sleeping before finding John. Again he was able to disarm the man without waking him. He gathered up his clothes and boots, then awoke John. The man saw the pistol muzzle. The sheriff motioned him to silently walk out of the house. Outside, Kinkead told him to get dressed. While dressing, John saw Joe walking back to the house.

"Joe, I'm being robbed," he yelled to his brother.

The entire household erupted. A crowd gathered. Kinkead secured John and told those gathering he was an officer discharging his duty. He had arrested John Squires on suspicion of train robbery. John yelled that Kinkead didn't have any jurisdiction in California. This view was generally shared by the crowd. It looked bad for Kinkead. But a team was being hitched to a wagon for Kinkead to leave town. When it was ready and standing behind the saloon, he and his prisoner rushed into it. Kinkead succeeded in getting them safely away from the crowd.

Eventually both Squires and Parsons ended up in the Truckee jail where Gilchrist already was confined. Gilchrist was kept separate from the other men. He broke completely under questioning and made a complete statement. He gave the names of all parties connected with the robbery.

A telegram was immediately sent to Wells Fargo in Virginia City, directing the arrest of Jack Davis. Another was sent to Reno calling for the arrest of John Chapman, Sol Jones, Chat Roberts and Tilden Cockerell. Davis was arrested in Virginia City. Jones, Roberts and Cockerell were taken in Long Valley by a posse headed by Chief Burke of Sacramento and Louis Dean of Reno. Chapman returned from San Francisco on the following day. He was arrested in Reno by Deputy Sheriff Edwards.

The entire gang was rounded up in less than four days after the robbery occurred. Most of the money was recovered. Gilchrist showed the officers where the money was cached. He said that it was the intention to let it remain there until the excitement of the robbery had subsided. Then they would dig it up and divide it. Kinkead earned an enormous reward for his efforts.

A grand jury was immediately called together. Indictments quickly followed. The trial began in mid-December. It was a memorable trial in the criminal annals of Nevada. Judge Charles Harris presided. The case was brought by District Attorney William Boardman. Thomas Williams appeared for Wells Fargo. Attorney General Robert Clarke represented the State. Central Pacific Railroad hired Jim Croffroth of California, a high profile criminal lawyer, to appear for them.

William Webster, who later become the editor of the *Reno Journal*, represented seven of the defendants. Judge Thomas Haydon appeared as special counsel for Chapman.

A tremendous legal battle ensued. It was primarily over Chapman's plea that he was in California the day of the robbery. Therefore, his lawyer argued, Nevada didn't have jurisdiction over him in these proceedings. For this court to convict him, first they had to prove a conspiracy existed and further prove the conspiracy evolved in Nevada. The confessions of Gilchrist and Roberts drove the conspiracy theory home. They were both promised immunity for their testimony. However, the law says no man can be convicted solely on the testimony of an accomplice, so it was necessary to have corroborating evidence.

This evidence was obtained from Gilchrist and included the fact the robbery was planned at Chat Roberts's Stage Station and Hotel in California. It was arranged that Chapman would go to San Francisco. There he would watch for a suitable shipment from Wells Fargo & Co.'s office. He would then send a cipher message to Jones at Reno. Jones would take the message to the gang members who were waiting word. They had holed up in an old tunnel in the Peavine Mountains north of Reno.

Jones testified on behalf of the State and explained the meaning of the cipher message. It read:

"Send me sixty dollars tonight without fail"

It was signed "J. Enrique".

Jones said this meant that a shipment would be on the train heading to Odgen, Utah and the gang should plan to rob it. Of course, Chapman said he never sent any such message. But to his surprise, the San Francisco Western Union operator brought the original message to court. He swore under oath that Chapman was positively the man who delivered it to him in the early morning of November 4. Judge Thomas Haydon, Chapman's attorney, asked how the operator could possibly remember every character that came into the telegraph office that day.

Much to his dismay, the operator simply pointed out it was the first message received that day and the sender requested and paid for a return message to notify him of delivery. Thus Chapman had to make two more trips to his office. By the third visit, the operator said he had taken particular notice of the man. Seeing his case eroding, Haydon went back to the question of

proper jurisdiction. He produced well known authorities from California to support his arguments. For a while, it was looking pretty good for Chapman. It was at this point that Nevada Attorney General Clarke took the floor of the courtroom. In an eloquent dissertation, he successfully combated the contention of Chapman's attorney. Chapman would be tried with the others. Basically, the trial was over. The defendants were all convicted.

John Chapman

36

Their sentences ranged from five to 23 years. Jones got the lightest sentence of five years, as promised, for his help in convicting the others. Squires and Chapman got the most severe punishment with 23 and 20 years respectively. Parsons was sent up for 18 years, Davis for 10. As agreed before the trial, Gilchrist and Roberts were allowed to go free because of their testimony at the trial.

It was noted with some interest by regional lawmen and Wells Fargo agents that the stage-robbing business in Nevada came to a virtual end with the imprisonment of these men.

Of course, others tried their hand at stage robbery, but none had the flair of Squires, Davis and Chapman. The others

usually got caught or ended up full of holes. The men began their sentences at the Nevada State Prison on Christmas Day of 1870. The other trio of train robbers joined them the following month.

Chapter Five
Serious Escape Plan Developed

Now in prison and hating every moment of incarceration, the train robbers wanted out. Obviously, they weren't alone. On Sunday, September 3 the constant escape talk took a more serious tone. Dangerous men openly spoke about the fact they'd been there long enough. The old expression "this place isn't big enough to hold me" gave them a common bond. The meeting was not attended by the meek. Soon they got around to the important discussion as to who would plan and lead any subsequent break.

The first name tossed in the hat was Jack Davis, who was serving time for train robbery. He had a reputation for being a shrewd man. He had arrived at the Comstock strike from the East in 1859. Here he led a double life. To his fellow Gold Hill neighbors, he was a successful livery stable owner and a claims recorder for the Flowery Mining District. This was a perfect cover. He had an exciting "hobby". He enjoyed robbing the bullion wagons in Six Mile Canyon. He then laundered some of his ill gotten gains

Gold Hill not far from Virginia City

through his legitimate businesses. A significant amount of gold and silver was hidden away in a very safe place in Six Mile Canyon. To help with his cover as a leading citizen, he even taught Sunday school in Virginia City.

Fellow train robbers Parsons and Chapman spoke out against Davis. They wouldn't take part if Davis was the leader. They felt Davis had co-operated with the prosecutors at their trial. Maybe he did, but rumor had it there were thousands of dollars in ill gotten spoils hidden away in Six Mile Canyon. Perhaps Davis had a good reason to try for a lesser sentence.

Cockerell, Squires, Baker, Morton, Taylor and Clifford agreed to pass on Davis. They knew the value of having Parsons and Chapman in on the break. These two were cunning and cool under pressure. Other men were suggested for the job. The pros and cons of each were considered.

Finally Leandor Morton was selected for the task. Most of the men knew he had thrown in with Charlie Jones in the failed plot with Guard Alexander Fleming. It was considered a very sound plan, even though it had gone south!

Morton, you'll remember, helped rob the train back in December with Baker and Taylor. He had on the gloves bearing the name of a missing U.S. Cavalry man. Morton did know exactly where the two army deserters were laid to rest. But no one would ever find them. He was 27. He had the typical temper said to accompany folks with red hair. At 5'8" and 160, he was well put together. Poor personal hygiene had caused him to lose a couple front teeth of which he was very self conscious.

Morton asked that Frank Clifford work directly with him in planning the operation. Clifford, also known as Francis Marion, was a 29 year-old Maryland native. He had chosen a life of crime and frequently ended up in jail. However, he never stayed very long. He was considered to be one of the best escape artists on the west coast. Morton thought him to be a natural to help plan the escape. The reason Clifford was in prison this time around was for his part in a stage robbery. He was convicted of rifling the Wells Fargo Express stage on the Len Lines between Hamilton and Elko. He had taken up residence at the Nevada State Prison on

April 22, 1870. His sentence was for 10 years. When not involved in criminal activities, he usually worked as a carpenter. Clifford was well educated. He wrote very well and was even known to have written some passable poetry.

Frank Clifford

During the week from September 4th to the 10th, Morton and Clifford spoke with several others at mealtime and after lights out. Clifford's additional input was carefully considered by Morton. Therefore, this jail break was ultimately a "team" effort.

The plans were fairly complex, but each element was rather simple. First, the escape would occur on a Sunday when the prison was only protected by the Captain of the Guard. A predetermined signal would alert those involved in the plan to swing into action. Next they would overpower the Captain. Other guards may be around outside the general area, but they usually considered Sunday to be a day off. Normally they didn't even carry their guns on Sunday. None of the guards would be expecting any trouble.

Third, they would gain access to the roof. Basically they were going to cut a hole in the ceiling above their jail cells. This had to be done so it could be covered up so the guards wouldn't notice the alterations when they periodically checked the cells. The inmates figured they could use some sort of cleat to help hold up a false ceiling as was necessary. Part of the wall would have to be dug out too. This would then give the convicts access to the roof. Once there, they could break through to the second floor of the prison which housed the Warden's family, the Assistant Warden, an office and the armory. Breaking open the armory, the men would take weapons and use them to fight their way downstairs, out into the yard through the main gate and over the fence. Finally, they would simply overpower any remaining guards and head for the Carson River. After that, it was everyone for themselves.

The plan was finally agreed upon. Actual work began Sunday, September 10. At night, the men worked on cutting out a portion of the ceiling above their jail cells. Once they made their way into the crawl space they dug a hole in the wall to give them access to the roof. Work had to be suspended when they had to do their regular prison jobs. While the men worked, the ceiling was replaced and held up by a series of invisible cleats. All in all, everything was going pretty well.

By Sunday the 17th, preparations were complete. Word spread amongst the prisoners that 6 pm was the time for action. A signal would be given by Pat Hurley. At the appointed time he would rattle his leg chains three times and drop his iron ball to the floor. As usual, that morning the prisoners were marched into the dining hall for breakfast. Nearly 70 of them assembled therein. The regular routine played out. The convicts would stay there all day. Some played cards or checkers, others talked about old and better times. Those that knew what was coming remained as calm as possible. They tried nonchalantly to eat their evening meal, but for most of them, the adrenaline was flowing.

❦ ❦ ❦

Meanwhile, orderly Bob Dedman was upstairs in Warden Denver's quarters. He had been assigned to help get things ready for a dinner party planned for that evening. It was nearly 4 pm. The guests would be arriving soon. Dedman had been sentenced to life for killing a man a year or so ago. At the time, the death was thought by many to simply be "self defense." But, he was arrested, tried and convicted for murder. The Warden knew the whole Dedman story. Once at the prison, the Warden had him assigned almost immediately to help run his household. Dedman even looked after the Warden's 9-year-old daughter, Jennie.

Mary Denver, the Warden's wife, entered the room where Dedman was preparing things. She noted that the guests were arriving. Dedman set things down and headed to the door to help greet the folks soon to be coming up the stairs. The guests expected included Mrs. Garner, mother of Mrs. Denver; Mrs. George Stew-

41

art of San Francisco, Mary's, sister; Mollie Youtz, A.C. Stewart and Fred Smith of Virginia City.

Dedman escorted the guests to the sitting room to allow them to mingle and wait for dinner. Pleasantries of the day were exchanged by the women. The men sipped an aged whiskey and sized one another up. They spoke about the progress of the Central Pacific Railroad. When Dedman concluded his dinner preparations, he entered the room and announced that dinner was ready. They all retired to the dining room for the meal Dedman had prepared. The Warden started the meal off with a toast to his guests.

⩗ ⩗ ⩗

Two hundred miles to the South, just outside Benton Hot Springs in Mono County California, Robert Morrison and his fiancé, Sarah Devine shared a kiss. The late fall afternoon was quickly cooling off. The two lovers snuggled close together. Morrison, the successful proprietor of the Benton General Store, knew he was a lucky man.

The object of his affections was a native of Pennsylvania. She came to Benton to be near her brother, Henry. Henry was a miner at the time, but had since come to work as a clerk in Morrison's store.

They both realized it was time to head back to town following what had become a regular Sunday afternoon affair. Bob enjoyed sharing his knowledge of this high desert region with Sarah. Usually they settled back in one of the hot springs for which the area was known. But this Sunday, he took her to the Crags. These were a series of interesting geological rock formations not too far from Benton. Nineteen year old Sarah was still a bit of a tom-boy. She enjoyed the outdoors and loved her time together with Bob, indoors or out. With 125 pounds spread over her 5'6" frame, she posed a striking figure. Her long Irish red hair, freckles and sparkling green eyes accentuated her beautiful face. Her skin was smooth and radiant. But what really impressed Bob was that her beauty was not just skin deep. She had a good heart and a deep passion. This was a special woman.

"Hey," he chuckled to himself; "she's a great cook too."

42

Bob realized he had gained a few pounds since they began spending time together. Today they shared a picnic of fried chicken, canned peaches, sourdough rolls and deviled eggs. Just when he thought he could eat no more, the apple of his eye unpacked a freshly baked apple pie.

"That was delicious Sarah," he said, "wiping some remaining crust from his mustache. "But if you keep feeding me this way, I'll have to buy a stronger horse."

SarahDevine and Robert Morrison near Benton

As the wagon wound its way down the steep incline, they looked forward to the evening ahead. Henry Devine, Sarah's brother, was having a dinner party in their honor to announce their upcoming wedding.

∽❀∽❀∽❀

Back at the prison, the warden offered his guests some fine French wine. He started the evening off with a toast to them and, of course, the great state of Nevada. Mary was very impressed with Dedman's culinary efforts. She considered him an excellent cook, but this time he had even outdone himself. The wonderful meal consisted of roast duck in a succulent orange sauce along with wild brown rice. From the prison garden were fresh green beans, flavored with bacon. A huge basket of delicious homemade sourdough rolls was on the table as well. This exceptional gourmet style dinner was washed down with even more wine. It came from the couple's private wine cellar at their Virginia City home.

Meanwhile, 14 convicts had crawled through the ceiling and worked their way through the wall and onto the roof over the living quarters of Warden Denver and Assistant Warden Zimmerman. There they waited for the Captain of the Guard, Volney Rollins, to come lead their fellow inmates back to their cells for the evening. Still others were now strung out along an opening in between the ceiling and the roof, waiting for the signal for the break to begin.

Dedman was clearing up the dinner dishes as he moved back and forth from the kitchen to the dining room. Soon he would take down Mrs. Denver's finest china to serve the special dessert he spent the afternoon preparing for her guests. Suddenly he flinched at the sound of a tremendous noise.

"What the hell was that?"

The women in the next room heard it too. They thought it was an earthquake and were unnerved.

"That felt like an earthquake to me," cried out one of the guests. "What should we do."

Hair stood up on their necks. Goose bumps appeared. Palpitations were felt. Jennie fearfully grabbed her mother's arm. They were all very frightened of earthquakes. The Warden noted his watch. It was 6 pm. Almost as a unit, the ladies gathered in the center of the room. The men moved in to comfort them. Then the ominous sound came again. That was enough for the ladies.

"Oh my God," yelled Mollie, "where can we go?"

She turned to follow as the other ladies immediately exited the room and headed downstairs. They ran outside the building opting for the safety of the yard.

The frightening sound was in fact the clanking noise made by the prisoners trampling along the roof dragging their heavy chains as they positioned themselves above the warden's quarters. The men knew they were making noise, but there was no turning back now. It was time to make a break for it.

44

Chapter Six
All Hell Breaks Loose

In the bustling mining town of Aurora, about 15 miles from Bodie, the Poor family was feeling anything but that. Today they had been enjoying a long-awaited reunion with their son William. His dad was the proprietor of a local hotel in Aurora and his mom was kept busy raising his brothers and sisters. Billy, as his friends called him, had been living in California. He had a couple of years experience working on river boats in Sacramento, Stockton and along the Delta. He also spent a year learning a lot about the railroad while working in Copperopolis, not far from

Copperopolis in the California Sierra Nevada foothills

Mariposa. The family had worried a bit when he didn't show up as expected yesterday. But he was here now. Billy had some trouble with his horse and it had been necessary to lay over in Bridgeport the previous evening. He got an early start this beautiful Sunday morning and had arrived just in time for the midday meal.

Naturally, his parents were pleased to have their 23-year-old son with them. They had really missed seeing him during the past two years. In their frequent correspondence, Billy had mentioned he was thinking of coming home to Nevada, but didn't want to if he had to work as a miner. He was thrilled when he received a recent letter from his dad telling him about a job that was opening up with a family friend. Billy Wilson operated both stage and mail routes in western Nevada. He was looking for a rider that he could rely on to cover an important mail route.

Young Poor decided right then and there he was going to take that job in Nevada. Billy didn't enjoy the work he was doing now anyway. Being an excellent horseman, he was more than qualified him for the job. Besides the young man was ready to try something else and what could be better than a life of excitement in the "wild west." Poor was happy to be around his family again. He was savoring a second bottle of sarsaparilla and was eyeing the huge cobbler on his mother's kitchen window sill. The dinner she had served was the best he had eaten in months. It consisted of roast goose with her famous corn bread stuffing. There were fresh vegetables from her garden. His mom's homemade bread rounded out this fantastic meal.

Since he didn't have to work until Tuesday around noon, he figured that tomorrow he'd hang out at the hotel with his dad. They could have lunch in town. His pop could fill him in on everything he needed to know about Aurora. Maybe his father knew a cute young lady or two he could meet. Billy was excited. He really did look forward to his first trip for Wilson on Tuesday.

⋖⋗ ⋖⋗ ⋖⋗

In the prison guard room, Volney Rollins checked his gold watch. He saw it was nearly 5:30 p.m. He remembered when his father gave him the time piece. He put it back in his pocket. The Captain of the Guards knew his workday was almost done. He folded up his newspaper and set it on the table at his side. Due to boredom he figured he read it cover to cover three times during the day. Now it was time to go through his usual Sunday evening ritual. He headed to the staircase and climbed up to the second floor. He did his routine check of the area. He heard the sound of conversation coming from Warden Denver's quarters. He knew the warden had company tonight, so he didn't stop to say "good evening". He passed by Assistant Warden Zimmerman's door and chuckled as he heard loud snoring from the room. Checking the armory door lock, he found it was secure.

"Hell, it always was," he thought to himself.

As he walked by the prison office he noticed a Henry rifle lying across a desk inside. That reminded him that it needed to be taken to the Carson City gunsmith for some minor repairs. No use putting it in the armory tonight, it wouldn't work anyway. He decided to cover it up with a coat to prevent moisture from getting into the workings. His rounds concluded, he descended the stairs. It was almost 6 pm, time to move the convicts to their cells.

He extinguished his pipe and knocked the instrument against the stone wall to remove any lingering tobacco. He shoved it back in his pocket and reached for the keys on the wall behind him. He headed over to unlock the iron gates of the dining hall. He would be glad to have the inmates return to their cells.

"It was a long day for everyone," he thought, "it sure must be awfully boring for them on Sundays. It's bad enough for me. It has to be worse for them. I'd better get to it,"

After the men were locked down, he planned to slip outside and across to the Warms Springs Hotel for a long awaited shot of whiskey and perhaps a card game.

He called to the men to get ready to return to their cells. As Rollins turned the key in the lock, many prisoners waited, as if spring-loaded, for the signal that Hurley was to give. It didn't come. Rollins started to swing the heavy iron door open. He stepped back. There was a momentary pause.

Some of the convicts thought "What now"?

For what seemed like an eternity, no one moved. But after 15 seconds or so Morton, never at a loss for action, decided to take the lead and got the game underway by yelling:

"Now, let's go now. Let's get the hell out of here!"

Suddenly, all hell broke loose. John Squires forcefully opened the iron door. He seized Rollins and threw him to the sawdust-covered floor. Others flowed through the open door like water escaping through a hole in a dam. Seeing Squires with Rollins, fellow prisoner William Russell pulled Rollins' head by the hair. Squires grabbed a bottle and swung it at the Captain's head. He missed and hit Russell's wrist forcefully instead. Russell yelled in pain. His wrist began to swell immediately. Squires took bet-

47

ter aim and broke the bottle over the Rollin's head. Blood rushed from a three and a half inch gash left by the blow.

Rollins' misfortunes were just beginning. Almost simultaneously he was struck just over the left eye with a slung-shot, cutting his face to the bone. Now bleeding profusely, the man, wounded badly, but not mortally, sunk to the floor. Other convicts saw Rollins covered with blood and sawdust, lying helplessly and still on the floor. As they rushed in for the kill, convict Pat Hurley dragged Rollins into a cell, locked the door and threw in the key. This move more than likely saved his life.

Hearing the commotion below, the prisoners atop the roof knew it was time to finish cutting the hole through the roof above the Warden's quarters. No one cared about noise now. The cat was out of the bag. Finally, the hole was completed. They poured through the roof and ended up in Assistant Warden Zimmerman's room. The man awoke to a frightful scene: striped men falling through his ceiling. They were armed with slung shots and fire was in their eyes. They quickly crowded through his door into the hallway. Dressed in bed clothes and completely defenseless, Zimmerman couldn't believe his good fortune. No one noticed him. Realizing the danger all about, he decided to flee. He scampered barefoot down the staircase and into the courtyard. No more was heard from him during the ensuing melee.

The frenzied prisoners bolted down stairs. They intermingled with and nearly knocked down the women from the Warden's dinner party. The terrified guests ended up in the prison yard without realizing what was actually occurring. They still thought an earthquake was in progress. It seemed natural these convicts were running for safety too. Even with all the commotion, only Rollins, Zimmerman, Denver and Dedman knew what was unfolding. No other prison personnel were aware of the break attempt.

Unfortunately, all this was about to change. A murderous gun battle was about to ensue in the prison courtyard. The terrified women were right in the line of fire.

The adrenaline-pumped convicts arrived in the prison yard. They realized they must get up and over the walls or out the main gate. No one had appeared to stop them. They knew lad-ders were in the storage shed. Some carried them to the wall and climbed over, dropping to the ground on the other side. Thinking ahead, Roth grabbed a pick and an axe, figuring they can be used to help him break the ball and chains hindering his movement.

Still upstairs, Morton, Jones, Clifford and Thomas Ryan led others to the armory. They broke in. For their efforts they were rewarded with two Henry rifles, two boxes of rifle cartridges, four double barreled shotguns and several six-shooters. Jones and Morton each took a Henry and a box of cartridges. For good measure they both tucked pistols in their pants. Thomas Flynn grabbed a revolver and some bullets. The shotguns and other pistols were grabbed up.

Now armed with Henry rifles, Morton and Jones were very dangerous. They went downstairs to the prison's main door. It was open. They saw women screaming in the yard. They saw someone running toward the Warm Springs Hotel. Some convicts were making a run for the sagebrush. It was dusk and the blowing wind had noticeably cut the visibility. They decided to wait a few minutes before venturing out.

Knowing a third Henry rifle was unaccounted for, Ryan figured it was in the Warden's quarters. Leading a group of convicts, Ryan set out to get the weapon from Denver. He had no idea that it was out of service and in the warder's office, waiting for repairs. Ryan stopped when he saw Denver and Dedman at the top of the stairs. Clifford was right behind Ryan. With only his Derringer to defend himself, Denver pointed it at the convicts menacingly. The surge towards him didn't stop. He fired and hit Clifford point blank. The others fell back. Clifford clutched his stomach and saw his hands were covered with blood. Feeling weak and nauseous, he stumbled back down the stairs. He slumped to the floor at the base of the stairway and lay there in intense pain. The shock he was suffering brought him in and out of consciousness several times over the next few minutes.

Seeing Clifford go down, Ryan yelled for more men to assist him in getting the weapon from the warden. He urged them to rush the warden and Dedman. He wanted that extra Henry rifle. For some reason several convicts blindly followed his orders with disastrous results. Denver had retreated to his bedroom where he saw his wife and guest hiding in a corner. He grabbed a loaded revolver. Returning to the main room he saw Dedman had his hands full. The orderly broke an oak chair into kindling and was using the largest piece to throttle anyone that tried to come through the door. A striped body was laid out cold in the corner. Another was writhing in the hallway from a blow to his back. He turned and fled down the staircase. Dedman was an absolute terror, thrusting his busted oak leg like King Arthur's sword at anyone venturing near. His blows definitely took their toll. He had successfully knocked several prisoners down the stairs. All the while, bullets whistled around him. One crazed convict, with a huge knife, rushed at him three times. He was repelled each time. The last time, Dedman sent him over the stair rails head first. He landed heavily on the floor below. He didn't try again.

Seeing that no progress was being made, Ryan was furious. He wanted control of that third Henry rifle. He was adamant in his resolve. He figured they needed it to secure their freedom once they finally left the prison. He swore to those around him that Denver had it with him in his quarters.

"Throw down that Henry rifle, Warden," yelled Ryan up to Denver. "Quit being stupid and throw it down. When you do we'll leave. No harm will come to you."

Denver naturally heard this request. He knew the rifle wasn't with him. He thought he last saw it in the office. He couldn't meet Ryan's request even if he wanted to. But he figured if he could stall the prisoners, help will soon come from outside the prison.

"No," the warden replied.

"Shoot him, shoot the warden," Ryan screamed. "Shoot him and we can walk up and get the Henry."

Several shots were fired. It appeared to Ryan that Tom Heffron was hit, but the man stood his ground. Denver got hit in the hip and was thrown back. Though wounded and in immense pain, he somehow got up. He planted himself just inside the door and stared right at Ryan, revolver in hand.

"If you want the damn rifle, why don't you just come on

up and get it," chided the warden.

Realizing they had spent too much time in the pursuit of the gun or fearing the warden, Ryan and the others left. In addition to his bullet wound, Denver suffered wounds caused by two slung-shot blows to the head. His scalp wounds bled profusely. He most likely would have been killed if not for the assistance Dedman gave him. Dedman was covered with cuts, bruises and abrasions. He sat down on the floor, physically drained.

In Benton Hot Springs, Henry Devine toasted the upcoming wedding of his sister Sarah to Bob Morrison. The three were among several friends gathered together for the formal announcement of the wedding plans. George Hightower, his wife Martha, along with James McLaughlin and his wife Mary, were among the prominent citizens of Benton Hot Springs in attendance.

Morrison, a native of New York, came to nearby Owensville around 1863. He partnered with some other men in a couple of early mining adventures. He had since expanded his holdings and now owned the Benton General Store. The store specialized in general merchandise along with wines and liquor. The 34-year-old Morrison was assigned the responsibility of regional Wells

Fargo agent this past year.

Hightower, a native of Kentucky, was a 44 year-old blacksmith. He also served as the local sheriff. He and Martha, a New Yorker, had two youngsters: eight year old George Jr. and Sarah, just five. Hightower also had a saw mill just outside town.

The McLaughlins were ranchers in the nearby Antelope Valley. They were pleased to go on the outing as they didn't get to venture away from the duties at home very often. Jim was all smiles from the toast while Mary fondly remembered how happy she was when they were married. It seemed so long ago.

Henry and Sarah Devine were from Pennsylvania. Henry came west, as many young men did, to strike it rich. After toiling as a miner for several months, he sought a more stable existence. After meeting Morrison, he was able to put his skills as a salesman to good use.

He was now a clerk in his friend's store. Sarah kept house for her brother, a task she would soon be doing for Robert or Bob, as friends called him.

Robert Morrison

Her first glimpse of Bob took place several months ago soon after she arrived in Benton. She saw a fine figure of a man at a distance on the steps in front of the General Store. She met him later in the week.

Henry had given her a list and asked her to run to the store for him. As Sarah entered the store suddenly there he was. He was writing down an order for an older woman at the counter. The lady had chosen a selection of mail order household goods offered by FA Walker and Co. This tall handsome man was soft spoken and appeared gentle. She liked that he appeared taller than she. She guessed about 5'11" and 160. Bob was well put together. Sarah decided to look through some of the order books on hand while she waited her turn. She saw stoves offered by Rathbone and Kennedy as well as Potter and Co. The Singer Sewing Machine catalogue interested her too. She was looking through the Christmas presents offered in the James P. Walke book.

Suddenly, she realized his attention had shifted to her. She

Sarah Devine

nearly melted when she looked up into his deep blue eyes.

"Good morning young lady. May I help you?"

She barely heard him speak. Sarah looked down and stumbled for words. She blushed a bright pink. Bob felt his pulse quicken. He was equally taken with her.

"I need to buy a few things," she blurted.

"Well you came to the right place," he said teasing her, "we actually sell a few things."

They both laughed and exchanged introductions. Their bond grew steadily every day. She was so proud of the man that would soon be her husband. They planned to have a big family. She loved children. She already had names picked out. Robert, of course, was her choice for the first boy.

She was currently looking forward to her upcoming trip next week. She was going to take the stage to Los Angeles for a visit with her relatives from Pennsylvania.

She was excited about her planned marriage to Bob, which would take place shortly after she returned near the end of the month. There was so much to do.

Chapter Seven
Murderous Gun Battle at the Prison

Back at the prison, one clever convict, John Watson, was formulating a plan. While all the commotion was going on outside in the yard, he was busy inside the prison. He found tools to cut off his irons. Cool as a cucumber, Watson was undoubtedly the shrewdest inmate in the prison. Freed from his shackles, he calmly went back to the dining room. He realized once he left, it may be quite some time before he could find provisions. Why not gather up whatever he could here, before he split?

John Watson

A glance around the room helped him locate a large flour sack. He went from table to table like a shopper in a general store. A lot of food remained from the evening meal. He soon had a full load.

In his head, a chess game was going on. He sat down at a table in the hall for a moment. He needed to out-think his opponent. So he considered his next move. Watson had always been pretty much a loner. He found out early on that if he didn't count on other people, they couldn't let him down.

But now, he figured he needed some companionship. But whomever he selected would have to fit into his grand plan. That plan was basically to get the hell out of there and never see the inside of a prison again. He quickly ran down in his mind who was available and how they might help him succeed.

He decided upon Daniel Baker and another man he only knew by the name of Jacks. Why these guys? Well, Baker told

54

him he had hidden $2,500 in gold dust in Skull, a place not far from Tacoma. Jacks, on the other hand, would be his map since he was well acquainted with the country eastward to Utah. Anyone looking into Watson's brain would see a pretty good plan being put into operation. He shouldered his sack and carefully set out to find Baker and Jacks.

Meanwhile, thinking he had a mortal wound, Clifford returned to the base of the stairway. He called out to Dedman.

"Bob, help me. I'm dying for sure. Please give me some water. I give up. Someone help me."

There was no answer.

"The others will kill me. Please come help me hide."

Again no answer. All he heard were the screams and the gun fire from the yard. He sat with his back against the wall waiting to pass out from his blood loss. Soon it became apparent to Clifford that he was not in imminent danger of dying. As a matter of fact, he felt his strength returning. His wound was no longer bleeding. He checked himself very closely. As he raised the cloth he had been holding on the injury he was very pleased to see that the bullet simply took a big hunk of his skin off as it racked across his stomach. He now knew he would recover in a few days. His entire mood changed. No longer wishing to give himself up, he was now intent on getting outside and a long ways away.

When the screaming ladies from the warden's dinner party entered the yard, they soon saw madly dashing convicts moving all about them. Naturally, this frightened them all the more and their already piercing screams intensified.

Guard Ed Langlois was relaxing on his day off when he heard screams coming from the prison yard. Muffled sounds of pop, pop, pop came to him as well. He stepped into his quarters where he grabbed his rifle and six shooter. He filled his pockets with cartridges. He stepped out of his quarters and ran into the yard. Langlois, a native of France, considered himself very lucky to be in Nevada. He was known as a brave man and his actions over the next 15 minutes would attest to that reputation.

Another off duty guard, F.M. Isaacs, saw Langlois in the fight. Not having his own weapon and knowing it would be very dangerous to try and get it, he ran up behind him and asked for a weapon so he could join the fight. He backed about 30 paces from the guard room window. Inside, he saw several prisoners trying to break out. It was hard to recognize them. Two stood on the front porch firing at anything that didn't look like a convict. He couldn't quite tell because it was nearly dark, but thought one was Charlie Jones. The other could be Thomas Flynn. The 38-year-old Isaacs used to live and work in Virginia City. He'd been a miner at the Yellow Jacket. When he got married last year, his wife insisted he find a safer occupation. They were very happy with his job at the prison. He was a good man and loved his wife plus the two kids she brought to the marriage. He fought bravely this hour. His shots were very effective. Close by Langlois, after reloading and firing several times, ran out of bullets. For some reason he grabbed a club and ran into the midst of the fleeing convicts.

When all hell broke loose, Carson City citizen Henry Phillips was at the prison. Fearing for his life, he quickly ran to his buggy. In a hail of gunfire, Phillips put the whip to his horse and sped to town to sound the alert. Miraculously, neither he nor his horse were scathed.

Nearby, Matt Pixley and his wife were just finishing their supper at the Warm Springs Hotel, where Matt was the proprietor. Although adjacent to the prison, the hotel was in a very quiet, peaceful setting. So they were naturally astounded to hear a tremendous commotion in the courtyard, along with terrible, frightening screams. Pixley told his wife to lock herself in their bedroom. He'd go see what was happening. He quickly peered through the window and was amazed to see convicts scurrying about the courtyard. Even more amazing was the sight of the warden's daughter, Jennie, standing there screaming. He immediately realized an escape attempt was underway. Running across his living room, he grabbed two pistols from the bureau drawer.

"Damn," he thought, "why don't I keep these loaded?"

He emptied a box of cartridges on the table and quickly loaded each one. He headed towards the front door knowing he had to rescue those women. He was a very brave man. His timing could not have been worse.

He exited the door and stood on the porch trying to determine his next move. Still inside the prison, Charles Jones shattered a window with his rifle barrel. In the fading light, he saw a man with pistols in each hand on the Warm Springs Hotel porch.

"That just won't do," Charlie thought.

He raised his weapon and sighted on Pixley. Thomas Flynn had already exited the prison and likewise saw someone on the hotel porch with pistols in hand. This was a threat to himself and others. He made sure a cartridge was in the chamber and sighted in on Pixley as well. Two shots rang out. A bullet caught Pixley just below the left eye, knocking him back into the hotel wall, killing him instantly. No one ever knew for sure whether Jones or Flynn fired the fatal shot. It really didn't matter; a brave young man lay dead on the hotel steps. It was reported that the grief displayed by his young wife at seeing his lifeless body was "heart rending." Jones chambered another round as did Flynn. The peaceful early evening surrounding the prison had been entirely disrupted.

Off duty guards dropped what they were doing and came to join the fight. It was amazing that there were still women standing and screaming in the middle of this battle. C.W. Burgesser, "Bergie" to his friends, the Warm Springs Hotel bartender, heard the gun shots. The 22-year-old Maryland native headed to the window to see what was going on. He was sickened by the sight of Pixley dead on the porch. He grabbed the double barrel shotgun along with a box of shells from beneath the bar and entered the fight. Matt had been his friend. Burgesser was immediately grazed in each ear by two errant shots. He fought on. A third shot tore into the crotch of his pantaloons, ripping away the whole seat of his pants as well as his drawers. Drafty, but undaunted, he continued to battle back.

Convict Ed Goyette didn't know what to do. He'd been sent up for "inflicting great bodily harm." This crime took place in Virginia City not long ago. He figured what he did was in self defense and it most likely would have been judged that, except for the extreme state of excitement in Virginia City at the time of the trial. Thus instead of going free, he went to state prison. He hated it here, as they all did. He considered the dilemma before him.

"Do I take advantage of this turmoil and slip out of here? Or do I lay low and stay here?"

In the midst of this thought he saw the Warden's daughter Jennie. The little girl was holding her hands over her face as if to shelter her from all that was happening. Bullets were flying everywhere. Fate took over. Goyette ran to the child and swept her up in his arms. Upstairs in her quarters Mrs. Denver was watching all this unfold. She was terribly frightened for her daughter. Petrified in place, she saw a convict run over and snatch up Jennie. She

was afraid he would kill her. But, instead the man carried Jennie to a safe place. She then saw Ed return to the danger zone where he grabbed the arm of a woman visitor and led her to safety too.

Unfortunately for Isaacs, the return fire was brutal. He had taken refuge behind a wagon but was hit anyway. The projectile entered his right knee. It broke as the ball torn through the knee bone, exited the leg and ended up embedded behind his left knee cap. Wincing in pain, and balancing his weight on his left leg, he

58

fired off two more rounds. An ominous "click" told him it was time to reload. Hopping on his left leg towards cover to reload, he was hit in the left thigh. The force of the shot whirled him around. He lost his balance and slammed into the dirt. He was now out of the skirmish. As he laid on the ground, clutching his damaged knee and writhing in agony, other bullets kicked up dust all around him.

"Bergie" saw Isaacs go down. He knew the man would not survive in the open. He rushed over to the fallen guard to render assistance. Goyette also saw Isaacs' situation was extremely dangerous. He cautiously worked his way over to help the bartender drag the wounded man to cover. Once Isaacs was out of harms way, "Bergie" noticed the man helping him was a convict.

"Thanks for the help," he said to Goyette, looking him straight in the eye, and asked "What are you gonna do now?"

"I was tryin to escape, but this is crazy. I'm gonna walk back in there and someday leave a free man."

"Best you come with me. I'll lock you up in the hotel. One of your fellow guests might have seen you help. They could do you harm. I'll tell the Warden that you were not trying to escape and needed protection."

In the yard below, Russell saw a figure in the upstairs window. He aimed his pistol at the person and fired off a shot.

The bullet whisked just between the heads of Mrs. Denver and a gentleman dinner guest. They immediately dropped to their knees to get out of the line of fire. Seeing the figure disappear so quickly, Russell figured his shot found its mark.

Guard Johnny Newhouse heard all the noise and was happy to join the gun battle with no regard for his own safety. He lived

William Russell

59

in Gold Hill, not far from Virginia City. With a pistol in each hand, he was really having a great time. He took aim at a striped figure trying to escape across the yard. The man was Parsons, one of the train robbers. Parsons grimaced in pain as he was hit by a volley from Newhouse. He fell down, but was able to crawl to the safety of some nearby cover. Newhouse rose up to fire again and was hit both in his shoulder and the back of the head. The force of the slugs knocked him off his feet. On the ground and losing consciousness, he was no longer a threat to the escapees.

Hanging around outside the prison, Joseph Parasich, another guard, could not help but hear the gun fire erupting and the screaming coming from inside. Joe ran across to the Warm Springs Hotel. He searched around for a weapon. He located a revolver and a box of cartridges. He quickly loaded it. He stuck more bullets in his pockets. He ducked out the hotel and entered the yard with his gun blazing. He could see the results of his shots taking place. Suddenly he was sickened as he felt a hot burning sensation from a ball hitting him in the groin. The bullet traveled some distance in fleshy tissue and lodged between his femur and nearby artery. Luckily it didn't hit the artery. His wound was very bad. He writhed in agony near the prison door. Like Isaacs and Newhouse, he no longer posed a danger to the convicts.

Langlois, the brave Frenchman, along with "Bergie," were the only deterrents remaining. Neither had any ammunition left. Langlois had been grazed by so many balls that his clothing had been cut to shreds. Realizing their fight was futile, they entered the prison to see what assistance they could render there.

Jones, the barrel of his Henry rifle hot to the touch, rested the gun on his shoulder. Behind him, Morton and Black noticed the absence of hostile gun fire. It was apparent to these murderous men that there was no one left to stop them from simply walking out. Many of the other prisoners had no stomach for the killing and fighting that had been taking place. They had kept safe in the cover of the prison until seeing it was prudent to leave.

Now they left their cover from behind the doors and windows of the prison. Some were carrying their ball and leg irons to make better progress. Others had worked themselves free from their bonds. Puddles of blood were soaking into the dirt. Bits of gore had landed everywhere. The yard looked like a battlefield. As they worked their way through the yard toward freedom beyond, they saw the dead and badly wounded lying in the dirt, suffering from their injuries. They too realized that there was no one left to stop them from walking right out into the darkness.

Jones had managed to remove his irons. As he shuffled along outside the prison, he casually glanced down at Pixley. He smiled for a moment and thought "better him than me!" Charlie saw Newhouse and Isaacs badly wounded. Hell, he was a compassionate man. He didn't like seeing these men in their present condition. Pruitt, the lone black man in the prison, watched from across the yard, as Jones walked over to Newhouse. He couldn't believe it when Jones pointed the muzzle of the rifle at the wounded man's head. With his finger on the hammer, he moved it back so it was ready to fire. Pruitt wanted to yell or something, but he was simply in shock that a man would do such a thing. Jones was about to put Newhouse out of his misery. To Pruitt's relief, another convict grabbed the barrel and moved it away from the man's head.

"That man fought bravely. If his wounds kill him, that's one thing, but to shoot him like a dog is wrong. Besides, you might need the ammunition later today or tomorrow."

Prone on the ground Newhouse barely understood what had just transpired. Fate had stepped in and neither he nor Isaacs would be assassinated tonight. Pruitt shook his head,

"Man, what is wrong with that white boy," he muttered to no one in particular?

Not far behind Jones came Watson, Jacks and Baker. Holding his stomach wound, Clifford was exiting the prison with Morton, Black, Roberts and Chapman. Ingram, Bigelow, Russell, Ryan, McCue and Hurley had already made it well past the prison boundaries. Cockerell, Burke, Willis, Squires, Roth, Pruitt and Lynch were not far behind. Thomas Carter, wounded during the fight, was struggling along. The wounded Parsons was moving slowly too. Blair and Lynch shouldered Carter to help him make his getaway. Forrest helped Parsons. Heffron was holding a bloody hand over his chest and slowly walked behind.

Daniel Taylor was lying just inside the prison door. Try as he might, he could not muster the courage necessary to break through the pain required for him to move his legs. Tears from the frustration of being left behind, not the pain, rolled from his eyes. They moved along his cheek, finally dripping into a pool of the man's blood on the floor.

Bernard Cosgrove was another prisoner that was injured during the initial moments as the escape attempt unfolded. Now he was back in custody and going nowhere.

Smiling Jack Davis had watched the action as it took place from a prison window. Once considered by his peers to be the man to lead this jailbreak, Davis now decided to render assistance to those that had been hurt during the past half hour. He was familiar with treating gunshot wounds and other injuries. He quickly moved from one incapacitated man to another. He made suggestions and helped to bandage a wounded man here and there. Together with other prisoners, guards and anyone else available, he helped move the injured men inside from the yard to the Warm Springs Hotel. Davis was actually moved to tears as he saw Pixely's wife kneeling next to her dead husband. Once he had done all he could, he returned to the prison to see what would happen next. Jack sat down in the main dining area along with the balance of the convicts that didn't try to escape. These men knew the magnitude of what had just transpired. Davis felt he had made a good decision. The cash, gold and silver he had hidden in Six Mile Canyon would still be there for the taking when he got out in a couple years.

About this time, Phillips' buggy was flying down Main Street in Carson City as he yelled at the top of his lungs about the prison break. The curious ran behind the buggy while Phillips rounded the corner and sought out Sheriff Swift. Hearing the news, he asked for able-bodied men to join him in riding to the prison. Swift was successful in rounding up 15 armed men. The posse saddled up and rode at a fast pace to the prison.

Naturally, they were too late to render any assistance. The sheriff ordered his men to fan out to check the yard and surrounding terrain. They found evidence of leg irons, but little else. While some of the men helped tend to the wounded, Swift assigned the rest to secure the prisoners that didn't or couldn't leave.

Meanwhile back in Carson City, Phillips asked the stable boy to tend to his weary horse. Phillips himself, tired and shaken, ran down the boardwalk to alert Doctors Simeon Lee and John Waters that there were severely wounded men at the prison. Upon hearing this news, Dr. Lee added several necessary items to his bag, while his son readied his horse and buggy. Soon Lee was racing toward the prison.

Dr. Waters had been getting ready for bed, but now instead was preparing a place to tend to the patients that would surely be forthcoming this night. He asked his wife to put on a big pot of coffee and boil some water so he could sterilize his instruments. She stoked the wood stove. It was going to be a long night.

Simeon Lee

Chapter Eight
Marching Along to the Carson River

Twenty-one former residents of the Nevada State Prison smiled wearily as they trudged away from that horrible place. The escapees kept together at first. There was strength in numbers. Each knew they needed to get as far away as possible as soon as possible. Several men had busted out of their shackles at the outset of the break. Now a few of them stopped for a short while to use the pick and axe that was carried away from the prison shed to remove their leg irons.

They headed due east away from the Nevada State Prison for about two miles. For awhile the men traveled along the high ridge. The wind was howling. The night was dark and it was getting cold. Even the wounded knew they couldn't stop.

Terrain convicts trudged through in the dark

Only Carter's wounds seemed to be really serious. He was helped along on the shoulders of two others. It was a painful trek for Clifford and Parsons as well. Soon the body of men turned to the right so they would reach the Carson River. Not all moved at the same speed. The string of men fanned out somewhat. A couple had lost their footwear in the fight. These men weren't used to walking very far anywhere, much less barefoot. Now they were walking over the rocky high desert terrain. The sagebrush scraped their prison clothes. The loose sand was unstable, making walking difficult. Their pace was slow.

⋙ ⋙ ⋙

While the trek towards the Carson River to the east was underway, two convicts, William Forrest and Chris Blair, decided to stop and lie low in the sagebrush. Forrest, a 22-year-old native of England was pretty smart.

He suggested they take a position about 100 yards from the prison gates.

They listened with great interest to the talk coming from the prison. It said all the convicts headed east.

Chris Blair

William Forrest

The early word was these felons would be trying their best to get to Arizona and Mexico. This was the information Blair needed to make plans regarding their escape route. These men decided upon working their way southwest toward Carson City.

When the lawmen came, and come they surely will, they would most likely head due east toward the river. These two planned to go directly where those that would be hunting them wouldn't think they would go. They would quietly move around the southern section of town. From there, they'd head toward Genoa and then over the Sierra to disappear in California.

֎֎֎

As the main body of men continued to move away from the prison towards the River, Marion Pruitt looked for an alternative route. He was the lone black man in the group.

"How can I get away from these others?"

Marion had nothing in common with any of them. There was nary a friend in this bunch. He had been serving time for burglary. He had four more years to go, but not now. The 21-year-old, Missouri native was jubilant. He was a free man. He heard others talk about him.

"They consider me as ignorant as a donkey," he thought to himself.

He didn't care what people

Marion Pruitt

thought. He was a lot smarter than they knew. He was an impressive black man at 5' 7" and 185, with huge muscles. He loved a good game of poker and loose women.

Marion could easily intimidate most folks, white or black, without much trouble. However his friends knew him as a kind, gentle man with a good sense of humor. Most of those friends were in Genoa. There was a good sized black community there. And that was where he decided to head tonight.

He quietly split off from the others near the Mexican ditch. He purposely left a trail heading north that was easy to follow. Then he stopped and began to carefully cover his tracks. Afterwards he headed south and west.

"Let all those white folks think I'm just a moke."

With any luck, he'd be in Genoa in a day or two. He knew a feisty woman there that was always mighty pleased to see him.

Early Empire Nevada

Five other escapees had a goal in mind before they left. They were going to head almost due north. Therefore they carefully worked their way toward the railroad line that ran between Empire and Carson City. It was only about a mile to the tracks. But the going was slow.

The wind was blowing and it was very dark. Now and then they had to lay low while a rider or two crossed their path. However, before 10 o'clock they had crossed the tracks and felt pretty good about their chances to remain free. They planned to bed down in the sagebrush for the night.

However, no matter whose party in which the escapees were traveling, each man was very cautious. No one wanted to go back to that miserable place again!

James and Mary had made their excuses to Bob and Sarah. The couple had known Morrison a long time and they liked Sarah from the start. They were very happy for them. They thanked Henry for his kind invitation and were now in the buckboard moving along at a steady trot along the dusty road to the ranch.

Mrs. Denver was torn between consoling Jennie and seeing if she could help with her husband's wounds. This had been the worse evening of her life. She had recently told her mother how safe it was at their home at the prison. Tonight her mother saw first hand how things could change in an instant.

∽ ∽ ∽

Sarah removed her shoes, gown and petticoat, exchanging them for her comfortable sleeping gown. She completed her toilet and settled back in her soft bed. She could not help but think that soon she'd be sharing her bed with Bob.

∽ ∽ ∽

Flynn, Hurley and Ryan left the prison together. They were part of the main body of men. Ryan was feeling the effects of his unsuccessful try to get the Henry rifle he thought was in Warden Denver's residence. His stomach was also giving him fits.

"What the hell did I eat?"

He stopped and sat down. The two others saw him sink to the ground. He saw their looks.

Thomas Flynn

"I'm sorry, but I can't go any further right now. I need to rest. I'll be just fine. Hurry and catch up with the others."

"Well don't hang around here for very long," said Hurley, 'there's bound to be somebody close on our trail."

"I'll be okay, get goin."

Flynn looked at him for a moment. He could care less whether Ryan continued or not. He said nothing and walked off to catch up with the others.

Hurley was close behind. After the two men walked away,

Pat Hurley

68

Ryan figured how to make his stay more secure. So he managed all the strength he left and stood up. He grabbed the closest hunk of sagebrush he could find and broke off a piece. He pressed it hard against the high desert sand and walked backwards in a zig-zag pattern for nearly 50 yards. He dropped back down from sheer exhaustion. He figured he had covered his tracks. Anyone following the main body would simply continue along the trail of the men ahead.

Thomas Ryan

ﷺ ﷺ ﷺ

Upon reaching the Carson River, the main party had thinned to 20. Some were exhausted. Others were in good shape and hardly fazed by this walk in the dark. The wind had died down, but still lingered. It was dark. It was a beautiful night. The stars twinkled brightly above. Most of them didn't notice. A few were on edge. Their nerves were frayed. Some sat down on the river bank to rest momentarily. Their feet and legs were weary. Those without proper shoes were really in poor shape.

The water was cold. It tasted good. Parsons and Carter used the water to help in washing their wounds. Parson's injuries were fairly minor. Not so for Carter. He was not sure how much further he would be able to travel. Many of them had some minor bruising as well as miscellaneous cuts and scratches.

None of these were of any real consequence. So far these men had just blindly headed to the river in a rush. At this point no one had stepped up as a real leader and assumed command. After all his crying and whining thinking he was mortally shot by Denver, Clifford's wound proved to be rather minor.

"For awhile, I thought I was dead for sure."

Now, however, his instincts had kicked in. He was weighing his options while washing off crusted blood. He knew he would be just fine. He had broken out of many jails. Getting out was the easy part. Staying out was the hard part. Like those around him, Frank had no intention of getting caught again.

"Hey, we can't stay here much longer," he said to the body of men. "After that battle back there, somebody's gonna be coming our way. Soon this whole river will be crawling with people looking to cash in on us. I think we need to head for the Mexican dam. It's not too far upstream from here."

The group rose up and headed south up the river. It was around 9:30 pm when they approached the cabin at what was called the Mexican dam. It was quiet, but the escapees were very weary. Clifford and Jones huddled together for a moment. Then Clifford stood up.

"I need three men to go up and see who's at the cabin."

"I'm game," said Burke

"Me too," Flynn said.

"I'm with ya," said Squires.

"Give a whistle when the coast is clear," said Clifford.

The three men went ahead to make sure it was safe for the rest. Seeing a light in the window, the scouts quietly crept toward the cabin. Suddenly a dog barked a warning. The men froze. The cabin door swung open and a tall man peered outside. The hound continued his barking.

"Quit that barkin, dog," yelled the figure in the doorway.

The big hound, his tail wagging away, stopped as commanded to do so by his master. The man walked outside. The scouts saw he was unarmed.

"Anyone out here," inquired the man?

"Good evening there partner, no need to be concerned, we don't mean you any harm," Burke called to the man.

A shrill whistle brought the other men to the cabin. It was home to a blacksmith that made his living tending to the needs of the local ranchers and teamsters. Six of the convicts had not yet been able to get out of their chains.

"Obviously, we're in a lot of trouble," said Clifford. "These men need their irons off. I need you to get that done."

"I reckon I can get that done," said the big man. "Follow me on down to the shop."

The blacksmith was followed to his shop by the six men still shackled. Some of the others sat and rested. A couple entered the cabin to see what they might be able to use. At the shop, the big fella opened a large tool box and gathered up his chisel and a small sledge hammer. He pointed to his anvil.

"Here," he said to young Roberts, the first man in line, "put you wrist up there."

The boy nervously followed his instruction. The blacksmith turned a chain link to the position he wanted. His huge muscles bulged and a single swing of the hammer split the chain link. The boy pulled his arm free and rubbed his sore wrist. He was pleased.

Bedford Roberts

"Thanks mister," said Roberts.

"No problem son. All right, who's next?"

In less than 20 minutes, the men were free. Fortunately for Carter, the blacksmith was a very compassionate man. He saw the severely injured convict resting on his porch.

"Let me look at that."

He inspected the wound in Tom Carter's leg. He could tell that a ball was still lodged in there. He knew that things would be much worse if it was not removed soon.

"If you can hold still for a few minutes I can get that ball out. It's going to cause a bad infection by staying in there."

"Do what you can, I don't

Thomas Carter

71

want to lose it."

"Bring him in the cabin and put him on the table," instructed the blacksmith.

Two men gathered Carter up and carried him into the cabin. They carefully put him on the man's table. The blacksmith had removed all kinds of things from man and beast over the years. His basic medical instrument was his pocket knife. He opened the knife and heated the blade over his oil lamp.

"Okay, this is gonna hurt him. I need four of you to hold him still for a minute or two."

Carter's arms and legs were held firmly in place. The blacksmith poured some whiskey on the wound and set the bottle down. Hurley quickly picked it up, took a swig and passed it around the room. The blacksmith probed the entry point. For a person his size, thought Clifford as he looked on, he was surprisingly gentle. The ball was found and removed. A poker from the wood stove was used to cauterize the wound. Carter winced in pain. The makeshift doctor applied a salve to the wound and dressed it with a piece of bed sheet.

"Hey doc," someone piped up, "what is that stuff?"

"Well I don't rightly know, but it works well on the horses I've doctored. It sure won't hurt the guy."

Carter was lucky to have made it this far. He was in no shape to travel further for a few days.

"Thanks for getting that thing out of my leg," Carter said. "I don't think I can walk on it. Let me stay here for a couple days. I can rest and then be on my way."

"This is the first place a posse is going to come hunting for the bunch of you," said the blacksmith. "Besides there's a number of folks that stop by each day. It would be impossible for me to hide you. As a matter of fact, you should leave here now."

"The big man's right," said Clifford to no one in particular. Turning his gaze to the blacksmith he said, "you tell any one lookin for us that we forced you to help.

It was around midnight when the 20 men rose up as a unit and slowly disappeared into the night. Being a man of meager means, the blacksmith was not pleased as the men took all the provisions he had. But he was very relieved after they left.

"Well old boy," he said looking at his dog, "might as well get some sleep. There's nothing we can do about it."

It was his desire to get along with everyone and to date he had succeeded. He felt no animosity towards any of those men. Damn, if not for a little luck a couple times during these past 10 years here in Nevada, he knew he might have been locked up there too.

Chapter Nine
Going Their Separate Ways

Jake Blount, a resident of Lake Valley, had always been a civic minded individual. Tonight he was in Carson City having a few drinks and playing cards with friends. When Phillips sounded the alarm, his card playing buddies mounted up and left with Sheriff Swift. Jake was older and didn't feel he could be of much help chasing after outlaws. However, when someone was needed to sound the alarm in Genoa, he shouted right out.

"I'll go."

Thus he volunteered to ride to the nearby town to warn the citizens about the escapees. It was around 9:30 pm when he stepped up to his horse. He checked his cinch and tightened it. Raising his boot to the stirrup, he swung onto his saddle. He reined his mount around and gently spurred his horse into a trot. He noticed the night air had cooled considerably. Just outside Carson City, Jake stopped for a moment, took his slicker off the saddle and put it on.

John Blount rides to warn the residents of Genoa

Not far ahead, Blair and Forrest were carefully making their way toward Genoa with plans on stopping before long to get

74

some rest. Their legs were fatigued.

"Man, I'm about all out," Chris said to Bill. "I figure we traveled far enough tonight," he continued. "No one will be looking for us in this direction anyway."

These last words had barely left his mouth when they both heard the sounds of a rider coming toward them.

About two miles out of town, Blount noticed something ahead of him off to the right side of the road. Reining in his mount, he peered through the dark to see what this might be. Jake felt the hair rise on the back of his neck. Goose bumps popped up on his arms. Suddenly, two men appeared out of the dark. Blount's horse reared up. He was forced to stop. The men were wearing prison outfits. He thought he heard voices in the brush. Fearing for his life, he immediately wheeled his horse around. He crouched down low in the saddle to present a smaller target. Forrest cocked his six shooter and fired at the rider.

Blount felt the wind of a ball as it whizzed by his left ear. The Englishman took another shot, but the bullet ripped harmlessly through the man's slicker. He cocked the gun again, but moved the hammer back down. The man was out of pistol range. He realized he might need his ammunition later. No use in wasting it. Blount spurred his mount all the way back to Carson City.

"Well crap," cussed Chris, "I guess that pretty much changes our plans for getting some rest."

"He's gonna be back this way with help in about an hour," said Bill. "They won't be able to track us while it's still dark."

"I figure we can cut off right here and let them just ride on by. No one will figure we'd stay right here," suggested Chris.

Forrest nodded in agreement. He couldn't see anything wrong with Blair's plan. They hurried off the road into the dark.

◈ ◈ ◈

As the body of men left the Mexican Dam, Watson motioned to Baker and Jacks. They came over to him.

"It's time we leave the others," he said. "This large a group will be easy to follow. We need to cut off here alone. This increases our chances of getting away. What do you figure, Jacks?"

75

John Jacks

Jacks was chosen at the prison by Watson to be his "map." The man knew which way they should go to get to Tecoma. This little town was founded by the Central Pacific Railroad in 1869. It was near the Utah border in Elko County. There were but 60 or so residents in Tecoma. Although there were a few mines not far away, it simply served as a train maintenance and railroad shipping center. Skull, the place that Baker said he stashed away some gold, was close to this little community.

The 24-year-old Daniel Boone Baker had been arrested along with Morton and Taylor for robbing a train in 1870. With a name like that, he was obviously from Kentucky. Hardly like his name sake, he was only 5'6" tall and a bit stocky. His face peered out from a black beard and hair. Watson always chucked when seeing D.B.B. tattooed on Baker's left arm. Poor guy had his initials there so he could remember who he was!

Daniel Boone Baker

Jacks figured the best way to get to Tecoma without being caught would be to head to Belmont in Nye County.

"We need to set a course for the northeast and strike out in an easterly direction. This should get us to the Mason Valley area in a couple days."

"How far is that from Belmont?"

"Belmont is a couple days from the Mason Valley."

Jacks would lead them a little south of Belmont in Nye

County. There were a lot of folks in Belmont. The escape news would be known there due to the telegraph. Unless they could get hold of other clothes, they were going to stick out like sore thumbs. It would be best to avoid contact with anyone for as long as possible. After slipping around Belmont, they would head north and east in a fairly direct line to Tecoma. Jacks figured it should take them about a week to make their destination.

While Watson waited for Jacks to formulate their travel plans, he considered what he knew about the man. He said he was born and raised in Pennsylvania. Watson knew he was sent to prison from Nye County, but didn't know what he did to end up in jail. He considered the 29-year-old man to be expendable. But he needed him until they got to Tecoma. Being younger, six inches taller and several pounds heavier, Watson felt he could get the upper hand against him if it came to that. Watson also figured he can find a way to outwit Baker when they got their hands on his hidden treasure. Once he had it in his possession, he would be off to Salt Lake City to lay low for awhile.

He was brought back to the real world as he realized Jacks was explaining how they were going to get all the way to Tecoma safely. After hearing the plan, he figured it would work well enough. Watson and his group left along the Carson River.

"We need to keep traveling as long as it's still dark. When daylight comes, we can find a suitable place to hide and get some rest. It will be safer that way."

Ryan had spent four hours in the sagebrush, suffering from the ague. He had gone through a miserable period of chills and fever. He was sweating in the brisk night air. This 26-year-old Irishman was tough. He was not about to give up. He had been sitting there thinking how stupid he was at getting caught for something the courts called "grand larceny." That sure was a big phrase for him being a thief. His dad was a thief, his uncle was a thief and he used to be good at being a thief. He reminisced about the past two years in prison. He was feeling much better. He knew it was important to get further away from this place. He got up and headed into the darkness. Ryan had only walked a few yards when he noticed something in the sand. It was a body. Rolling the figure over he saw that it was Tom Heffron. The front of the man's prison uniform was covered in blood. Evidently he had been shot. He must have wandered off the trail and died right here. The Irishman said a silent prayer for the fallen man and walked away.

The blacksmith was right. After Sheriff Swift and his posse left for the prison, the Governor's office was alerted. With Governor Bradley away, his Private Secretary Charles Belknap sent a telegraph to Virginia City around 8 pm. The sporadic clicking of the equipment at the telegraph office awakened the night clerk. He adjusted his glasses and clicked back that he was ready to receive a message. His eyes widened as he received and deciphered the

Governor Bradley

message. It was addressed to General Batterman of the Virginia City Militia. It explained the magnitude of the escape and the possible threat to citizens throughout the general region. It requested immediate military assistance. The clerk quickly took down the information, hurriedly moved his pen towards the ink bottle, and accidentally knocked it over. Ink ran everywhere. He didn't care. The heavy-set man grabbed his coat and started running as fast as he could to deliver the message to Batterman.

It was unfortunate for the clerk that the General's house was on a hill overlooking much of the city.

Charles Belknap

78

Exercise in any form was rare to the clerk. To say he was racing up the hill to the General's house would be a great exaggeration. After the first two hills, his pace had slowed considerably. As he neared the General's house, his heart was pounding and his lungs felt as if they'd explode. He tried to yell out to the occupants, but his breath was way too busy to create any sounds, except for a loud puffing. He knocked heavily on the door.

The General was busy enjoying *The Celebrated Jumping Frog of Calaveras County*, a book written by his friend Samuel Clemens, now better known as Mark Twain. His wife was knitting some items for Christmas. Suddenly, they heard a thundering noise at the door. He arose and hurried to the entrance to see what all the commotion was about. His wife set her needles down and followed him to the door. As the door opened, they observed a large man making noises like the locomotive that ran from Carson City to Virginia City. The man was obviously trying to say something but couldn't. The man extended his arm and the General retrieved the paper from his hand. He unfolded the note and read it with care. It was pretty straightforward.

He looked at his wife and said, "there's been an escape at the State Prison."

He told the clerk to go to town and have the alarm rung to call out the militia. Then, the clerk was to go to the train station and alert the station master. A special train would be needed to carry the General and his troops to Carson City this very night.

The clerk departed down the hill. Batterman closed his door and asked his wife to set out his uniform. Removing his shirt and pantaloons, he moved across the room to where his wife had laid his uniform and put it on. As he was buckling his belt he heard the bells sounding the alarm. His militia men would be assembling shortly. He adjusted his hat and kissed his wife.

"Please be careful, I want you home safely."

She knew he had no idea of when he might return so she didn't inquire. After he left, he sat down and picked up her Bible. She closed her eyes and held the Good Book in her lap as she silently said a prayer asking for his safe return.

The station master was astounded when the clerk told him

of the escape. This was as horrifying news as when he heard the Piper Opera House was on fire. He walked to the caboose on the side track where he knew a conductor and his train crew were asleep. He quickly woke them up and explained the situation. The men realized the importance of their quick action. They got dressed. Sizing up the situation, the conductor ordered railroad cars that could accommodate about 30 saddled horses. The militia could ride in regular passenger cars. To the credit of his crew, the train was assembled and ready to go in about 30 minutes.

To the General's amazement, the train was loaded with his men, members of the both the National and Emmet's Guard along with all their provisions by 9 pm. What a feat! He boarded the passenger car at the end of the train. He saw Major General Von Bokkelen alongside Captain Richard Arnold. There was an open seat next to Lieutenant Lyman. He settled back on the hard wooden seat.

"Evening gentleman."

"Evening General," the men chorused.

"Well, Major, this will make for an interesting evening."

"That it should."

Batterman reached into his long coat to take out his pipe and tobacco pouch. He prepared a bowl and struck a match. He brought the flame to the top of the bowl and sucked air through the stem. After a couple quick puffs it was lit. He settled back in the seat to determine a course of action to use once they reached Carson City. The whistle sounded, the engineer pushed the throttle forward. The big wheels spun for a second and then grabbed hold of the rails. They were on their way. The special train arrived at the Carson City Station around 10 pm, just three short hours after the alarm was sounded by Secretary Belknap.

Major General Von Bokkelen

Chapter Ten
The Search for the Desperados

Russell, McCue, Ingram, Bigelow and McNamara were the five convicts that headed north across the railroad tracks that lead to Empire earlier in the night. William Russell was serving time for six years for a burglary committed in Stoney County a little over a year ago. He was a skinny 5'11." This 31-year-old Ohio native didn't look like a thief. He looked very intelligent. Working their way through the dark in the sagebrush was tough going. They crossed the Carson River.

The Carson River

"I don't know about you guys, but I'm bushed," said Russell. "Let's stop and rest for awhile."

The other men agreed. They were all dead tired. Russell laid down and fell asleep almost immediately. A couple of hours later, Russell rolled over and winced in pain as he put weight on his wrist. It was double its normal size from the hit it took when Squires missed Rollins' head and whacked him instead.

"I'm not sure that old bastard didn't break my damn arm," Russell thought to himself. "I wish I had some whiskey to drink to dull this pain a bit."

He noticed a fire had been started while he was asleep. It now glowed in the dark. As he wiped the sleep from his eyes, Russell saw some men on horseback silhouetted against the darkened sky quite a distance away. He quickly threw dirt on the fire, putting it out.

◆◆◆

When the main body of men, now numbering 17, left the Mexican Dam, they traveled down stream. About a half mile below the dam, they crossed the river. They moved away from the water and up a hill in an easterly direction. The men had covered another half mile when some stopped. Flynn looked around at the others. He was an Irishman by birth and was also known by the alias, Matt Rafferty. The 31-year-old was sent to the Nevada State Prison from White Pine County to serve five years for grand larceny and two more for attempted robbery. He soon broke out and committed another burglary in Washoe County. He was caught and received two additional sentences of nearly 17 years.

"Listen up. We need to start splitting into smaller parties to make it harder for any posse trying to track us," said Flynn. "They can't follow all of us."

Several others looked around. No one else said anything. Jones stared off into the night. Flynn and Lynch peeled off to the right and headed up the river. They took Carter with them.

"I'm heading over to Six Mile Canyon," said Squires. "Anyone with me?"

"I'm with ya, John," replied Hurley.

Squires took a look at the stars above. He got a bearing for the direction he wanted to take. He would head off to the left which would take him back down the river towards Dayton.

Willis looked at Hurley and Squires, then back at Jones. Jones looked menacing. He felt more secure following Squires.

Squire looked over at Jones.

"Give em hell Charlie," he said.

"You too John," replied Jones.

Willis trailed behind Hurley as they sought to catch up with Squires, who was several yards away and moving quickly.

The 10 remaining convicts stood there silently. This group was composed of Clifford, Parsons, Roth, Chapman, Burke, Jones, Morton, Black, Cockerell and Roberts. No one moved.

"All right," said Jones, assuming command, "let's get out of here."

William Willis

This band kept going straight. The route would take them through the Pine Nut range toward Pine Nut Valley. The mountains rose up to nearly 8,000 feet. The slopes were basically covered with a grand forest of Pine Nut trees, thus the name. This forest showed the signs of heavy logging operations. Clear cut areas easily stood out. The fallen lumber was used for firewood and to make charcoal. Lots of timber in this region had been taken in the past few years. This was due to the demands of the miners to cook and keep warm. It was also caused by the need for charcoal at the quartz mills. The loggers were methodically denuding the forest.

A few miles into the Pine Nut range, Morton stopped the party and turned to Jones.

"When the hell are we gonna turn and head straight toward Bishop Creek," he demanded?

Back in prison, Charlie had shared letters with Lea from a Mrs. Hutchinson, who lived in Bishop Creek. Jones had told Morton they would be able to get help from this kind lady and other friends he had in Inyo County once they got there.

Jones looked around the group of men in the party. He didn't like the way Morton just brought up the current topic of discussion. The last thing he wanted was for these other men to know anything about what he had in mind. Realizing he had to answer Morton's question, Jones purposely said,

"I'm pretty sure we're close to the turn off point."

The "pretty sure" comment got the response he wanted from several men in the group gathered around him.

"Hell," Roth cursed, "Bishop Creek's a long ways off?"

Parsons popped off with, "Charlie, if you're not sure, I'm not going that way. I can't afford to get caught!"

Several others uttered in agreement.

"I don't care who comes along," Jones sneered at them. "If most of you were shot dead last night, it wouldn't bother me."

Hearing the retort, Parsons and Roth looked at each other in utter amazement. Chapman mumbled something to Clifford.

"Lighten up Charlie," said Morton. "We're all in this together."

"I wasn't talking about you Lea," Jones replied looking at Morton. "I know I can count on you. You were blazing away back there at the prison. Others were too. But I don't recall seeing any of these guys until the gun fire stopped."

Parsons and Clifford took great offense at this comment. Roth was standing apart with Roberts. Clifford turned towards Charlie and said:

"Sorry ya feel that way Charlie. I got myself shot and Parsons, here, was wounded too. I'm not sure you know what you're talking about. But hey, no hard feelings. I wish you luck."

With that said he turned and addressed the others.

"A friend of mine runs cattle not too far from here. We could be there in a couple days or so. It's a hell of a lot closer than Bishop Creek. Anyone that wants to come with me is welcome."

"I'm with you Frank," mumbled Roth.

"Me too," said Parsons.

"Count me in," Chapman said.

No one else said a word. With that Clifford started off into the darkness. Chapman, Parsons, Roth and Roberts turned and followed him.

At this point "The Jones Gang" included Morton, Cockerell, Black and Burke. As young Roberts moved away with Clifford's bunch, Cockerell yelled after him.

"Hey, Bedford, don't go along with that bunch. Charlie's got a great plan. Get back here!"

Tilden Cockerell

He tried to run and catch up to the boy. This was no easy feat. He had been barefoot since the escape. Naturally, his feet were nearly raw. Roberts heard him. He slowed up and waited. Tilden Cockerell was a very good friend of Roberts' dad Chat. Chat took part in the infamous train robbery in 1870 with Cockerell, for which Tilden was doing a 22-year stretch. Chat had gotten off by telling the court what he knew of the event. Tilden had spent a lot of time at Chat Roberts' Antelope Stage Hotel nestled in Long Valley over in Lassen County, California.

He had known young Roberts from the time he was a mere lad. Tilden knew the young man very well. On his periodic visits to the hotel, he would bring the boy candy and gifts. He kind of looked on the kid as a "pet." He liked having him around. As he was growing up, the boy looked up to Cockerell. He knew the boy looked forward to robbing stages and other exciting adventures of which Tilden spoke. At 38, Cockerell was amongst the oldest of the escapees. He had come west from his native Illinois several years ago. Up until that train robbery, he had been a very successful highway man. He was tall at 5'10" and still solid at 175. He was considered a man of great physical strength. He was also smart. His good looks turned the head of many young ladies over the years. He imagined he was still quite charming to the ladies.

Roberts didn't need much persuasion. He never did. He rarely did any original thinking. Cockerell's influence had definitely left his mark on him. As a matter of fact, his stay in prison was a result of Cockerell's teachings. He was serving 10 years for robbing a stagecoach this past January. He was just 17 when he and Charles Beaver, a really unfortunate boy who was even younger, stopped a coach near Susanville in Lassen County. After demanding the driver throw down his shotgun, Beaver kept a shaky six shooter on the coach. Roberts dismounted to take whatever he could get from the passengers. Opening the door of the coach, he first took $93 in coin from a passenger named Walter Thomas. As the heist unfolded, the driver correctly read the characters behind the masks as inexperienced highway men.

While the outlaws were busy with their quarry, the driver slowly and carefully reached for the concealed Derringer located in his breast pocket. Fingering the tiny gun, in one quick motion he drew, cocked and fired. The shot hit young Charles, knocking him off his mount. The gunfire spooked both horses. They ran off into the darkness.

While the driver reloaded, Roberts fled the scene. His gravely wounded accomplice was left to die in the sagebrush or be captured. The horses hadn't run far. Roberts retrieved his mount about 50 yards from the coach. It was then he realized that during the excitement he'd dropped the stolen loot. Stepping aboard his horse, he gathered up the reins of his companion's mount and went home.

Beaver survived and turned on his former partner in crime. Roberts was arrested. Imagine his surprise when he learned during his trial that an Army Major inside the coach had a $7,000 payroll on him that went unnoticed! Now 18 years old, the thin, 5'7" young man was an escaped convict.

He mulled over what Tilden had been saying. He really didn't have any idea of what he was going to do in the future anyway. Why not tie in with a guy that seemed to have a plan and knew what he was doing? He turned around and walked with his mentor back to join the Jones' gang.

The special train carrying General Batterman's Militia, the National Guard and Emmet's Guard sounded it's whistle about a half mile out of town. A large group of citizens gathered around to watch the train pull in.

The event at the nearby prison had gotten everyone's attention. Rumors flew that gangs of convicts were descending upon the town. A wholesale pillaging was expected. Men feared for their lives. Women feared for their virtue. Merchants were concerned their shelves would be emptied and their town burned. It stood to reason these people were relieved as the train packed with military personnel slowed to a stop at the Carson City Station around 10 pm. While Major General Von Bokkelen and Batterman conferred to formulate a battle plan, their officers saw to the unloading of the men, horses and provisions.

Around half past midnight, 11 mounted guardsmen started south under the leadership of National Guard Lieutenant Lyman. They were accompanied by Gold Hill Constable Thomas Harkin. General Batterman himself, with 13 of his mounted men, left shortly thereafter at 12:55. Several local citizens offered their services to help capture the escapees. They accompanied the General's detachment. His mounted column headed out in the same direction as Lyman's group. General Batterman had left orders requesting that most of the Emmet Guard ride to the state prison. This detachment would make sure the rest of the prisoners were well guarded until daylight. The balance of this group would remain in Carson City and help patrol the streets. No one knew for sure if the town would actually be attacked by the very men that they were trying to capture!

When Blount returned in Carson City around 10:30 pm, he quickly rode to the Sheriff's Office. It was locked. There were no lights on inside. He pounded on the door. There was no answer.

He realized no one was there. He knew Sheriff Swift was away on the hunt. Frustrated, he wondered where he could find the town deputy. He saw lights a couple of blocks away. There was quite a commotion down the street in that direction. As he neared the spot, he saw it was a local saloon. Inside, he found young Deputy Sheriff Gus Lewis. The inexperienced lawman was desperately trying to enlist more volunteers to help go after the convicts.

"Hey quiet down," Blount yelled at the crowd. "There's some convicts on the road to Genoa. They tried to stop me, but I got away. They shot at me. Here look at this hole in my slicker!"

This outraged several men in the saloon. Blount's news really stirred them up. This was just the help Deputy Lewis needed to form his posse. Several of them offered assistance.

"All right men, I need six of you to ride with me to get the word to Genoa," the young deputy yelled over the din.

Lewis led his posse outside. As the men mounted up, word came down the street that the State Armory was opened to provide Henry rifles. Not to be outdone, one of the towns' leading citizens, E.B. Rail, opened the doors of his store offering all the ammunition needed for the capture of the murderous convicts.

Therefore, when Deputy Sheriff Lewis and his six volunteers rode out of Carson City on their way to warn the citizens of Genoa, they were armed to the teeth!

⊷⊷⊷

The Jones gang kept moving through the mountains as silently as they could. Cockerell was having a tough time trudging along without any shoes.

"It's good to have people afraid of you," Jones thought.

Charlie knew the others were aware of his actions during the prison break. He heard whispers about his near execution of the guard on the ground in the yard. He knew the men in his party were also leery of Morton. That worked well to his advantage too. The two of them should be able to lead these other mutts safely out of the Pine Nut Range. He figured he would take them through the Adobe Valley and then skirt around Aurora. They would closely follow the Aurora Owens River Toll Road to Long

Valley in Mono County. From there it was just a few more miles to Bishop Creek. There Jones figured help would be available from his friends. Then they would slip up and over the Sierra.

Abruptly Charlie stopped. The wind had shifted and his nose detected the scent of a campfire. He sniffed the early morning breeze while he turned his head to help him pinpoint the likely direction of the fire. He figured the source was about a quarter mile ahead. His companions had smelled the smoke as well. Charlie and Morton lead the way as the party of men altered their course and headed into the wind.

Soon they observed a low glow ahead of them. As they moved forward they could see the faint outline of a freight wagon

silhouetted by the fire. A team of horses was tethered to the wagon. They watched a moment to see if they could tell how many men might be at the camp. No movement was observed. They couldn't tell if anyone was asleep on the ground. Silently the men edged closer.

Suddenly, embers flickered into the air. They heard a sound. They could see someone, partly hidden by the wagon, was stoking the fire. One of the horses sensed their presence and whinnied. Another pawed the ground. The man stood up and looked around. Charlie's men saw the outline of a rifle resting against the wagon wheel. The man told the horses to settle down. Charlie whispered to the group that he and Morton were going to rush the man. He ordered them to stay put. Morton and Jones inched their way forward. Now just feet from the wagon, they rushed in. The man was tackled by Morton as he dove for the weapon. Their captive turned out to be a Dutchman. He struggled with his assailant, cussing loudly in broken English. The others came in to help. Burke and Roberts dragged the old man over to the wagon. Morton dusted himself off. Black grabbed a rope from the wagon. Soon the man was secured to a wheel.

"Hell, why tie him up?" questioned Morton. "He shouldn't be tied up and left here. Kill him. Once I tied up this bastard, real tight too. What'd I get for being merciful? I got 19 buckshot pellets in my back for not killing a man that I had left tied up."

This conversation unnerved the Dutchman. After this tirade he expected the worse. Instead Burke spoke up

"We don't need to kill him in cold blood. That's the best way to get more people riled up about us. Now we just have the law after us. We don't need citizens after us too. Think about it."

This made sense to the Dutchman! He babbled on in his broken English that he wholeheartedly agreed. Much to his relief, apparently so did the others.

The episode over, Cockerell realized he was cold. So were the others. He told Roberts to build up the fire. Black had gone through the wagon to see what they could use He found a few provisions, an old rifle, two six shooters, some ammunition and some clothes. "Not bad," he figured. The men tried on the clothes to see who could wear the stuff they found. They knew it was important to get out of the prison duds as soon as possible. All this time, Jones had been looking over the stock. They looked good to him. Charlie came over to the camp.

"Hey men," he laughed, "we got ourselves some horses."

✍ ✍ ✍

After leaving the others, Squires, Willis and Hurley had made good progress towards Dayton. Hurley was thinking he could get himself lost in Virginia City.

"I need to rest here for awhile," he said, sitting down.

Squires disagreed with the idea. His intent was to move on under the cover of darkness throughout the night.

"While it's still dark, I moving on, come on Willis."

He was driven. He wanted to get to Six Mile Canyon as fast as he could. There, near the Flowery District, he had cached lots of loot. He figured once he got his hands on it, he could buy his way out of trouble. He continued on. Willis followed him.

During his entire 21 years on this planet, William Willis rarely had a thought of his own. The entire break took him by surprise. He really liked the prison food and was busy finishing off his dinner when the break started. Actually, he was licking his plate. He knew it was about time to leave the dining room and go to bed. He heard the Captain tell them to assemble. Then, in the next minute, the Captain was getting his ass kicked. Screaming women and gun fire came next. Truth be told, he wet his pants. Why was he in jail? He liked fires. He was an arsonist. He set a fire that burnt down much of Virginia City. Why? He liked to watch things burn. You could understand why no one mentioned the break to him. Can you imagine the guy walking up to the Captain and asking:

"Hey Captain, I forget, what time does the break start?"

Obviously, no one really wanted him around. Now he was just blindly following along after Squires. He tried to stay with Hurley, but Hurley shouted at him

"Get lost ya dumb bastard."

Hurley might well have sized poor William right up. The

91

Georgia native looked dumb, acted dumb and was even considered rather stupid by his parents before he ran off.

Squires took no notice as the kid followed close behind. He inched along as quickly as possible in the dark. He realized that once the sun came up, he needed to be very careful. Squires had been born into one of the most prominent families in Connecticut. He wondered what dear old mom and dad would think of him now? He remembered every second of the recent break. It was nothing like the score of stage robberies he committed over the years. The 38 year old was still bitter for being pinched for a train robbery. If some loud mouth named Gilchrist had just kept his trap shut, he wouldn't have been in prison in the first place. He told the others at the time they planned the heist they didn't need that guy. They didn't need the stage station either, who gave up information during their trial to avoid prison himself.

The old stage robber considered his criminal life behind him. With all the cash, gold and silver he had stashed in Six Mile Canyon, he planned to live like a king. As the sun began its ascent over the horizon, Squires got his bearings. He'd made it to about a mile east of Dayton. It was probably best he rest most of the day and set out again after dark. He found shelter in some nearby rocks. It wasn't until he covered up the tracks to his hiding place that he realized he had a shadow: Willis. The man looked at him with a blank stare, the type a dog gives you when they don't know what's expected of them.

"Sit down over there."

The young man immediately obeyed.

"This could work out just fine," thought Squires, "I can have him do all the things that might draw attention to me."

Chapter Eleven
Which Way Did They Go?

Weary from a night of constant vigil and no sleep, Sheriff Swift and his posse rode into the prison yard around 5:30 Monday morning. Despite a long and hard ride, they found no sign of the escapees. It was chilly. Both the sheriff and his men were hungry. He swung his leg over the saddle and stepped down. He tied his horse to a post. The others dismounted and secured their horses.

"Head on over to the Warm Springs Hotel and have something to eat," said the sheriff.

The mood was somber. Most men knew Matt Pixley and some knew his young wife as well. Due to the horror of the previous evening, Bergie, the Warm Springs bartender, was forced by circumstance into assuming many of Matt's duties. He had gotten some rest and was helping out. He saw the posse enter.

"Hi boys. Get yourselves settled. I'll bring some coffee."

He soon returned with cups and a big pot of hot coffee.

"I've got flapjacks, eggs, bacon and spuds cookin in the kitchen. What can I get ya?"

He jotted down their requests and returned to the kitchen.

Swift spoke for a moment with the guardsman left in charge. The man reported that all has been quiet through the night. Swift took a hurricane lamp from a table just inside the prison. He raised the wick and lit it. The sheriff walked through the prison, the dining hall, up the stairs and back down. He was pleased to see the men left in charge had everything well in hand. Most of the prisoners were still asleep. He was told that Denver's family had left. Jennie was taken by her grandmother to their home in Virginia City. Mrs. Denver was in Carson City with her husband. To his relief, he found everything in good order. He walked over to the Warm Springs Hotel to get something to eat. While relaxing for a moment with a cup of coffee, he chatted with the officer in charge. Both men would really like to catch some convicts.

"I figure if you and your men rode eastward until daylight you might trick someone hiding nearby. This could give them a false sense of security. They may move about in the open if they think you're gone. So, about an hour after daylight have your men reverse their course and return toward the prison. It's possible this course could turn up a few unsuspecting escapees."

"That could just work. If they see us pass by them, they may figure they'll be clear to travel more out in the open."

The man barked some commands to his troops. They all mounted up.

"Good hunting."

"Thanks."

The sheriff watched as the men rode out.

"Morning sheriff," Bergie said bringing the sheriff a cup of strong coffee as well as some sausage, eggs and bread.

"Morning."

He looked down at his breakfast. He wished he could get some sleep, but the meal would have to suffice. Those bastards needed to be caught. After Swift finished his meal, he walked to the kitchen to find Bergie.

"Thanks for finding something for my men to eat. They have another long ride ahead of them."

"Glad to be of help."

"I heard you got a bit drafty during the gun fight."

"Oh you heard about that too," said Bergie turning a bright red, "Oh yeah, there for awhile it got real drafty."

"Well, I'm glad you made it through all right."

"Thanks sheriff."

Meanwhile prison guard Ed Langlois, the feisty Frenchman, couldn't believe no one found any dead convicts. He knew that several were wounded. Dan Taylor was one of them. He was now up in the infirmary. Ed swore he heard Clifford moaning about his imminent death as he struggled away from the prison. The man had blood all over his shirt and pants. Ed didn't believe the man could have made it very far. He had to be out there dead or dying in the sagebrush. From his hospital bed, Isaacs had said that he knew Parsons and another convict were shot at almost point blank range. He couldn't imagine why they were not dead in the yard.

Swift called his posse together. He suggested they find fresh mounts if possible. He asked them to assemble back at the hotel about 9 am. They were going to ride out from the prison to try to pick up the convicts' trail.

By the time they stepped into their stirrups, the sun had come up enough to put a full light on what occurred this past evening. This was frontier country and these men had witnessed several unpleasant scenes during their lives. However, what they observed here sickened them. It was appalling. Pooled blood stains greeted the eye everywhere. It was along the porch and inside the hotel. It graced the main gateway and could be seen on the stones of the inner walkway. More was on the prison porch, door, steps, windows, door sills and facing. Even the wainscoting, walls, bars, bolts, beds, floors and stairs were covered. Riding thru the yard, they noticed that not even the shade trees and the green grass of the front yard were spared.

The group rode silently to Carson City. Upon returning to town they loaded up with provisions for a couple days ride.

Watson's party has been carefully picking their way through the Pine Nut Mountains. Once through the range, they could get to Mason Valley. The terrain was sometimes difficult, even dangerous. The three men were tired. They would stop and rest all day once the sun began its ascent.

"You're sure you can find that $2,500 in gold you hid?" Watson pointedly asked Baker. "Exactly where is it?"

"It's right where I left it," replied Baker, "at Skull near Tecoma. I don't know what else to tell ya. You'll see."

"Baker might be smarter than I thought," mused Watson.

He couldn't help but notice the man was being a bit evasive about the location. He remained confident he would outwit the man when the time came. Jacks had done a good job of leading them along the trail. So far he was a wonderful "map". Suddenly, Watson realized it was daylight. Thank God, he said under his breath. He stopped and looked around. He saw some jagged rocks off to their left about 50 yards.

"Let's settle down over in those rocks for the day. We'll be safe here. After dark, we'll get goin again."

John took the sack from his shoulder and put it on the ground. He opened it up and rummaged through the contents. He found something to his liking. Pointing to the sack he said:

"Here, find something to eat."

❦ ❦ ❦

Around 7:30, Storey County Sheriff Atchison and his posse rode into Carson City for a well deserved rest. They pulled up to Amos Judd's livery barn and dismounted.

"Howdy Amos, please feed and water the horses for us," the lawman said to stable owner. "They're as tired as we are."

"Sure thing sheriff. Did ya see anything?"

"Not a thing. Any possibility of getting fresh mounts?"

"I've got a couple here, sheriff. I'll see if I can round up two or three more for ya from Dawson's place ."

"Thanks Amos."

Aside from Atchison, the group included Virginia City's Chief of Police George Downey and Constable Ben Lackey. While Atchison saw about fresh mounts for the group, The 31-year-old Ben led the men down the dusty main street to the local dining room for breakfast. Many times he had wondered how he ended up in Nevada. But this New York native loved his job. The large body of men moved several tables together and pulled up chairs. Soon they were savoring bottomless cups of coffee.

"Here boys," a giggling young waitress said bringing

them a huge basket of biscuits, a plate of butter and some fresh preserves. "I'll be back with bacon and eggs shortly."

As Atchison walked down the street to join the others for breakfast, he saw Sheriff Swift ride into town.

"Any sight of them," he called up to the man?

"Nope. How about you," said Swift reining in his horse?

"Nary a one. We rode northeast of here with no luck."

"We just came from the prison. I had a talk with the officer in charge and everything's quiet there. Some guardsmen are working their way to the river now."

"They're out there somewhere. After breakfast, we'll get provisions for a couple days' ride and get after them again."

"We ate at the Warm Springs Hotel. We came here for supplies too. We'll find them. It's just going to take some time."

Amos Judd followed up on Atchison's attempt to procure fresh mounts for the men. He was successful. He obtained two pack animals as well. The mules were loaded with enough provisions for three days.

Ben Lackey showed up with the rest of the party around 8:30 am. The men moved their gear to the fresh horses. In about 30 minutes the group headed out for the prison. The sheriff planned to track the prisoners from there to the Carson River. He would move along the river until they found where the convicts might have crossed. On foot and without food, how far could these felons get? His experience told him they would be found in a few days. He wished it was winter. It was always easier to catch escapees in the winter. Tracks stood out in the snow and usually they got so cold they allowed themselves to be captured.

❧ ❧ ❧

Eleven weary mounted National Guardsmen, Constable Harkin and Lieutenant Lyman rode into Carson. They tied up their horses near the diner just as Sheriff Atchison and his party were leaving. The riders were hungry and tired as well. They were savvy enough to know a good breakfast was all they'd get at this time. The Lieutenant told the sheriff that he had led this party far up the Lake Bigler Road in pursuit of the convicts. They hadn't

97

seen any track of the escapees, much less seeing any of the felons themselves. After eating, he planned to contact his commander and get further orders.

     Following Sheriff Swift's suggestion, several mounted Emmet Guardsmen had left the prison following the huge trail left by the fleeing prisoners. Based on the account of the French prison guard's description of Clifford's wounds, they expected to find the man somewhere in the sagebrush. About a mile from the prison they discovered a coat lying in the sand. A guardsman gave it to his commanding officer. The man looked it over. It was easy to tell that it belonged to one of the prison guards. After another mile they retrieved a disabled rifle. In addition, not far from where they found the coat, they observed a short prison shoe print. It showed that whomever wore it, left the main track of the convicts by himself and headed off to the left. This direction led to a road that went north along the Mexican ditch.

     The guardsmen got all the way to the Mexican Dam without seeing any trace of Clifford or anyone else. The blacksmith was thoroughly questioned. The man said he was aroused from his bed the previous evening by the barking of his dog. He grabbed some pants and stepped outside for a look. He was almost immediately surrounded by a large band of convicts. Concerned for his safety, he did exactly as they told him. They demanded he help get the shackles off those still bound. He was also instructed to tend to the wounds of one of the men. He said they weren't violent, but they did take a shotgun and two old pistols. He said he didn't have much ammunition, but they took that too. They also took all his food. All his clothing, except what he was wearing at the time, was taken as well. It was his recollection that the party left somewhere around 10. The whole group headed down river.

     Dr. Lee had tended to the wounds of the convicts that were hurt and unable to escape the previous night. This all took place after tending to Denver, Dedman, Rollins and the other officers of

Daniel Taylor

the guard. Daniel Taylor was one of the most severely wounded inmates while attempting to escape. He had been jailed for his part in the train car robbery at Pequops. He was resting in the infirmary. He was found just inside the prison door, near the dining area. He was hit by a shotgun blast.

Dr. Lee had removed all the buckshot from Taylor late last night and dressed the wound. The doctor told Taylor he would make a full recovery.

"Big deal," thought Taylor. "I still have nearly 28 years left in this hell hole."

Anyone watching him in his hospital bed would try to figure if his grey-blue eyes were slightly crossed or if he constantly was wincing in pain.

❦ ❦ ❦

As the members of Russell's party awoke, a discussion began regarding what they should do next. McCue and Bigelow wanted Russell to lead them to a safe place. He agreed, but Ingram and McNamara didn't go for it. While waiting for someone to come up with an alternate plan, Russell considered what he should do next. He knew Pat McCue, alias Peeping Tom, pretty well. McCue was a very large 6'6" Irishman. He weighed nearly 203. He caused some kind of mayhem in

Pat McCue

White Pine. He was in the midst of a seven year sentence. He was known for having a fairly short fuse. That could lead to danger in the days ahead.

Ed Bigelow was well known to Russell as well. He had come to Nevada from Maine. He had worked as an engineer on the outside. He was serving a five year term for grand larceny.

Ed Bigelow

"Hell," he questioned, "I robbed the Stamford Mill. What's grand larceny anyway?"

Ed was 29, stood 5'8" with a medium build. He had a well marked crease in his upper lip. Russell wondered what "stupid" comment might have caused that fat lip. Bigelow had a wrinkle between his eyebrows. His habit of chewing tobacco with a short rapid sheep like gnawing motion disgusted Russell. The man even pursed his lips tightly at times and resembled a sucker fish when he did. Russell realized he really didn't care much for Ed.

Elijah Ingram and Tim McNamara were unknown to Russell. He'd seen them in the prison yard and around the dinner hall. He never spoke to them. After careful consider-

Tim McNamara

ation, He decided these men would most likely hinder his own successful escape. As the day progressed, the others hadn't formulated any plan for what to do next. Russell, however, knew what he was going to do. After the others fell asleep that night, he'd quietly slip into the darkness. He didn't care what they did. He figured the four of them would leave an easy trail for someone to follow.

Elijah Ingram

With first light the men with Clifford decided they needed a rest. They looked to find a place to hide far off from any trail or cattle track. They would be able to lay low and stay out of harm's way. Clifford had been told by an acquaintance that he had a ranch in this general vicinity. It was his plan to find the place and get provisions so he and the others could leave Nevada.

Frank had a pretty good idea in his head where to find his friend's property. The others in his group just hoped he could find it. All four of them were very hungry. They hadn't eaten anything since dinner time on the night of the prison break. Fortunately for them the body craves sleep over hunger. The men found a spot off the beaten track and rested all through the daylight hours.

అ౯ అ౯ అ౯

In the morning, Dr. Lee came in and talked with Warden Denver. Mrs. Denver was at his side.

"Well Frank, how do you feel," he asked.

"I'm awfully sore, doc. But if it weren't for Bob Dedman, I probably wouldn't be talkin to ya."

Neither Frank nor his wife had seen Dedman since the Warden was taken from the prison Sunday night and moved to the doctor's office in Carson City.

"From all accounts I've heard, you may be right. I attended to him last night. He'll be just fine. He's been praised widely by the Carson City community for his heroic efforts."

"There's no need to convince me," Frank said. "I was there. Doc, I'd like a pen and paper. I need to write out an order for the officers at the prison."

While lying awake the previous night, Denver thought about how he could properly thank Dedman for saving his life. He decided to begin the process of gaining a pardon for him. That would take awhile. Meanwhile, he planned to give the man the privilege of staying in the Warden's quarters indefinitely. Dedman wouldn't be required to be under lock and key. He could cook his own meals. He'd be allowed to come and go within the confines of the prison. All this the Warden committed to paper.

"Here, doc. Please see that this gets to the prison as soon as possible."

"I certainly will," said the man as he folded the paper and put it in his coat pocket. "I'll take it personally to the prison later this afternoon."

Dr. Lee returned his full attention to explaining what had happened to the Warden.

"Now let's get back to you. The bullet that entered your hip traveled upward through the fleshy tissue and muscle about 10 inches from the point of entry. It's now lodged near your spine. It needs to be removed. The surgical procedure is a little tricky, but must be done. You should be just fine."

"That's easy for you to say doc," Denver said to the man. "I'm more than a little afraid of this scheduled event. I know if the bullet doesn't come out, I could get an infection and die. But what about the pain I'll have during the procedure? How do I stay still while you get that thing out?"

"We'll use a substance called morphine. It's now being widely used, even here, way out in the 'wild west.' The drug is injected into you painlessly with something called a syringe. This greatly reduces any pain during and after surgery. We're gonna get to you in about an hour. Meanwhile, you need to rest."

With that, the doctor and the Warden's wife left the room. She was concerned about her husband and had lots of questions.

"Dr. Lee, is Frank going to make a full recovery?"

"Mary, he'll be just fine. He's strong. He'll have to take it easy for a month or so. But there's no permanent damage."

"I'm so relieved to hear that."

"How's Jennie doing," he inquired? He'd heard what happened all around the girl in the prison yard during the break.

"Jennie was taken home to Virginia City early this morning. We want her as far away as possible from the horrible events she witnessed. I can only imagine what must be going on in her young mind. She's presently with my mother. I'm returning to Virginia City this evening."

"I'm very glad Jennie's in a good place. I really need to join Dr. Waters. I'll let you know how Frank's surgery goes."

"Thank you for everything," she said, reaching out for his hand and holding it momentarily.

Mary Denver had her own vivid picture of the night before. It focused on Jenny standing in the courtyard and the man that whisked her up and carried her to safety.

"I really need to find out who that was and thank him," she thought with a tear in her eye.

Dr. Waters was in assessing Isaacs' wounds. As Dr. Lee stepped into Isaacs' room, he heard Dr. Waters talking with the wounded man about the extent of his injuries. Mrs. Isaacs was listening in. Dr. Lee remembered seeing how awful his right leg looked last night when he first saw him. He was very glad that Isaacs seemed to be holding his own. Dr. Waters told Isaacs that they would be removing the ball in his left leg a little later in the day. He took Mrs. Isaacs aside and told her of the grave nature of his wounds. She knew she must be strong, but worried what she and her two children would do without him.

৵ ৵ ৵

Ingram awoke with the sun in his eyes and realized it was long after sun up. He reached over and shook his friends awake. McNamara looked around and wiped the sleep from his eyes. McCue got up, walked a few paces and stood behind a bush to relieve himself. Bigelow leaned up on one elbow and looked around.

"Hey, where's Russell," he inquired?

The others looked at him blankly and were surprised to find him gone. They told McCue when he rejoined the circle.

"Bastard just up and left us here on our own," he said.

The two Irishmen looked at each other in disgust.

"Better off without him" sneered McNamara.

"Well, what do you think we should do now?"

"The best thing we can do is head over to Placerville," replied Bigelow, still resting on his arm. "We'll keep off the regular trails and travel mostly at night. There're several encampments along the way where we can get something to eat. The first thing we need to do is find some clothes so we don't look like this."

The others agreed to follow Bigelow's suggestion. They would head west toward Placerville.

Chapter Twelve
Tom Carter Has Some Bad Luck

Life in Genoa was going on as usual. The citizens were alerted the previous night of the prison break. Collectively they kept a weary eye out for strangers, especially anyone wearing stripes! Genoa was among the oldest settlements of Nevada. The region first attracted attention in 1848. Mormons traveling to the gold diggings in California from Salt Lake City stopped over there. Therefore it was known as Mormon Station for several years. Now the town was the Douglas County seat.

Genoa, Nevada. Once called Mormon Station

Robert Bollen and his wife, Sarah, enjoyed living in Genoa. That beautiful morning they were out on personal business. Bollen had been the County Sheriff since late 1868. Douglas County was fairly peaceful, especially Genoa. They even had a lively "colored" population. But folks there got along. They were good law abiding citizens. Now at 43, the Virginia native decided he wouldn't run for sheriff again. He'd rather do something else now. He wanted to spend more time with his family. He and his wife thought Genoa was a great place to raise a family. What a pretty spot on the western side of the Carson River with a willow-fringed stream meandering through it! Here was a picture of extreme beauty in the foreground with rugged majesty behind.

During the night, Flynn and Lynch had been trying to help

the wounded Carter get far away from the Carson River. They figured that would be the region the lawman were going to scour come morning. To his credit, Carter kept telling them to leave him. He hurt too much to move and just wanted to lay somewhere peacefully until he felt better.

The three were just off a well used road about five miles from Genoa near the Cracklebaugh Bridge. Flynn heard something and the men stopped. Just up the road they saw a man and woman in a buggy heading toward them. As they watched, a reflection flashed off the driver. Flynn squinted and saw it came from a tin star on the man's chest.

"Sorry partner," Flynn said to Carter. "I've got to leave ya. I can't get caught now."

David Lynch

"Me either," stammered Lynch running into the brush.

As the Sheriff rode along in the buggy with Sarah, they saw movement ahead to the right of the road. There were two figures running away from the road as fast as they could. From his experience this meant something was amiss. A more careful scrutiny told him they were wearing stripes. He urged his horse forward at a gallop. Sarah held on tightly. Seeing a man lying off the road, he slowed the horse up. The man was trying to move away, but was obviously injured. The other two had made wonderful progress away from him, so he decided Sarah was safe in the buggy for the moment. He jumped to the ground, gun in hand, and ran over to the man. The man was hurt and posed no danger. Bollen holstered his weapon.

"You're one of them," said the sheriff.

"There's no fooling you," remarked Carter. "Was it the striped outfit I'm wearing or what," he joked through his pain.

Carter was actually relieved to be in custody. He'd known for some time that his wounds weren't going to enable him to get away freely. He figured he'd either get caught or die out in the open. He preferred to get caught. He knew he'd get proper medical attention.

Bollen admired the man's spirit. He helped him to his feet. Together, they slowly made it over to the buggy. He and Sarah lifted him up and in. It was only meant to carry two people and a few items in the front. They carefully set him on the floor with his back against the seat. She opened the man's dressing to look at his injury. Being the wife of the county sheriff, she'd seen plenty of awful wounds. This was one of them, but far from the worst she ever saw. It was apparent that someone cauterized this injury and dressed it. She closed the dressing back up. There was nothing further she can do for him here.

"Well, it looks like you're gonna survive," she remarked, "but these wounds need proper tending. Oh, by the way, I'm Sarah and that guy behind the badge is my husband, Sheriff Bollen."

Carter looked up and back over his head toward Sarah.

"Pleased to meet ya, ma'am," he drawled. "I'm Thomas Carter. I stepped out of the Nevada State Prison last night. I sure wish I hadn't. I thought the firing had stopped and the coast was clear. Then somehow I managed to walk right into a slug. It's hasn't gone well for me since."

Both the Bollens smiled as the sheriff circled his buggy back toward Genoa. He expertly flicked the reins. The town was only about three miles down the road.

Flynn and Lynch stopped running. They stood in the sagebrush with hands on hips, trying to catch their breath. They watched as the man in the wagon jumped out. He pulled a gun, headed over and knelt down by Carter. After awhile, they saw the man lift their companion and carefully help him to the buggy. He was lifted into the rig. The lady with the man seemed to be looking him over. They were glad no harm had come to the injured man and watched in relief as the buggy turned and headed away.

"He'll be better off going back and getting medical help," said Lynch.

"Yeah," countered Flynn, "out here he'd probably get that wound infected and die."

106

Silently they both counted their lucky stars. They hadn't been caught. No one was coming after them. They no longer had to worry about Carter. They headed back the same way the buggy went. They figured they would keep a wary eye on the road ahead in case someone was sent to inquire as to their whereabouts.

❧ ❧ ❧

Billy Poor was very happy. He spent the night in a very comfortable feather bed. The young man was pleased to be with his family once again. Today, his dad would show him the town. Aurora was a bustling place. He looked forward to their day together. He was also very excited about his new job.

"Just think, I'll get paid to ride horses," he thought.

There was no danger from Indians. No one was going to rob a mail rider. It would be just him and his horse on the open road. His daydream was ended by his mother's request that he join them for breakfast. He sat down to a huge plate of pancakes with three over easy eggs nestled on top.

"She remembered," he thought.

As he did when he was a kid, Billy poked the yokes with his fork. He liked the yoke to spill all over his pancakes. Most folks preferred syrup. If any pancakes remained after the yokes disappeared, he would just add syrup to the pile.

"I'm looking forward to a day in town with you, pa," Billy said. "Maybe you can introduce me to a nice young lady."

"How about the lovely Miss Chapin," his brother teased.

His dad laughed, "that won't be such a good idea."

"Why can't I meet her," questioned Billy?

"Well, Miss Chapin's no lady. The character isn't even a woman," his dad chuckled. "It's the name some of the rowdy men in town gave ole Tom Chapin. Tom's all right. He's an honest businessman and teaches Sunday school. But since he won't drink with them they decided they'd make fun of him. You know how some people are."

"Yeah, I reckon," said Billy. "I earned a couple nicknames working back in California."

A shrill whistling interrupted their conversation.

"Enough of all the nonsense," his father said. "It's time to head on down to the hotel."

While he and his dad walked up the street to the hotel, Billy was not surprised to see nearly every man armed. Having spent the past few years in California, he was used to men carrying guns. Billy noted his father wasn't armed.

"Dad, why don't you carry a shooter?"

"In my profession, I don't feel the need. There's a double barrel shotgun under the hotel counter just in case. But no one there has ever had occasion to use it. Back at the house we have a couple of pistols, an old rifle and a shotgun, but they're for rabbits and birds and such"

He went on to explain to Billy that guns had a lot to do with the character of the men of Aurora, and the west in general. Their value system was built around fighting when provoked. When you mix that mentality with a liberal consumption of alcohol, that fighting could easily prove fatal.

"However," his dad continued, "with the citizens armed as they are, the incidence of robbery, burglary, and theft has been highly reduced. Carrying a gun is never questioned in Aurora. Men believe they have a right to self-defense. Guns have proven to be a most effective tool in exercising that right."

Typical gunplay in the street

Nearly every man in Aurora was armed. Even humorist Samuel Clemens worn a pistol when he lived there. He had worked as a miner and wrote for the Esmeralda Star.

He once remarked that "he had never had occasion to kill anybody with the Colt Navy revolver he carried, but he had worn the thing in deference to popular sentiment, and in order that I might not, by its absence, be offensively conspicuous, and a subject of remark."

Not even the high homicide rate was a subject of great

concern. Town folks usually accepted the killings. They figured those killed, with few exceptions, had it coming. Hell, they agreed to fight in the first place. Anyway, most of those killed in Aurora had reputations as bad men. So when one died in a shoot out, so what? Their sudden death was simply a job related hazard. No one asked them to become gunmen.

Billy's dad had pretty much given his son a run down of

Aurora. He was the proprietor of a hotel simply known as The Esmeralda. This was a two-story brick building with five impressive columns holding up the popular balcony. The older man opened the door for his son and followed him through the entrance.

Esmeralda Hotel

   ᢁᢁᢁ

The Bollens and Carter returned to Genoa in quick fashion. Seeing the convict lying injured in the buggy, curious onlookers gathered. Sarah explained what happened to the ever expanding crowd. Bob stepped off the buggy. Slowly coming toward him was the Carson City stage. He was in luck. He raised his arms and flagged down driver Wellington Bower as the man slowly maneuvered the coach down the street. Bower reined in his team.

"What's up sheriff," inquired the driver?

"I've got another passenger for ya," Bollen replied. "I'm sure Governor Bradley will pay the price of his return ticket."

With that, he and a couple of others assisted Carter out of the buggy and put him in the coach. The only other passenger this morning was a member of the National Guard called back to duty because of the escape. The sheriff was glad to see him on board. Naturally he figured he'd make sure Carter got to Carson City. Wellington saw his new passenger was on board.

"Come on Blackie, come on girls," Wellington sang out, "let's get this stage on up the road to Carson City."

The big mule and his girlfriends dug in. The stage moved on out. Carter figured he would be back at the prison for dinner.

⋧⋧ ⋧⋧ ⋧⋧

About 10 miles east of Carson City in Dayton, Justice of the Peace Bryant was reading over a few land documents. His office was over the saloon at the Union Hotel. Momentarily he was going to get a bit of interesting news. He heard riders on the street. He peered out his window and saw several men dismount outside his office. They appeared to be cowhands.

Brant went down the stairs to see what the men might want. Seeing him upon entering the saloon, one of the men said:

"Where's the sheriff?"

"I'm in charge here," replied Brant, sizing up the group.

The Dayon Nevada Union Hotel and Saloon

110

"How can I help ya?"

"We were traveling from Carson City to Virginia City," their spokesman said, "when we observed several men off in the distance. We continued and before long we could see they were convicts. Hell, they were close enough so we could see their prison outfits, even their numbers. We counted 18 in all."

"Exactly where did you see these men," Brant asked.

"They were on a large hill by the Smith Ranch," came the reply. "The ranch isn't far from the dividing line of Douglas and Ormsby Counties. When we stopped, the men on the hill motioned for us to come on up. At that point we feared for our lives, took a wide berth around the group and came here as soon as fast as we could ride to tell you."

Again Brant asked about the location. The man repeated himself. Brant thanked him. The men left his office, mounted up and rode off down the street. The Justice of the Peace sat there and laughed.

"How could these men have been heading from Carson City to Virginia City and seen these men near the Douglas/Ormsby County Line," he thought to himself. "That point was south and east. If the men had left Carson City, there was no way they would have traveled in that direction to get to Virginia City."

He figured this was a grand hoax or worse, purposely told to throw off the lawmen. Just in case, he walked over the telegraph office. He had the clerk send a brief note to the command post set up at Carson City. The note made its way to General Batterman. He ordered 12 armed soldiers to head in that direction just in case the report was true. The region they wanted to scour was about 11 miles from the prison, east of Carson City.

Chapter Thirteen
Saying Goodbye Is No Fun

Robert Morrison wasn't looking forward to this particular day. Sarah had made plans to visit some friends and relatives in Los Angeles for a few days. He loved her and didn't like the idea of her traveling without him. He also didn't like the idea of her being absent, period. Since her arrival in Benton several months ago, she hadn't traveled anywhere. She was precious to him and he knew he'd really miss her while she was gone. She was scheduled to leave that day. He would be taking her to the stage that traveled from Aurora to Fish Slough. They would meet the stage somewhere around noon at Adobe Meadows on the Aurora to Owens River Road. It was a nice clear day, and Bob figured they needed to leave by 10 am to rendezvous with the stage. Sarah would make Fish Slough by late afternoon. She should be there in time to catch another stage that would transport her to Independence for arrival later in the evening. She would stay there overnight. The regular stage to Los Angeles from Independence ran on Tuesday. He was already looking forward to her return. That was when they would be married. She lit up his life and he felt an uneasy emptiness when she was not around. Oops, there she was. She looked radiant. But then, she always did.

"Good morning," she said.

"Hi honey," he replied, as he leaned over to kiss her full on the lips. It was awhile before they came up for a breath!

The energy created by the meeting of their flesh swept through them both. It was good they were to be married shortly. One or both may burst if this union were to be postponed much longer. He helped her into the wagon. She adjusted herself as he climbed in himself. He unwrapped the reins and urged the horse onward. She talked nonstop during the trip. He figured she had covered about every subject imaginable. No matter. As long as she was close by he was happy. They reached the meeting point around 9:45 am. They were early. He offered her some water from their canteen. She took a long drink and offered him one. He replaced the stopper and put the canteen back in the wagon.

Neither of them looked forward to saying goodbye. Each knew it was temporary, but they had grown accustomed to one another's company. The next few days would be hard on them both. Not knowing what to say, neither said anything. He looked to the north when hearing the rumbling sounds of the stage coming over the rise. The coach slowed to a stop followed by a cloud of dust. They had both turned there heads to avoid a mouthful.

"Howdy, Pete."

"Hi there, Bob. I can see you have some precious cargo there for me. Let me set these brakes and I'll help get the young lady's luggage loaded."

"No need to jump down. I'll put Sarah's stuff in the back and secure it."

Sarah remained seated as Bob took the luggage. She looked up at Pete and smiled.

"Good morning. You'll have to forgive Bob. He's so preoccupied with me leaving that he's lost his manners. I'm Sarah."

"Pleased to make your acquaintance young lady. No one else is with me this morning, so you've got the place all to yourself. Bob will get you all settled inside in just a moment."

"Do you mind if I ride up there with you? I'd rather sit with you and talk instead of sitting in there alone and bored."

"Well I would sure like the company."

"You might be sorry," offered Bob. "She can talk on any subject at length. You might not get a word in edge wise."

He helped lift Sarah from the wagon. He gently set her on the ground. They looked deeply into each other's eyes. Their eyes were a bit moist with tears of sadness. They shared a big hug and several goodbye kisses. Then he assisted her as she climbed onto the wheel and into the boot next to Pete.

"See ya soon sweetheart," said Bob trying to hold back his emotions. "Make sure you keep that thing on the road, Pete. You have someone very valuable to me aboard."

Pete knew exactly what he meant. Everyone was aware of

the love between the two of them.

"Sure enough, Bob. She'll be at Fish Slough before you get back to work."

The big coach started on down the wide road. Bob's heart felt heavy as he climbed back into the wagon by himself. He watched for a moment as the stage rolled up the road. Sarah looked over her head and waved at Bob. She was really going to miss him. But she would be back soon. They would be married and live happily ever after! Bob saw her turn and wave. He raised his hand and waved back. He was glad no one could see him. He was a bit embarrassed. He was too old to have tears in his eyes.

"You'll be just fine," he said to himself while he wiped his eyes. He circled the wagon around and headed back to Benton.

❧ ❧ ❧

In Carson City, Dr. Lee and Dr. Waters readied themselves for their afternoon operations. First, they would remove the ball from the Warden that was resting near his spine. It was in the lower part of his back. They planned to have him lay face down

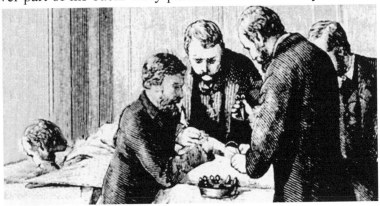

on the operating table. His head would extend over the table edge. This will keep his back in a more relaxed position. The morphine injection would keep Denver still while the doctors cut into his back to remove the ball. They had enlisted two young men to help. They would use their strength to make sure the Warden didn't move his back during the procedure. Dr. Waters prepared the syringe and injected Denver. The effect of the morphine was almost immediate. They reassured the man. A small two inch incision was made above where the ball was lodged. The capillary bleeding was minimal. The skin was carefully peeled open. The grey metal of the ball was seen. Dr. Lee took his instrument and carefully lifted the ball out. The whole procedure took less than 15 minutes. His wound was dressed. Dr. Lee left to tell Mrs. Denver everything had gone fine. Their nurse set about boiling the instruments just used. She knew that they would be operating on Isaacs next.

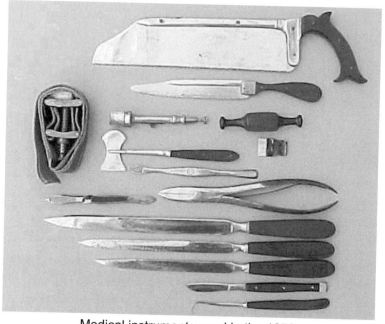

Medical instruments used in the 1870s

Morrison arrived back at Benton around 2:30 pm. He left his wagon at the livery stable. No one was about, but they knew whose rig this was. It would be properly cared for. He dusted himself off and headed over to the General Store. Henry saw Bob as he came in the door.

"Howdy Bob, you get sis off on time?"

"Yeah, no one else was on the stage so she insisted upon sitting up with Pete."

"That sounds like sis. While you were out that package from San Francisco you have been waiting for arrived. It's over there under the cash register."

Bob hung up his coat. He went over to retrieve the package that Henry referenced. He could see from the packaging it was indeed what he had been expecting. He ripped off the wrappings. Under it all was his new suit.

"Well Henry, it looks pretty good. What do you think," said Bob, holding up the coat.

"It looks awfully formal. I think Sarah will be pleased with you all dressed up in that outfit."

"She better, it sure did cost enough."

"Oh well, you only get married once."

"I guess so. I'll probably get buried in it too!"

❧ ❧ ❧

Pete was a bit off. The Aurora stage didn't make Fish Slough until 3 pm. He and Sarah had a wonderful chat while they bounced their way along the road. He could certainly see what Morrison saw in the young woman.

He imagined the pair would have a long and rich life together. Fortunately, the stage to Independence wasn't scheduled to leave until 4 pm. The station master secured the horses as Pete jumped down off the coach. He extended his hand to help the young woman down.

"Thank you Pete," beamed Sarah.

"My pleasure ma'am," replied the weathered stage driver. "I'll make sure your belongings get on the Independence coach."

Sarah walked over to the stage office and purchased her ticket. She sat in the office for awhile. It was so quiet. Only the clickety click of the telegraph broke the silence. She already missed Bob. She couldn't believe her good fortune at coming west to be near her brother. Just think, if she hadn't she would have never met the handsome Mr. Morrison.

Puron "Wild Man" Dow walked into the stage office. He was a towering man at 6'7" and weighed well over 250 pounds. Sarah was mildly startled when she first saw him. His well-developed paunch completely hid the fact he was wearing a belt. He looked right at her and said in the most gentle voice.

"I guess you're the little lady I'm taking on to Independence this afternoon."

Sarah liked him immediately. "You're right, that's me."

"Pete has all your stuff loaded and ready to go. If you're all set we can leave now. The wife won't mind me being home early for once."

Sarah was a bit tired and didn't mind being alone in the coach during the short ride to Independence.

≈ ≈ ≈

Isaacs was lying in great pain as the doctors told him what they hoped to accomplish. The ball that went through his right knee had done severe damage. It was lodged in the back of his left knee at present. He had a couple of other flesh wounds. But compared to his leg injuries, these were really of no consequence. Dr. Lee told the man they were attempting to save his right leg. Both doctors had concurred. They didn't think they could save it.

However, they knew that he had a better chance of surviving if he had a good positive outlook. So they held back the bad information. Isaacs was made comfortable on his stomach like they did with Denver. The assistants were again available to stabilize his legs.

The syringe was loaded and an injection was administered to each leg. Dr. Waters undid the dressing on Isaacs right leg. The wound was ugly. The knee was shattered. Even if they didn't have to remove the leg, it would never bend correctly again.

They didn't expect and didn't find any trace of a ball in the wound. A new dressing was applied. Moving to the left knee the wound was gently opened. A long probe was inserted. The ball was located. Another instrument was inserted to retract the offending object. Dr. Lee dropped the ball into a bowl. The wound was washed and rinsed. A dressing was applied. Isaacs was made as comfortable as possible.

Dr. Lee washed up and looked in on Warden Denver. The man was sleeping peacefully. Mrs. Denver was sitting close by.

He walked over and gently touched her shoulder. Neither said a word. Dr. Lee could now go home for a richly deserved rest. Dr. Waters would remain in the office for the night.

⤜ ⤜ ⤜

Darkness had set in. Clifford, Chapman, Parsons and Roth had spent most of the day resting. The men had found a pretty secure place in some rocks. They had been entertained most of the day by the antics of a young coyote. They soon learned this was the coyote's method of catching its dinner. The animal would wander around sniffing the terrain. It was trying to locate a hole where a mouse or squirrel might be hiding.

The fun started when it did. Motionlessly, it watched and waited. When a potential meal appeared, it slowly rocked back on its hind legs and then suddenly sprang forward. With any luck it grabbed its prey.

If successful, it usually sat right there and enjoyed its meal while they watched. Their friend was five for eight on the day. Roth's stomach actually growled loud enough to be audible.

"Hell, I'd be happy with a squirrel myself," he thought.

As this little group rested and enjoyed their animal friend, they became aware of being watched from a distance. Those looking them over never attempted to get closer. None of these men had very keen eye sight. But after awhile, they saw the interested party were Indians.

The little band actually came around four or five times

118

during the day to observe them. As the day went by, they came a little closer. It was a bit unnerving to the four of them. What did these Indians want? Would they tell someone about them? Each time they returned, the men felt even more uneasy.

They knew it was too risky to have a fire. The smoke or the glow could give them away. Being cautious worked well for them this particular night. Sometime around 10 pm, the men heard something. Quiet as mice, they waited to see what it was. They were relieved when a buck and three does walked within 30 feet of them. About an hour later something else grabbed their attention. The faint sound of conversation came to them. It sounded like men talking. It slowly became louder. Then, not 50 yards off, appeared the distinct silhouette of 11 mounted men passing along in front of them. Clifford felt like one of the mice the coyote had stalked all day. But he was not about to let anyone pounce on him anytime soon.

To the north and east, Squires and Willis had continued during the day toward Six Mile Canyon. They were fortunate to find water along the way. It was almost fall and many of the springs were nearly dry. By late afternoon, they had reached the hills above the Carson River across from the eastern edge of Dayton. This town was built on the banks of Gold Creek. It was established as a trading post in the early 1850s. Thousands had passed by Gold Canyon seeking their fortunes.

In 1856, Chinese laborers were imported to dig a water ditch. This irrigation ditch ran from about two miles west of town to Gold Canyon. It was called Chinatown back then. In 1861, residents changed the name to Dayton. This was in honor of the town's surveyor, John Day. Water from the Carson River operated mills that processed the ore from the Comstock. The Pine Nut Trees he and Willis had just traveled through, provided firewood as well as charcoal for the smelting furnaces. There across the river were shops, a hay yard, blacksmith, hotel, general store, hotel, saloon and a lot more. He planned to move east of Dayton and then north to catch the road to Six Mile Canyon.

The two men watched as a couple of people crossed the river in front of them during the afternoon. Squires very was careful not to let anyone see them. Willis was like a puppy, following Squires wherever he went. After a night and day giving nearly constant instructions, Squires noticed after awhile he needn't. It seemed that whatever he did, Willis would automatically do too.

"I could jump right over that ledge, smash myself on those rocks below and Willis would simply jump over after me," Squires thought, looking back at Willis.

Squires was hell bent on getting to Six Mile Canyon as soon as possible. He knew he could find a safe place to hide there for as long as he needed. He figured the loot he had stashed would assist him in enticing someone to give him whatever he needed. Squires stood up and continued on his way. Fido followed along.

⊰⊱ ⊰⊱ ⊰⊱

Ryan had made good progress along the west side of the Carson River since his bout with the ague. The weary escapee wasn't exactly sure where he was. He wished he had the rifle that he spent so much time trying to get from the warden. Here he was, free, but without any weapon, dressed in an itchy prison suit with uncomfortable shoes which left a distinct print.

He decided he needed some rest. He saw a horseman coming along the river. He remained undetected. Then he waded across the Carson River heading southeast. He was nearly played out from the long walk. Off about a quarter mile were a corral and

120

a barn. As he continued, he saw a ranch house on the other side of the barn. He nestled in some bushes to watch the place. He observed a man and a boy tending livestock around the barn. Dusk was setting in. The tempting smells of a home cooked meal were caught by his nose.

"Damn, I'm hungry," he thought.

As a great weariness set in and his stomach reminded him of how long it had been since his last meal, he threw caution to the wind. Ryan slowly stood up and slowly walked the 100 yards to the house.

"Hello the house," he called out.

Shortly, a man came out of the barn. He looked Ryan up and down. Ryan was a bit nervous. What would this man do?

"No way he can't see this striped outfit," thought Ryan.

"I'll bet you could use a good meal mister," he said.

Ryan relaxed and smiled. "Yes, yes I sure could."

"Well come on up to the house, supper's about ready."

Chapter Fourteen
Hot on The Trail of the Outlaws

The Atchison party traveled with Sheriff Swift's posse all through the day. Their Indian guide was an excellent tracker. In the early afternoon the Virginia militia and their local citizens joined them. The guide saw where a party of convicts had split off the trail. Evidence showed him they had split and went in three different directions. The posse chose to follow the larger group.

It was fast going for the Indian guide to follow them through the sand hills where he could easily see the tracks. But when they got to the rocky ridges, he had to proceed much more slowly. He figured the convicts were heading though the Pine Nut Mountains on toward Pine Nut Valley.

In the mountains they came upon an unfortunate soul that was tied to a wagon wheel and gagged. It turned out to be a Dutchman. In broken English, punctuated by lots of cursing, he said:

"Someone snuck up and jumped me early this morning. Before I knew it, I was grabbed and tied to this wagon. In all, there were six men. One of them they called Morton, wanted to kill me to make sure I didn't say anything. Another one, who they called Burke, didn't want me killed. Lucky for me, the others agreed. Then they gagged me, took my horses and rode out."

He also told the lawmen they took his weapons, extra clothes and provisions. He figured they were probably five or six hours ahead of them by now.

"I'm going with you," the Dutchman told the men gathered around him. "I want my stock back. We need to be careful though. They have a couple Henry rifles and pistols too."

The load on one of the pack animals was passed out among the posse members so the Dutchman could ride along with them. It was late in the day when the group left the Dutchman's camp. The Indian tracked the convicts until some time after dark.

It was obvious no one could follow the escapees over this long rocky ridge. Hell, it would be nearly impossible to find any tracks in the daylight. The guide looked at the stars above him. He scanned the distant mountain peaks.

He knew that three or four miles ahead of them, well up the side of a rugged peak, was a spring. He had a hunch the men they were after would go by there.

"Men go to spring near mountain top," the guide said. "I know this place and can lead you there safely in the dark."

Several men were tired. They wanted to rest. The leaders insisted they move on. The Indian led them through the darkness. He led them over rocks and through sagebrush. They went over precipices at the risk of life and limb. At length, after much misgiving amongst posse members, the Indian stopped at the spring. Atchison told the party they would rest there until daybreak

✺ ✺ ✺

Sarah Devine pulled the covers around her as she settled in for a good night sleep. The ride from Bishop Creek to Independence didn't seem long at all. "Wild Man" Dow sang at the top of his lungs all the way.

"How can a man so big and scary, be so gentle," she wondered? His wife must be a lucky lady.

She longed for Bob's comforting hug. Before long she wouldn't be sleeping by herself. She knew she was ready for him and wanted lots of children.

Their kid's future would be secure. Look at what Bob had already accomplished. She fell asleep thinking of his gentle arms wrapped around her.

Russell had left the others just before midnight. He cut directly across the sagebrush where he was less likely to be trailed. He stumbled over something in the sand. Sitting for a second where he fell, he dug around to find the item. It was an old musket. He checked it out. It looked good, but it couldn't possibly be fired. The lock was broken. That made no difference. He didn't have any powder or balls for it anyway. But he decided to take it along. Hell, he could swing it like a club if he had to. He felt very conspicuous.

After stopping at a mountain spring for about an hour, Jones took his party through the Pine Nut Valley. They reached the Hot Springs on the Walker River in the early morning. Charlie knew he was about 10 miles north of Wellington on the Dayton Road. Things calmed down since Clifford's group split off. Horses taken from the Dutchman helped them make better progress. The men were in good spirits. Jones started toward the outpost.

"Rest here boys. I'll go in and get us a few things."

He had some coins stolen from the Dutchman so he could carry on a regular transaction. This would lessen any suspicion of them. Charlie hoped to put off anyone on his track while he was there. He entered the store, gathered up a few items and took them to the proprietor behind the counter to pay for them.

"Excuse me sir," he said, "which way is Dayton?"

The man gave him the directions he needed. Charlie thanked the elderly gentleman and walked out the door.

"Man, I sure can be personable when I need to," Charlie thought to himself.

Jones then led his band down the road toward Dayton.

"This ain't the way to Bishop Creek," said Cockerell. "We're heading north. Bishop Creek is south."

"Shut up, Tilden," commanded Charlie. "I'm trying to get

anyone interested in us to follow this track from the Hot Springs towards Dayton. So just shut your mouth and try to keep up."

The party left plain tracks toward Dayton for a couple miles. Jones felt anyone following will take the bait and track them to Dayton. At this point they turned and would now pass north and then east. This would take them near Pine Grove and then on the Aurora Road between Wellington and Sweetwater. Being on a horse was a lot easier on his feet. Since his days in the Civil War, he was never one to walk a lot. The hiking from the prison to the Dutchman's camp had really wore on his feet. Like Cockerell's bunch, they were being watched by Indians. That didn't bother Jones. Indians were a curious lot. A light was seen in the distance. It came from a ranch house. The men decided to swing off the road and rode far around the ranch. During the detour, they saw the evening fires of the Indian camp to the east.

"There's a little switch," Charlie thought, "now I am watching them."

❦ ❦ ❦

Ben Lackey arose from a deep sleep at first light. For a moment he just lay there on his bedroll, trying to gather his senses. He didn't recall where he was. He and the others got there when it was dark. Naturally he hadn't ever seen the place during daylight. He pulled his boots on over his socks and stood up to answer nature's call.

He walked a few yards from the camp. Watching the morning sky as he took care of business, he was shocked when he looked down. There, not 10 feet from where he slept, were signs of the convict's tracks.

"Hey," he yelled. "Wake up. Look what I found."

Their guide quickly verified what Lackey had seen. He said the tracks were about six hours old. The posse saddled up and set off after the Indian. He was already a quarter mile ahead.

❦ ❦ ❦

Billy Poor awoke to the noise of an early morning rooster. He rose from his comfortable feather bed. Barefoot, he wandered

outside to make use of the little shed with the half moon on the door. Back inside his mother had hot coffee on the stove. He poured himself a cup.

"Good morning ma. That's a mighty loud old bird out there."

"That he is son. I've got some breakfast for ya. Your father had to leave late last night. His night clerk got sick so he had to cover for him. He said he'd see you tonight after you get back."

The young man was very excited. Today he would take his first trip as a mail rider for Billy Wilson. He knew he didn't have to be there until noon.

However, he was going early for no other reason than he was really excited! His mother had another pile of pancakes covered with three fried eggs, just as he liked them.

"You're the best ma. You always remember my favorite breakfast. You're gonna spoil me."

"Nope, I'm just setting a good example so you can train yourself a good woman to take care of you."

After a little chit chat with his mom, Billy got dressed and pulled on his boots. He took the new gloves his father gave him out of the box. He stuck them in his saddle bag. They were great. They even had his initials on them! He was going to take the morning stage from Aurora to the Sweetwater station to meet Billy Wilson. This was where Billy wanted him to start his mail run. He kissed his mother goodbye.

"See ya, ma. I'm as excited as a little boy at Christmas."

"Good luck Billy. Have a safe trip."

He walked up the street to the stage office.

First light found Russell several miles from his sleeping

126

former companions. He was glad to be rid of them. The sun's glare was intense as he headed east. He looked behind him. He was a careful man and often looked back. He figured he'd go a few more miles and then find a place to hide till later that night.

He heard a noise coming from up ahead. Someone was whistling a tune. It was a catchy little tune. He'd heard it before, but couldn't remember the name. Obviously, there was someone on the trail heading his way. Soon he saw two mounted men. They pulled up in front of him.

"Morning stranger," said one man pleasantly.

Russell felt he must have made an impressive sight. A man dressed in a black and white striped outfit standing in the road with an old musket. He just glared up at them, saying nothing.

How could they not see he was a convict? The two men sized him up. He cocked the hammer and fingered the trigger on the weapon. The men naturally took this as a menacing gesture.

"Well, stranger. I'll guess we'll just be on our way."

They gently nudged their mounts and slowly rode around Russell. They gave him a wide berth. He smirked. They obviously didn't see the weapon had a broken lock.

He figured they would tell someone about seeing one of the escapees, first chance they got. This could be real bad. Thus, he reversed his trail and crossed the Carson River again. Now he was headed toward the Sierra Nevada. He found himself whistling that catchy little tune. He couldn't get it out of his head.

�� �� ��

In Independence, Sarah was up early and ready to move on to Los Angeles. She hadn't seen her relatives for almost nine months. She was getting excited. She was anxious to get started. She knew it was still quite a distance and she was somewhat impatient. The stage from Independence was scheduled to leave at 9:30 sharp. She was at the office and raring to go. She was nearly giddy when the Concord coach pulled up in front of the office. She joined the other passengers inside the coach.

"Just think, by tomorrow I will be having dinner with my mom and sister. I have so much to tell them about Bob."

127

She then realized that she hadn't thought about him at all for at least the past two hours. That was the first time that happened since she met the man!

৵ঌ ৵ঌ ৵ঌ

Those trailing Jones and his five comrades reached the Hot Springs on the Walker River in the early morning. The weary men dismounted. They looked forward to a hot meal and black coffee. They were served beans, eggs and tortillas. They asked a young Mexican boy to water their horses. If possible, they wanted them fed as well. While eating, the officers learned the six convicts had passed that point sometime after midnight. They found they were still six hours behind their quarry. It was reported they had set out for Dayton to the east. Swift, Downey and Atchison discussed the situation at length. Sheriff Swift gathered his group together.

"Men, I've decided that we need to turn around and head home. There's no way for us to catch these men. They're still at least six hours ahead of us. Our mounts are tired and so are we. I inquired here about fresh horses. None are available. We just don't have any choice."

Swift was very disappointed. It wasn't in his nature to give up. But what else could he do? With a heavy heart, he asked his group to mount up. They were turning back. Wishing the others good luck, Swift and his men were on their way.

Ben Lackey was driven. He was a bulldog. He wanted to catch these men. Atchison wasn't so sure. Downey and the Virginia militia leader sided with Lackey. The Dutchman was hell bent to stay on the convicts' trail. The men had been able to give the horses water and feed, plus a little more than an hour's rest. They thanked the Hot Springs proprietor for his hospitality and hit the trail. They headed east toward Dayton. Jones was smart, but not smart enough to fool experienced trackers. The posse saw where Charlie's party had turned south. They followed.

The stage from Aurora arrived at Sweetwater around 10 am. Young Billy had ridden up top in the boot with Billings, the driver. He quickly stepped off the coach. Billings threw down the young man's saddlebags. He had told him where to meet with Mr. Wilson. Billy could feel his heart pounding as he opened the door to the man's office and entered. The man behind the desk sized the young fellow up.

"Why I imagine you're young Poor. Welcome to Sweetwater. You're a mite early, son. Come on in. Sit down."

"Thanks. I just wanted to get off on the right foot. I'm really excited about this opportunity."

"Well we have plenty of time to go over everything. You want some coffee? It's over there on the stove."

"Don't mind if I do. It'll help clear some of the dust out of my throat."

He took a cup from a hook on the wall and filled it.

"Can I freshen up your cup?"

"Naw, I don't drink any this late in the morning."

Billy sat the pot back on the stove and resumed his seat. He looked around the small office. Aside from the man's desk and the wood stove, he saw wall maps and posted announcements. He noticed one of them told about a Nevada State Prison break at Carson City the previous Sunday night.

Watson, Baker and Jacks reached the Mason Valley in the early morning. They had followed the Walker River into a large fertile valley. It was named after its first settler, "Hock" Mason. He first saw the valley back in 1854 while on a cattle drive to California. Hock was so struck with the land that he returned five years later. It was then that he established the valley's first home-stead and called it the Mason Valley. At 4,380 feet, this was an area ripe for farming, surrounded by high desert terrain.

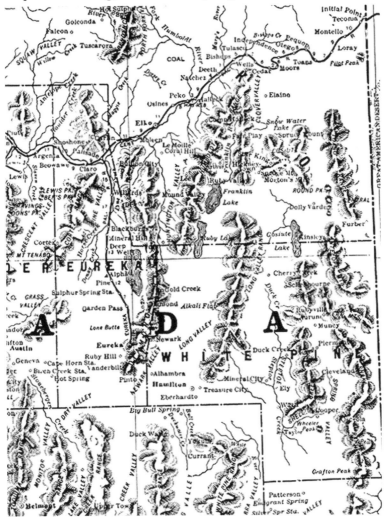

The map to Tecoma Nevada

Watson and his party hadn't seen anyone following them. They needed to get to Skull to so he could con Baker out of his gold. Skull was a mere mining camp close to Tecoma. It was near the Utah border, east beyond the Mason Valley and past Belmont in Nye County. During their overnight journey they came upon a gruesome sight. But it sure worked to their advantage.

They found the remains of two men and a mule. They were spotted at the base of a cliff. Apparently the dead men had been traveling along the top and lost their footing. This find gave the three of them an advantage. They removed the clothing from the men. They also found other duds on the dead pack animal. One rifle survived the fall. Both corpses had gun belts and pistols. In the dead men's gear they found shaving items, a few dollars in coins, bedrolls, cooking equipment, an axe and more.

They packed the non perishables and other items to take with them. No more prison garb. Watson decided to shave. He got out the shaving gear and a wash basin. Baker and Jacks looked at him in amazement.

"You don't want to shave," said Baker.

"Why not?"

"Cuz right now we all look like all other miners roaming around these parts. If you're clean shaven you'll stand out. We don't need to stand out."

"You're right, what was I thinking?"

He was amazed he hadn't realized this himself. Maybe Baker wasn't as dumb as he originally thought. He felt much less conspicuous and more confident they would succeed with his overall plan. Looking at the other two he said:

"If anyone asks, I'm John Martin. Baker you're Frank Cunningham and Jacks you're Isaacs Biggs."

With their present gear and get ups, there was no need to hide anymore. They decided not to skirt Belmont. They would go right through. Perhaps they could get an updated report on the prison break.

෨ ෨ ෨

The Jones gang had passed Pine Grove, skirted Wellington and was now on the Aurora Road moving toward Sweetwater.

"Hey Morton," said Charlie, "doesn't that guy Dingman

ride the mail on this trail."

"Yeah, I think he does, last time I heard anyway."

"Wouldn't it be great if he happened along today?"

"That would really make my day."

Dingman was hated by the convicts. This was due to the prison escape attempt in 1870. During this failed breakout, three convicts were killed. It was rumored Dingman shot them. The truth was two were killed by Wellington Bower. Dingman did get one. No matter - in typical prison bravado, the convicts had vowed to kill this man if the chance ever came their way.

After the incident, Dingman thought it better he leave his prison job. It was rumored he had taken a job as a mail rider out of Aurora.

Chapter Fifteen
Billy Poor Rides Out of Sweetwater

Billy Wilson had started his stage line and mail run several years ago. At first, he did everything. He fed and watered the stock, loaded the coach and even drove the routes. Little by little the business grew. It had become rather successful. Now he didn't have to work so hard. After he finished his morning paperwork, he took young Poor out to the stable.

He asked the boy to pick out a mount. Once Billy had chosen a horse, Wilson told him to saddle up. Young Poor asked Wilson which saddle and tack belonged to the horse. Wilson liked the kid. The boy knew that the horse would be paired with a saddle. Wilson was pleased with the young man's knowledge of what he was doing. He had hired the kid sight unseen as a favor to his father. He was glad to see it was going to work out.

The young man led the horse over to the office. He tied it to the porch rail. Wilson stepped out of the office with the mail pouch. It was almost noon, time for the rider to leave for Wellington. Poor tied the mail pouch to this saddle. He checked his cinch and tightened it. He patted the animal that was about to speed him on his way. Billy opened his saddle bag and took out the gloves his dad had given him. He felt very proud. He pulled them on. They fit perfectly and felt good, real buckskin. He grabbed the saddle horn and swung onto the horse. He turned toward the end of town and rode out. Poor was confident he would make the 22 mile ride to Wellington in record time.

༺ ༺ ༺

Ben Lackey's horse had come up lame. He stopped and checked his mount. The news wasn't all bad. The horse had thrown a shoe as well as picked up a rock. Ben removed the rock. He realized he couldn't continue trying to catch someone so far ahead with this horse.

"Damn, the luck. I can't go any further on this horse."

Downey, Atchison and the Virginia militia leader looked around their combined group. It was evident that none of them should go on. They were far from supplies and their animals were weak from this continued pursuit.

"Well, Ben," said Downey, "this must be some sorta sign. We'd all better head back."

Once a final decision was made to turn back to Virginia City, the Dutchman was livid.

"We can't stop now," he yelled in his broken English. "I won't stop until I have them. I'll get some help in Aurora."

"Sorry," said Downey, "we just can't go on. Good luck."

With that Downey, Atchison, Lackey and the rest slowly rode east toward Dayton. It was closer than riding to Carson City.

∽§∽ ∽§∽ ∽§∽

"Good morning, Dr. Lee," offered Mrs. Denver as she saw the doctor enter her husband's hospital room. "My husband is quite uncomfortable. What can be done about that?"

"Well, we cleaned out the wound again early this morning. Apparently when the ball entered Frank's body it carried little pieces of cloth in with it. Since cloth has germs, these germs had caused further infection. I feel I have been able to get all the dangerous material out of his wound."

"Will he make better progress toward recovery now?"

"Yes. He should be able to go home in a couple of days. By the way, how is Jennie?"

"Jennie's back in school. Fortunately she seems to have returned to her normal routine. She was able to sleep through the night and that's a good sign."

"I'm pleased to hear that. That whole experience had to be very traumatic to such a young child."

∽§∽ ∽§∽ ∽§∽

The Jones gang had stopped to rest, again. These frequent stops were caused by Cockerell. Charlie knew Cockerell's feet were in terrible shape. He could see the man was barely able to

134

walk. This was slowing down their movement considerably. He needed time to think. He took Burke aside.

"You know that we'd be better off if Tilden just stayed here by himself," said Charlie.

"What do you mean," inquired Burke?

"He can hardly walk and is slowing us up. We need to get rid of him. I think I'll just shoot him. That'll solve the problem."

Burke was shocked. He walked over to Cockerell to try and prevent Jones from taking any action. Jones dropped the subject.

"We're gonna rest here awhile," said Charlie. "Roberts take a horse and scour around to see if you can find something to eat or anything of use to us. But don't be gone too long."

"All right Charlie. I won't be long."

Bedford rode toward Sweetwater. About a mile from the others, he saw a small structure about 50 yards from the road. He cautiously rode up.

"Hello the house."

No one answered. Roberts figured this must be the Milk Ranch that the folks at the Hot Springs had spoken about. He dismounted and tied his horse to the hitching post.

"Anyone here."

Again no answer. He opened the front door and entered the house. Roberts looked around the place and found some useful items. In the bedroom was an old cedar chest. Inside were several articles of clothing. The kid quickly stripped off his prison duds and put on a pair of pants and a shirt. He gathered up the rest of the clothes for the others. He left the house and headed for the barn. He figured he had been there about five minutes. He heard something out on the road. It was hoof beats. Someone was coming from the south. He hid himself in a cornfield. He watched as a single rider approached and rode on past.

Billy Poor was enjoying his ride. It was a pretty day and not too hot. His mount was an easy ride. The gait was comfortable. Billy wasn't getting sore. He'd been a little worried about that. He hadn't ridden much for the past couple of years. He had saddle sores before and remembered they were no fun. Billy was now about 12 miles out from Sweetwater. The actual spot was a half mile north of Sulfur Springs. He saw a stream crossing the road. He slowed to a walk. Perhaps he would water the horse. He looked up and saw a group of men.

The mail rider heads toward Wellington

Burke was the first to hear the rider.

"Hey, maybe that's Dingham!"

The rider slowed down and was riding toward them.

"Afternoon," he said.

Morton reached up and pulled Billy off the horse. The kid landed hard on the ground. Morton held him there with a knee on his chest. He took a six shooter from the Billy's belt, tossing it to Jones. Billy looked up at the others watching him. He was petrified. Morton went through his pockets. He found $20 in coins and a pen knife. Seeing two rings on the man's fingers, Morton removed them. He then stood and pulled Billy up. The frightened boy was wild eyed.

Burke sized him up. "What's your name? You look like that bastard on the jury that helped convict me."

"Poor," the boy gasped. "Billy Poor. I'm the mail rider from Sweetwater."

"That's it," he replied. "You look just like your old man, the bastard on the jury that sent me to prison. I'd like to kill you son, just to make your old man suffer for what he did to me!"

"Where's the regular mail rider, Dingman," said Jones? "We want Dingman. We want him so we can cook his goose!"

"There you go you son of a bitch," Morton yelled at Jones. "Now you let the cat out of the bag."

"I don't know anyone named Dingman," cried Billy.

"No matter," laughed Jones. "Hey Lea, bring that guy with you and follow me."

With that, Jones walked off parallel to the road. Morton followed, dragging Poor behind him. Burke, Black and Cockerell looked on apprehensively. They figured that with the mood Charlie was in, it was better to leave him alone. They heard poor Billy, arguing for his very life, as Morton pulled him down the road. Jones stopped about 200 yards away.

"Take your boots off," ordered Morton.

"What."

"You heard me. I said take your boots off. Take your pants and shirt off too."

"Why?"

"You ain't gonna need them, that's why. Hurry up."

Billy sat in the dirt tugging on his boots to pull them off. He removed his jacket, then his shirt. He stood up and undid the buttons on his pants. He slid them off. He just stood there in his long johns. Charlie and Billy were about the same size. Jones had removed his prison shirt and pants. He took Billy's clothes and put them on. He threw his prison garments at the kid.

"Here," ordered Jones "put these on."

"Why?"

"I don't want ya to catch cold," he snickered.

Billy pulled on the pants and pulled the shirt over his head. He stood there looking at Morton and Jones not knowing what to do next. Morton looked at Billy and teased him.

"Hey, aren't you one of those Nevada State Prison escapees? Maybe I better shoot ya and get me a reward."

For several minutes the two men took turns tormenting their captive. Billy was treated like a toy they were playing with. Finally they tired of this sport. Jones picked up his rifle and opened the breech to see if a cartridge was ready to fire. Morton checked the rounds in his shooter. Billy's eyes showed terror as he watched his captors. Both men fired fatal shots at his head. Poor fell like a stone into the sagebrush.

"Well Lea," said Jones, "it looks like one of those convicts got what was coming to them."

"Sort of. But he doesn't look like any of us," said Lea.

With that, he walked around until he found a large rock. Barely able to lift it off the ground, Lea carried it over to the dead boy and dropped it on his head. The huge rock bounced off the young man's head. It torn the skin on his face and broke his nose. Morton's intent was to deform the face beyond any possible recognition. This horrible act didn't achieve the desired result.

"Hell, that didn't help," said Jones, "he still looks just like the guy we killed."

"I know what to. This will help a lot," replied Morton.

He grabbed the dead boy's legs and drug the body over to some sagebrush. He broke off other pieces of sagebrush and put them all around the kid's face. He pulled a match from his pocket, sparked a flame and lit the brush on fire. In a moment it flared up and burned rapidly.

Morton starts brush fire to hide the body's identity

"That'll do it," said Morton.

"Man, Lea, I never want ya to get mad at me!"

Morton looked at the rings he took from Poor, as Charlie watched to see what this crazed man might do next. Lea took a gold ring and tossed it to Jones.

"There ya go. I'm keeping this one If I get caught, I'll just toss it away."

"Thanks. Not me. I'll wear this one to hell," said Jones.

Morton and Jones watched the fire play out. Morton had Poor's gloves and his boots. Together they calmly walked back to the camp.

⚜ ⚜ ⚜

The monthly shipment from San Francisco arrived at the Benton General Store around 11 am. Morrison and Devine had worked all morning to rearrange things. Bob wanted to make sure he had enough room for all the items he was expecting. He was glad he had lots to do. It was hard for him not to think about Sarah. It was even harder to have to wait a week for her return. He had grown so used to Sarah, especially her hugs and kisses. He really missed his future wife.

"You've got that look again, Bob," Henry joked.

"What look is that?"

"The silly one you always get when you think about sis. She'll be back before you know it."

"Have I ever told ya how pleased I am that ya came out here to make your fortune? Just think, if ya hadn't, Sarah would have never showed up here in Benton. Thanks, my friend."

"Ah shucks. I didn't know ya cared!"

139

Chapter Sixteen
Desperate Men on the Run

After the rider disappeared, Roberts continued to rummage around. He was able to find a few potatoes and other useful things. It had taken him about 20 minutes. He saw some chickens and chased after them. They outmaneuvered him so he left them alone. He went back to his horse, undid the reins and climbed aboard. He took his time riding back to the others.

Returning to camp, he saw three men near the horses. Two others were approaching the camp from a hill nearby. He saw some smoke in the distance. He reined in to look further. He didn't recognize the two coming off the hill. Soon he could tell this was Morton and Jones. The latter no longer wore prison garb.

"Where'd ya get them duds, Charlie," Roberts asked.

"Oh I got a raise. Looks like you found some duds too."

"What's that smoke back yonder," Black asked.

"That kid must be cookin his dinner," laughed Morton.

With that, Morton and Jones settled into camp. They told the others how they played with the kid, dressed him in the prison outfit, shot the boy and then set the him afire.

"There the kid was, begging for his life, but we didn't give him much time to beg, hey Morton? I can't believe you smashed in his face with that rock and then set him on fire. Man, you boys better steer clear of ole Lea here or he'll probably roast ya!"

John Burke

Burke remarked, "I don't give a cent on such cold blooded murders as that, we'll have the whole country after us. I'am going to leave this crowd."

"Leave if ya want too," said Lea.

"I'm taking a Henry and a horse."

"You aren't taking either."

140

"I'm taking both and if any of ya bother me I'll shoot your guts out."

"Boys, there's no use for this," Cockerell interjected. "We've got to stick together."

Burke sneered at the cutthroats, "Ya couldn't kill him with one shot, ya had to shoot him twice!"

"We both shot him," said Morton, "because I'd offered to pull the trigger with any man and Charlie said I'm your man. So we both shot him!"

"Hey Burke, take these," said Morton as he threw Poor's boots to the man. Then he put the kid's gloves on.

"These are brand new," he thought, nice buckskin.

Burke sat down to take his boots off and put on the new ones. Cockerell watched with great interest. Having been without shoes since the break, his feet were torn up. Burke knew this.

"Here ya go," he said handing his old boots to Cockerell.

"Thanks," he said, "my feet are killing me."

"It's probably best we think about getting on down the road," said Charlie. "Hey Roberts, what'd you find?"

"Aside from some clothes, I got a few potatoes and a couple cans of peaches."

"Where'd ya find them?"

"There's a small ranch about a mile up the road. I think it was the Milk Ranch they spoke about at Hot Springs. No one was about. It looks like a man and woman live there."

Roberts purposely phrased his reply to place a man and a woman at the ranch he visited. Morton and Jones had set a rule for the group. If they found a place run by a single man, they'd kill him and take everything. If he was a family man, they'd let him live. The others didn't want to have anyone else killed. The mail rider was bad enough. After the party had moved some distance from the Milk Ranch, Roberts said that only a single man lived there. Morton and Jones were both furious with Roberts. He shrank away from them. The others prevented him from getting a severe beating. Morton and Jones wanted to go back and kill the guy at the Milk Ranch, but they continued on their way.

The men had gone a short distance down the road when

Morton felt his saddle move. He was riding Billy Poor's mount. He stopped the horse and stepped down. He slipped off his gloves so he could fix his saddle. He set them on the horse's haunch. Finding the problem, he worked to fix it. Satisfied his saddle was okay, he placed his boot in the stirrup and swung aboard. A couple hours later, 10 miles down the trail, Morton cussed out loud.

"Shit, I set those damned gloves on the back of this horse when I adjusted the saddle. They must a fallen off. I'm goin back to get them."

"That's crazy, Lea," Jones said. "Forget them."

They continued on. Morton thought of the Poor's gloves in the middle of the trail covered in blood with his initials on them. He still thought he should go back, but continued with the others. Before long they got to a place called Dexter's Canyon. Charlie figured this would be a good place to camp for the night.

❦ ❦ ❦

Parson's wound was healing nicely. Roth and Chapman were getting impatient with Clifford. They'd walked all day and accomplished nothing. Roth wanted to know where the hell Frank's friend and his ranch were. He now wished he'd gone with Jones and his group.

"Frank," he said, "we're all thinkin this. Where's this friend of yours? We could die out here if we don't get some help."

"I know what you're all thinkin," Clifford apologized. "I'm sure we're close by. We'll probably find it tomorrow."

The men hadn't eaten since the meal they had at the prison the night of the break. It was late in the day and they were all weary. Parsons found a good spot with shelter from the wind and cold of the evening to spend the night. They hadn't seen anyone all day. Not even the Indians had bothered them. They were all seated on the ground, resting.

"Hey look," whispered Roth pointing off to the east "There's another coyote looking for his dinner."

"That, my friend," said Parsons, "will be our dinner."

He sighted his shooter at the animal and fired. The coyote yelped, flopped on its side and tried to stand. Parsons shot it again.

142

This time it lay still. In a moment the old stage coach robber had the animal back at their makeshift camp. He skinned it. Chapman and Roth had quickly gathered up some kindling. Roth sparked a flint several times in a pile of leaves. Soon he had a small fire. Chapman added some small sticks. Parsons waited until they had some good coals. Then he cooked a long awaited meal.

Afterwards, Parson remarked, "that was the sweetest tasting meat I ever had."

☙ ☙ ☙

The mouth of Six Mile Canyon looked just like home to Squires. He and Willis had been slowed up most of the day by all the traffic that moved in and around Dayton. They were finally able to get across the Carson River. They'd moved down river on the north side until they reached their current position. Squires

Virginia City Nevada above Six Mile Canyon

figured it was just a matter of time before he'd convince someone to give him a stake. He'd just offer part of the cache he'd hidden away here in the canyon as an incentive. The two continued on up canyon for about three miles. Squires noticed something and figured he'd located a place to hold up. It looked like a mere coyote hole. Squires stuck his head in. It opened up into a space about 8 feet deep and nearly 12 feet long. He crawled in. When Squires disappeared inside the ground, Willis was puzzled. He stuck his

143

head in, quickly looked around and pulled it back out. Squires stuck his head out.

"Get in here."

"No, you're nuts. That's like a prison cell."

"Fine, don't come in. Go find your own place to hide."

Soon Willis crawled inside as well.

⚘ ⚘ ⚘

The stage agent at Wellington was mildly agitated. He had some mail that needed to go to Aurora in the morning. Normally the mail rider from Sweetheart would have been here by now. He was aware a new rider had been hired and was scheduled to work today. Where the hell was he? Some regular customers had come in to see what mail might have been delivered. He simply had to tell them the mail rider hadn't arrived yet. If it had been raining or snowing he could understand why the rider might be late. But today had been sunny and bright. Finally in the late afternoon, the agent walked over to the telegraph office.

"Hey there Horace," he said, "I need you to send Billy Wilson a message."

"Just a second," the man replied, fumbling with his instrument. "Okay, what's the message?"

"The mail rider from Sweetwater didn't arrive yet. I have return mail to give him once he does arrive. Don't expect him until late tonight as it is now nearly 6:30."

Horace keyed the instrument and sent the message. The words quickly ran through the wires to Sweetwater. The telegraph operator wrote down the message and took it over to the stage office. He found the door locked and a note saying Billy had gone to Aurora for the night. Knowing Billy would want this information, the operator returned to his office and sent the information on to Aurora. The message was soon received. The Aurora clerk had seen Billy just a while ago going into the saloon just down the street. He walked over and delivered the message to the man.

"Thanks," said Billy to the operator.

The information disturbed him. What in the hell could have happened to that boy. It was too late to go looking for him

144

now. Well I had better go over to the Poor's place. His parents must be wondering where he was.

"Good evening Mrs. Poor. I dropped by to let you know that your son didn't get to Wellington yet. He probably had some trouble with his horse. If he doesn't turn up tonight we will go look for him tomorrow."

"Thank you Billy, please keep me posted."

"I will. I'm sure he's just fine."

Billy walked off the porch and back toward the saloon. Mrs. Poor grabbed her shawl. She left the house and headed to the hotel. She had to tell her husband this distressing news.

✒ ✒ ✒

Tom Ryan had been welcomed with open arms. He couldn't have been more surprised. When he approached the ranch house last evening he didn't know exactly what to expect. The ranch was owned by James Horton. He and his wife Hanna had been there for five years. They had two young sons, Brett and Morgan. Without as much as a howdy do, Hanna had found him clothes to wear. He was about James' size, so they fit just fine. The man even had an old pair of boots.

Ryan joined them for dinner. Afterwards the two men enjoyed talking and smoking on the porch. His past never came up. He had been given a blanket and was still wrapped up in it when he heard the animals near him fussing. He noticed young Brett with his milk pail. While he watched, the young fella expertly milked the old girl. The boy noticed he was being watched.

"Morning sir," the lad said.

"Morning son," replied Ryan.

The boy returned to the house. Ryan got up and stretched. He had no idea of what to do. He walked over to the house and knocked on the door.

"Good morning Tom," said Mrs. Horton. "How about a nice hot cup of coffee."

"Thanks ma'am."

"James already left for Shorty's place. He helps Shorty and Shorty helps us. Today, they're moving steers down from the Pine Nuts to the flats here. He asked me to set out some provisions for you. What are ya planning to do?"

"I'm not sure. But, I'd like to help out for a few hours to thank ya for your kindness. How can I help?"

"Well after a little breakfast ya could chop some wood for us. It's starting to get cold in the evenings. That would save James some work."

Ryan enjoyed a wonderful morning meal. She had prepared pancakes, fresh sausage, three fried eggs and pan fried potatoes. He couldn't remember when he'd eaten such a fantastic meal. He spent the day cutting and stacking wood. There was more than a cord on the porch for the Hortons.

James returned just after sunset. Ryan joined him at the barn and asked how his day went. Then they went to the house for dinner. Hanna had steaks, potatoes, fresh vegetables, bread and cobbler for dinner.

Ryan thought he'd died and gone to heaven. Sitting on the porch again after dinner, James thanked him for the wood. He asked if he'd like to stay on for awhile. Ryan was tempted. But figured he'd end up getting caught. He thanked the man and retired for the evening. He went to the barn to sleep.

He rested comfortably for about four hours. A little after midnight he headed to the mountains across Jack's Valley. He hated to leave, but felt he had too.

⋞⋞⋞

When Pat Hurley left Squires and Willis, he blatantly went right back to Virginia City. This could have been very dangerous. Pat was fairly well known in the bustling town. But, he figured, why not? He felt much relieved after looking up some friends. They told him the County Sheriff, City Chief of Police and nearly every other lawman was reported out of the region looking for the escapees. Old Pat Hurley was a hoot! His buddies thought it was great that Pat had come back to them. They enjoyed themselves, gambling, drinking and generally carrying on. What could anyone expect? They were Irishmen!

⋞⋞⋞

Bergie Burgesser, the brave bartender from the Warm Spring Hotel, was now hailed by locals as a hero. He had told the story countless times about his experience in the courtyard. With bullets flying everywhere, his pantaloons were torn to ribbons. Soon he was standing there with his fanny hanging out in a blaze of gunfire. He'd no idea why he wasn't hit. On a very sober note, he missed his friend Matt Pixley. He'd taken over most of the duties that Pixley had handled. The dead man's young wife had left the hotel and was staying in Carson City with her brother-in-law's family. Burgesser was hoping for the return of his revolver. Some one took his ivory stock, silver barreled, six shooter from the hotel during the melee. He was very sentimental about the weapon. The stock has the head of Shakespeare on the side and CWB on the end. He considered it to be a highly prized as a memento and its return would earn his lasting gratitude.

⊰∽⊰∽⊰

The stage to Los Angeles had traveled a long way that day. Sarah was enjoying her conversation with her fellow passengers. One was a Mr. Hopkins. He had an interesting story. Just six months ago he was nearly penniless. Then one day he was working his sluice box at some old tailings by an abandoned mine near Monoville. To his astonishment, he found 17 fairly good sized nuggets in just five hours. He packed his mule, rode to Bishop Creek, bought a new suit and a ticket to Los Angeles. He was excited to show his dad that he had amounted to something!

Sarah told her story, too. It was Bob, his business and all about the plans they had for the future. As she talked of Bob, she felt very close to him.

The two other passengers were Henry Barther and Benjamin Remany, both Privates of the U.S. Cavalry. They were posted at Camp Independence. They were traveling to Los Angeles to be with Henry's mother. He had received word that his father had passed away. The elder Barthers had raised both boys back in Pennsylvania. Sarah was sad to hear of their loss, but she was pleased to hear they were fellow natives of Pennsylvania.

Having these good people to talk with during the long trip made it much more bearable. She didn't mind any of it. She just wanted to get there and see her family.

⊰∽⊰∽⊰

"It's getting dark," said Jones as he slowed up in Dexter Canyon. "We'll stay here tonight."

Charlie dismounted. The others followed, except Cockerell, who was still afoot. The horses were hobbled. Black and Rob-

148

erts looked around for some firewood. The men were hungry.

"See those cattle out there," pointed Lea? "I say we have one for dinner."

He mounted his horse and rode toward them. Soon a single shot rang out. Morton was back in about 20 minutes with some nice looking steaks.

"Where are those potatoes you found," he said looking at Roberts?

"Right here."

"Good, I'll cook them up with these steaks. We'll eat like rich folks tonight!"

∝ঙ ∝ঙ ∝ঙ

Billy Poor's father took the news of his missing son hard. It was no secret to anyone in Aurora that 29 convicts had escaped from the Nevada State Prison on Sunday night. Rumors had convicts going everywhere, including toward Aurora. Poor's father feared his son had become a victim of foul play. He shared these concerns with the sheriff and others in Aurora.

Consequently a party consisting of Deputy Sheriff Palmer, J.S. Mooney, P. Kelly, Ned Baker, Horace Poor, John McCune and about a half dozen others was gathered. The men started in pursuit just before nine that night. They rode south toward Mono Lake and Adobe Meadows.

Chapter Seventeen
Stories of Life Along the Trail

Two miles south of Carson City, Henry O'Leary had spent another night on the road. He thought about home. The 17-year-old lad had run away from his stepfather's farm. The old man hated him. Everyday he was beaten. Enough was enough. He wanted to kill him, but he couldn't. So he left to seek his fortune. He wondered if he'd made the right decision.

Just a few more miles and he'd be in the hills of Virginia City. He'd get a mining job. In his spare time, he'd look for a claim of his own. The cool breeze brought him out of his dream. He grabbed his makeshift pack and headed toward town. On the outskirts in the southern section of Carson City, the young man walked in from the high desert. As the trail became a street he

saw several quaint houses lining the road. It was cold. His stomach was growling. His coat collar was pulled up around his neck. Spotting a home ringed by a picket fence he altered his course. He opened the gate and entered the yard, closing it behind him. Continuing on to the porch he knocked on the door. He heard a voice yell:

"Just a minute."

He stood there waiting, not knowing what to expect. He

150

heard footsteps coming toward the door. To his surprise his knock was soon answered by a striking young woman.

As she opened the door, Amanda Eberhart, saw a young man wearing a thin coat and black pants. He had a light stubble beard. She sized him up. He looked harmless and very cold. The boy was very good looking.

"Excuse me ma'am, I'm really hungry and wondered if ya could give me something to eat."

"Sure. Come on in. Sit over there at the table. Do ya want some coffee?"

"Yes, please." An aroma of breakfast hung in the air. He noticed the table standing in the back of the room. He went over and sat right down.

Amanda was so very excited. Here was a handsome fella right in her house. Her parents had left early and wouldn't be home until late this evening. She was a flirt and she decided to turn it up a notch. She tried everything she could to make him notice her.

She bent over seductively when she poured his coffee. She brushed his shoulder with her body as she brought a plate of eggs, sausage and biscuits. She wanted to treat him to a hearty meal. She batted her eyes. Nothing seemed to get him to notice her. She was disappointed that he kept his head down during his stay.

Why wouldn't he look at her directly? She knew she was pretty. Everyone said she was. What was wrong with this one? She wasn't sure if he was painfully shy or trying to hide something. Just when she was going to ask him if he'd like her to draw him a bath, her little brother wandered into the dining room. Darn him. Why does he have to spoil my fun?

"Hey Amanda, who's that?"

She just glared at him as he went on to ask the man:

"Where do ya live?"

"Nowhere in particular."

"Where did ya stay last night?"

"Out in the sagebrush."

"Wasn't it cold outside?"

"Yes it was, for someone dressed as I am."

As suddenly as he appeared the little guy disappeared. Her guest stood up. She wondered why he was in such a hurry?

"I'd like to thank ya for that delicious breakfast."

"Why don't ya sit here with me and talk for awhile."

"I really need to be getting on. Thanks again."

With that he looked directly into her sparkling eyes. She was mesmerized. He had never felt this way before. He reached out with his hands and gently touched her cheeks. Her eyes closed. He slowly bent down and kissed her on the lips, ever so gently.

"Thank you Amanda for your kindness," he whispered, breaking their kiss.

"He knows my name," she thought as her heart fluttered.

The young man turned, opened the door, exited and closed it behind him. The young lady was flush with pink. She could hardly get her breath. Her brother ran in and said:

"I'll bet that's the escaped convict they call J.B. Roberts. He's the only one that's young like him."

Henry continued toward Virginia City. He hoped to catch

a ride on a freight wagon to hasten his journey. He thought of Amanda. Wow, what a girl. Maybe one day he'd return this way.

Fifteen miles southeast of Carson City, two enterprising prospectors, John Ludwig and John Wheeler, toiled in the hills. Like nearly everyone else in western Nevada, they'd heard of the murderous prison break. These were hardy men. They'd turned a buck in many ways. Now they wanted to cash in on this event. Yesterday a posse rode through. The leader said several escapees were heading south. The convicts figured freedom would be found in Arizona or Mexico. The 33-year-old Wheeler convinced

his partner he knew how to get some of that reward money. They were very familiar with every foot of the region from Belmont to the Coast Range and from Carson to the Colorado River. They'd been mining in Nevada and California for the past seven years.

"We'll cut off their escape route to Arizona and Mexico, forcing them back this way," said Wheeler to his partner. "I'm gonna ride south to the Armagosa Mines. Once I tell the men there to be on the lookout, they'll spread the word clear to the Cajon Pass. I'll get word to the Paiute and Armagosa Indians too."

"That's a great idea, John," said Ludwig. "When the convicts know they can't safely go south, they'll head back this way. With any luck we should be able to catch a few."

The two packed provisions for John's trip. Wheeler, secured he gear, hopped into the saddle and spurred his mount towards the south and the Armagosa Mines.

Ludwig waved as his partner disappeared in a cloud of dust. He pulled out his tobacco pouch. He took a paper and slowly filled it with tobacco. He carefully rolled the cigarette. He replaced the pouch. He struck a match, ignited the paper, took a puff and sat down for a relaxing smoke.

He would gather up their gear and take it back to town this afternoon. He told Wheeler he'd let Sheriff Helm know of their plan. Perhaps the sheriff would form a posse and work with them. Once he'd spoken to the sheriff he'd ride out toward the White Mountains to meet up with John on his return trip. He figured that John should be back in about a week.

Wheeler rode along as fast as he could. He had three swift horses. The route he had planned was nearly 150 miles one way.

Deputy Sheriff Palmer and his posse took a long detour toward Mono Lake from Aurora. During the day an Indian told him that six men were camped in a canyon about five miles away near Dexter.

Eventually they were rewarded with tracks left by the convicts near Adobe Meadows.

Hope that young Poor was still alive and well was also found. It was in the form of his gloves in two different locations.

The men figured the young man had left them so someone following them could locate him. Thus their desire to continue and help save him spurred them on.

Burke was the first of the Jones Gang to awaken this morning. The group had thoroughly enjoyed the beef Morton cooked for them last night. Cockerell woke up and wiped the sleep from his eyes. His feet were feeling better. Ever since Burke told him what Charlie had said about him dragging behind, he'd been very careful. There was a shooter in his pants and he wouldn't hesitate to use it if Jones made any move to eliminate him. Burke and Cockerell exchanged glances. Roberts rolled over, farting loudly in the process. The noise actually woke Black up.

"Geeze kid, take it easy, you're gonna soil yourself," teased Burke.

"Golly boy, what crawled up your backside and died," ventured Cockerell.

Morton had been taking all this in when the wind shifted and his nose picked up what Roberts had put in the air.

"My Gawd," he said sitting up and looking at Roberts. "Get up and move away from camp if ya have to do that."

Black too had a keen sense of smell. The foul odor from Robert's direction actually drove him from his bed roll.

"Damn, what is that?"

The object of ridicule didn't say a word. But unfortunately for the others, he wasn't done yet. He thought this was funny. Raising his fanny at bit, he purposely forced out another.

"Okay, Roberts," yelled Charlie, "that's enough."

"Sorry," lied Roberts. "It must be something I ate."

In Carson City, the county district attorney held an investigation into Matt Pixley's death. A jury was quickly assembled to hear the proceedings at the Coroner's inquest. Most of the testimony came from the guards involved in the murderous shoot out.

Members of the Coroner's inquest went to the hospital to hear from Isaacs. Speaking slowly from his bed, he said he observed Charles Jones and Thomas Flynn fire their weapons at the same moment in Pixley's direction. He couldn't say who actually

The Corner's Inquest at Carson City

killed Pixley, but placed both men in a position to appear guilty.

The jury heard from Newhouse, the Warm Springs bartender and others. It didn't take the jury long to come to a conclusion. They found that Pixley met his death by a gun shot wound inflicted by Charles Jones or Thomas Flynn.

The court clerk was directed to issue warrants for these two. The jury wanted it read into the proceedings that the other escaped convicts were to be held as accessories.

It pained the men in the Coroner's Jury to see how poorly Isaacs was doing. They admired him for his courage in mustering up the strength to tell his story. One of the men, Peter Rochi, was a friend of Dr. Lee, who had been caring for Isaacs. Once the inquest was over, he sought out his friend to inquire about Isaacs.

"Howdy doc," Peter said, "is Isaacs going to recover?"

"Unfortunately, he's in a very perilous condition. I'm afraid his right leg will have to be amputated. But at this point, Dr. Waters and I don't feel it prudent to tell him. That information could further demoralize the man. I feel terrible for his wife.

156

She's taking it real hard. But enough of that; how are things down at the blacksmith shop?"

⊰ ⊰ ⊰

The men with Clifford were impatient. He'd promised them help would be close at hand. They'd get food and clothes. Provisions and horses would be forthcoming, too. They'd spent two days roaming around in circles.

"Frank, we need to find your friend's place today," said Parsons. "If we don't, then we need another plan. We'll freeze or starve up here if we keep wandering around like this."

"Yeah Frank, this isn't good," said Chapman. "The only thing we've eaten since we broke free was that coyote. Sleeping outside under the stars isn't what I had in mind when I joined up with you. It's too damned cold."

"I'm sorry boys," he replied. "But we can't get side tracked. His place must be near here. Give me another day or two. We'll find it. We can't give up."

"I want to find this guy's ranch as much as you, Frank," said Roth, "but we need to think about other options. We're too hungry and the nights are too cold to do this much longer."

"It's okay Frank, we know you mean well. I'm still with ya," said Parsons. "With any luck we'll find the place today."

"I'm with ya, too," said Chapman.

"Thanks," replied Frank. "I'm frustrated too, but I can't give up. Let's head up that draw and over that rise. His place just can't be too much further."

With that, Clifford started for the draw. The other three followed him up the trail.

⊰ ⊰ ⊰

Down along the East Walker River, Joe Schreck looked over the beautiful land that surrounded his way station 17 miles north of Aurora. The station was situated at the foot of a canyon. He vividly remembered the day back eight or nine years ago when he first saw this place. There was fine bunch grass all about. The river provided plenty of water. Just because I live on the bend

157

of this river, he thought to himself, I ended up with the nickname "Elbow Joe". He had to admit, the bend does resemble an elbow. He'd never regretted "squatting" here back in the 1860s. He first established a stage station. He then bought some cows to built up a dairy herd. His cattle ate the natural feed. Each year he mowed the fine meadow grass and stored it for winter feed.

Well enough of that he told himself. He'd better get the milk containers and butter ready for the daily stage. It was due in about an hour. The stage took his butter and milk into Aurora for sale. As he finished, his wife called him to supper.

Again he remembered the early years. At first it was lonely by himself. His old dog was fairly good company, but died back in 1868. He wanted a wife and family. That was a problem. There weren't any women out this way, except those passing by on the stage. So he tried a long shot. He answered an advertisement in the Territorial Enterprise for a mail order bride.

To his surprise, he received a reply the following month. Letters were exchanged for about five months before he had the courage to ask her to come to Nevada and be his wife. To his further surprise, she agreed! Then it was two more months before she arrived. Imagine his surprise when a very lovely young lady stepped off the stage two years ago. Julie was just 16 then. She came all the way to Nevada from Prussia. She looked so fragile when he first saw her, but not now. She milked the cows and churned the butter every day. She was a great cook and warmed him up on those cold winter nights.

"Elbow Joe," he thought, "you're a very lucky man."

On the way to the station, Joe heard hoof beats. He looked

up the road and saw a cloud of dust. It was too early for the stage. In a moment, he saw six men passing nearby the station. Five were riding, one was walking behind them. It was unusual for folks to pass him on by. They must be in a real hurry. He scratched his head and recalled what a rider said yesterday. Twenty nine convicts had broken out of the Nevada State Prison. Maybe these were wanted men. If so, he was glad they passed him by. He entered the house.

"Hi sweetheart," he said smiling at Julie.

"Sit down, Joe. Who's out on the road?"

"I don't rightly know," he answered, not wanting to alarm her, "but if they knew what was on this supper table they'd probably double back."

∽∽∽

"Charlie," said Morton, "why are we passing this place without stopping?"

"This is Elbow Station. Joe, the owner, knows me real well. He's a great guy and has been good to me in the past."

"We should stop then," remarked Burke. "Let's have a drink and see if he has an extra horse."

"We can't stop here. It's a busy station. Someone may drop in while we're there. I'm not taking any chances. So forget it. I don't want to talk about it anymore. We'll just keep moving."

"Sometimes I don't know what to make of you Charlie," said Morton shaking his head. "One minute you're ready to kill everybody in sight and the next you just want to ride on by."

∽∽∽

The stage to Los Angeles had moved through the Walker Pass and on over the Tejon Pass. Sarah was now just a few hours from her destination. She was getting more excited all the time. She and her fellow travelers slept on the stage as it moved on.

"Just think," she mused, "tonight I get to have dinner with my mom."

159

Chapter Eighteen
Searching for the Mail Rider

Billy Wilson had a restless night. He couldn't stop think-ing about the mail rider. He hoped the boy hadn't met any of the escapees on the road. There had been reports that six of the men were heading toward Aurora. If the kid did run into the convicts they probably took his horse and guns, maybe even his clothes. But what good would it do to hurt him? At first light he saddled up and rode to Sweetwater. He arrived around 8:30. He went directly to the telegraph office to see if there were any messages from the Wellington Station. There was.

"It's midnight. No sign of the mail rider. I'll send the mail pouch with the stage in the morning. I hope he didn't get tangled up with those escaped convicts heading toward Aurora."

He replied with the following:

"I'll find a rider to bring the mail today. If the kid doesn't show up by noon, wire me. Jim and I will set out to find him."

Billy asked the operator to send another message to Mr. Poor in Aurora.

"No news on Billy this morning. He's probably walking into Wellington as you read this message. I'll send word when I know more."

Wilson thanked the telegrapher and left. He needed to fig-ure out who could carry the mail to Wellington for him today.

෯ ෯ ෯

The command post set up in Carson City was a constant hub of activity. Since the break out, numerous convict sightings had been reported. General Batterman's staff worked to separate the credible from the false reports. Just today, Lieutenant Lyman and his troopers were sent to scour the willows along the Carson River. News came that two prisoners were seen near the Cradle-baugh Bridge. They were reported to be a short distance from the east and west forks of the river. The teamster making the report said they looked exhausted and weary. They didn't appear to be armed. He thought they should be fairly easy to catch.

Some reports had a humorous touch. One came in yesterday. Pat Hurley was reported to be in Virginia City. That news wasn't all that significant. He resided there for years. What was significant was the report said he was dressed in women's clothing. The man making the report was sure it was Pat.

"He's parading around with his friends like a dance hall girl. He shaved off his mustache. It didn't help. He still looks like a big dumb Irishman. Go have a look for yourself. When you find the girl with the India ink flower bouquet tattooed on the inside of the right elbow, that's him."

A telegraph was sent to the Virginia City Police. Virginia City was a big place with lots of saloons. If it were true that Hurley was hiding out there, it could take days to find him. Anyway, the commanders never received any word concerning the report.

≪§ ≪§ ≪§

A man coming over the head of the Kingsbury grade from Lake Bigelor to Vansickle's during the night reported he saw prisoner Tom Heffron. Naturally such sightings had to be taken seriously. A squad of the militia was dispatched to follow that lead.

An excited little boy stopped in on his way to school one morning. The kid said that the young convict, Roberts, had stopped and asked for food at his house.

"My sister gave him breakfast. He told me he slept out in the desert last night. She wanted him to stay. But he said he couldn't. Then he kissed her. I told her she kissed the convict guy. I told her to tell you, but she wouldn't. She doesn't believe me. She liked him. I could tell. But I know where he went."

Riders were sent to follow up. Just outside Dayton they did find a young man meeting Robert's description. The fellow caught a ride on a freight wagon heading to Virginia City. It was the person that had breakfast at the boy's house. But it definitely wasn't Roberts.

A report arrived saying that Chris Blair and William Forrest appeared at the Philadelphia Brewery, two miles beyond Virginia City on the Geiger Grade the past Wednesday. It was said that Blair ate a can of oysters and then went into the Brewery and got a drink. The command dispatched Ben Lackey and Chief Downey to pursue them. Again, the report was false

Not one of these leads had helped in tracking down the escapees. It was frustrating for the men in the command and in the field. As far as they knew, not one group of lawmen, the National Guard or the Virginia City Militia had even seen an escapee, let alone caught one. The sole exception was Sheriff Bollen's capture of Carter on Monday morning. There were newspaper accounts that said those on the run had outside help. Fingers were being pointed. Other reports put the number on the loose at better than 40, not 29 as reported by prison officials.

❧ ❧ ❧

Russell moved along the trail slowly heading towards Lake Tahoe. Normally, if he heard something he ducked into the trees to avoid detection. He'd finally been able to get that catchy tune out of his head. He was getting hungry. Around midday his nose told him about a cook fire nearby. Cautiously he made his way forward. He saw two men at a makeshift camp.

"Good afternoon," he said, walking up quietly.

The two sized him up. He knew they couldn't help but notice his black and white stripes.

"Come and sit," said one. "I'm Jake and that's Bob. You must be one of the escapees. Don't worry about us. We don't mean you any harm. Fact is, we're wanted ourselves."

"Thanks for the invitation," said a very relieved Russell. He instinctively knew they met him no harm. "It's been awhile since I had something to eat."

"Well, it ain't much, but it'll help fill ya up. Where ya headin? Sorry. Forget I asked. I'm just makin conversation."

"That's okay," he said. "My intention is to get all the way to the coast and sign aboard a ship. It pays okay, the work's easy, and nobody can find me. This tastes wonderful. What is it?"

"Of all things, Bob took a shot at a rabbit this morning. He

162

missed the rabbit but hit a fox that was stalking the rabbit. Some tough luck for the fox, huh?"

"I'll say," replied Russell. He noticed that Bob hadn't said anything. "Thanks for sharing your grub with me Bob."

The man looked up and nodded.

"Bob doesn't talk," said Jake. "He was tortured by some Mexicans who cut out his tongue."

Russell looked at Bob. The man just smiled back at him.

"He's a great saddle companion," Jake said. "He's a good listener and he never argues with me!"

Russell laughed at the remark and nodded back at Bob. He figured he'd hang around with these two for awhile before continuing on to Lake Tahoe.

∾ ∾ ∾

Billy Wilson couldn't stand waiting for news about Billy Poor any longer. He found his friend Jim Peel.

"Jim, I want you to come with me this afternoon. We need to ride to Wellington and see if we can find any sign of young Poor. I'm worried about him."

"No problem, Billy. I'll just be a few minutes. I'll meet you at your office."

"Thanks Jim."

The men left the stage office in Sweetwater at noon. Billy had a real bad feeling about the boy. He figured he was either hurt real bad from a fall, or worse yet, had a run in with those men on the run. Billy and Jim rode slowly. Each took a different side of the trail to make sure they didn't miss any sign of the boy.

∾ ∾ ∾

George Hightower stopped into the Benton General Store for some freight delivered for his blacksmith shop. Henry was busy stocking shelves behind the counter. Bob was helping a lady with a catalogue selection.

"Afternoon George," called out Henry. "We've got your order stacked and ready for your wagon. I'll meet around back and we'll get ya loaded. How's Martha and the kids?"

"They're just fine, Henry. How's Bob doin with Sarah outta town?"

"Well sir, he's just plain miserable. I'll be glad when she's back and he can carry his fair share of the load around here. Heck, I've been around that girl longer than he has. She never bothered me like that."

"Gee, wonder why," laughed Hightower?

The men went around back and loaded the freight into the blacksmith's wagon.

"Thanks, Henry."

"No problem, George, I'll see ya later."

Thomas Ryan spent most of yesterday and all of today wandering around aimlessly. He considered returning to the Horton place to take them up on working there for awhile. Each time he came back to that thought, he figured it'd just be a matter of time before someone recognized him. He knew the Horton's would never say anything. But he couldn't count on those he didn't know. It was better that he move on down the road.

His thoughts wandered back to the Hortons. That, he said to himself, was the life he wanted. Suddenly, he missed his mom and dad back in Ireland. He ran off at the age of 15. The trip to America was really no fun. He was seasick on the ship almost the whole trip. But he'd reached the land of opportunity. The only real opportunity he had thus far was robbing the folks that he'd been working for in Nevada. That got him a four year prison sentence. He knew better, but he was so tired of everyone telling him what to do. What he really wanted was to find a real job, a good woman and happiness. Hell, that wasn't so much to ask for. He decided to head toward Placerville. No one knew him there. He'd find work and start fresh.

The hole Squires and Willis called home left a lot to be desired. Willis seemed content. He always did. But Squires wasn't happy spending his days under ground like a rodent. Their routine was rather simple. During the day they laid around and rested. At night they crawled out and stole useful things. They had managed to eat regularly with the vegetables growing in the region. They stole some clothes and a few provisions. The late evenings and early mornings had turned quite cold. Therefore they tried to return before it was too bad. They slipped firewood into their hole and could keep themselves warm with a small fire during the night. They tried to do without a fire during the day for fear that someone may see smoke coming from their hiding place.

Squires ran through a list in his head of people that might help him in return for some of his loot. He wrote a note to the first merchant in Virginia City he felt might assist him in getting some needed provisions. He explained he would exchange some of his cached gold for items he wanted, including three good horses, clothes, provisions and weapons. He was offering $7,500 in exchange. He planned to walk to Virginia City during the night and leave it where the man would find it. He figured it would just be a day or two before he was out of here. He expected a return note from the man the next evening.

Morton had been riding Billy Poor's horse since they left the scene of his murder. He and the Jones Gang were traveling through the Adobe Meadows region. He quickened his pace until he was next to Charlie.

"Hold up a minute."

Jones reined in his horse. The others slowed as well and wondered what the man was up to this time.

"What's up, Lea?"

"I've got a bad feeling about this horse. Someone's bound to have missed that guy by now. I need to get rid of this horse. It's bound to be recognized before long."

Morton dismounted. He walked the horse over behind an outcropping. He drew his shooter and put the barrel to the horse's head just between its eyes. He fired. The animal fell in a heap. It kicked and writhed for a minute and then lay still.

Burke and Cockerell looked at each other. How could

someone be so cruel to an animal, they thought independently.

"Roberts, step down off that horse. Since you and Tilden like each other so much, now ya can walk along together."

The boy immediately obeyed. He was afraid of both Lea and Charlie. There was no telling what either of them might do. They continued on and before long, arrived at a pretty little canyon. Charlie led his men to the far end. It was very secluded. There was running water and shade trees.

"I know this place," said Jones. "We'll bed down here tonight. You rest. There's a sawmill about a mile from here. I'm going up there and see about getting us something to eat. Don't go wandering off. Just stay put. I'll be back in about an hour."

Charlie turned his mount and rode off down the trail. While he was gone, more than one in this little band silently thought about heading away in a different direction. Burke, Roberts and Cockerell was very leery of Jones. Morton was just like him. They really couldn't get a good read on Black. He was a very quiet person and kept to himself.

Jim Peel and Billy Wilson arrived at Wellington three hours after they started. They hadn't seen any trace of the mail rider. They tied their horses at the hitching post in front of the stage office. The news from inside was no better. No one in Wellington had any news on the boy either.

"Well Jim, I'm going to have a drink over at the saloon. They have some good sandwich fixings there too. Then I'm going to ride to Aurora with my eye on the trail again."

"I'm with ya Billy. But it'll be good to wet my whistle and get a bite to eat."

Charlie rode up to Hightower's sawmill late in the afternoon. He tied up his mount and looked around. He knew lots of folks here about, but didn't see any of them here now. He walked over to the mess hall to see what might be available.

He exchanged pleasantries with the cook. No one else was

George Hightower's sawmill

about. He asked for and obtained some bread, meat and salt. He thanked the man. Charlie mounted up and was back at his camp just before dark.

"No potatoes tonight, boys, but I did get some bread and salt to go with this meat. How about it Lea, will you cook this up for us?"

"Glad to, Charlie. We'll eat in about an hour. You boys gather up some firewood so I can cook your supper."

It was a frustrating ride back to Aurora for Jim and Billy. After leaving Wellington, they'd slowly, criss-crossing the trail to make sure they didn't miss anything in the brush. Billy's voice was hoarse. He'd yelled the boy's name while riding more than 40 miles. He could hardly speak. Upon arriving in Aurora, Billy stopped at the hotel to tell Mr. Poor he hadn't been able to find any trace of his son. While there he heard Sheriff Palmer had taken some men to look for the convicts and young Poor.

Sarah's stage was on it's final leg of the journey. She hoped it would arrive in Los Angeles on time. To her relief it did. Mrs. Devine and other family members met Sarah at the station. They shared hugs and kisses. It was a wonderful reunion. They asked about the trip to Los Angeles. Mom wanted to know how Henry was. She inquired what Benton was like. Sarah answered all their questions. Then she told them all about Bob. It took the excited young lady nearly two hours to do so.

∽∾ ∽∾ ∽∾

Squires was fuming. He crawled back into the dark, damp hole he shared with Willis. He left the latter at the hideout while he went to Virginia City just after midnight. He'd concealed himself in the shadows, waiting for a message. Just before dawn a figure silently passed nearby. An envelope was left under a barrel in the alley. He retrieved it. He expected acceptance of his $7,500 for horses, guns, clothes and other provisions. To his dismay he was turned down flat. Instead a demand was made for $15,000. Willis could see Squires was mad.

"What's the matter, John?"

"I offered some money in exchange for provisions to someone I thought was a friend. I found out last night that he's no friend to me. He'd just as soon rob me. The hell with him. I'll just find someone else to help me."

He didn't figure Willis had to know the amount or any other particulars he had in mind. Willis didn't figure in his future plans anyway. He'd just have to find another "master".

"No way I'm gonna pay somebody $15,000. I worked too hard and took too many chances to get that loot. I'm not gonna just give it away."

The old stage robber began formulating another plan that might work if he couldn't get assistance from someone in Virginia City. He felt it'd be easy enough to steal a couple of weapons on one of his nightly visits to town. His new idea was certainly going to be more hazardous, but he might not be left with any alternative. With gun in hand, he could steal a good horse, lead it quietly outside town and ride to Six Mile Canyon. Squires would grab some of his hidden loot and ride east to Utah. Salt Lake City was a large enough place for someone to lay low for while. In a few months, he would come back for the rest of his earnings.

Chapter Nineteen
Ordeal at the McLaughlin Ranch

Sheriff Palmer's group was having some terrible luck. Several posse members had taken sick. This was highly unusual. Perhaps it was the food they ate. Maybe they just had the ague. Nobody really cared. They were feeling awful. It's hard to ride and concentrate when your body's constantly threatening the expulsion of something foul at any second.

They'd managed to follow the six convicts into the Adobe Meadows region. This was wide open territory. They knew their adversaries were not far ahead. Sheriff Palmer felt his posse was in no condition for a shoot out with the bunch ahead of them. Both men and horses were fatigued. Finally he raised his arm to halt the column behind him.

"Men, we need to stop here and rest. I can tell most of you are just miserable. I admire your spirit, but we're after some dangerous men. Even at our best, we may be no match for them."

"Sheriff, we can't stop now. Those men have my brother," said Horace Poor. "How can I stop here and go back? I just can't. Anyone with me?"

Horace looked amongst the posse members. The sheriff looked on as well. No one said a word. Finally one arm was raised. It was Mooney.

"I'll go with ya, Horace."

"Wait a minute Horace," said Palmer. "I'll write a note to Sheriff Hightower in Benton Hot Springs. It's not far. He can get men together and join us in the morning. None of us are prepared to move forward now. Not even you and Mooney, Horace."

So Palmer wrote: "From Adobe Meadows, September 22, four or five escaped convicts from the Nevada State Prison are now concealed in the hills back of this place. They are undoubtedly headed for Long Valley. If you can raise a posse and go there you will surely intercept them. I think they will travel tonight. We

169

have tracked them beyond a doubt to this place. They have, I think, four animals, which must be nearly given out. They have with them Billy Poor, the pony rider. Should you go, please be careful not to injure him. My men are very much fatigued and some have taken sick or I would be riding tonight. There is a reward of $300 each, dead or alive. Send me an answer immediately, as I expect to start early in the morning. If you think it advisable to join me here, use your discretion. But if you do anything it would be good for you not to get lost."

Since Mooney seemed free from any ill effects of the other men's ailments, Palmer asked him to carry the note to Sheriff Hightower. As Mooney wheeled his horse and headed for Benton Hot Springs, Horace Poor and the others dismounted. Over the next few hours, most of them drifted off back to Aurora. At last only Horace remained with Palmer to wait for Hightower's men.

ℕℕℕ

John Wheeler had made good time. Every time he met someone along the trail he told them to be on the lookout for the escaped convicts. He said that if they couldn't catch them, to try and force them to retreat back toward the Sierra or the White Mountains. He explained this concerted effort would prevent the men from fleeing to Arizona and Mexico.

He hadn't stopped except to water his horses and exchange mounts periodically. He ate jerky from his saddlebag while he rode along. He figured he'd reach the mines by late afternoon.

Ludwig had kept his part of the plan moving forward. He'd gathered all their supplies and returned to town. He found

the sheriff and laid out their plan. The sheriff was more than happy to throw in with Wheeler and Ludwig. He'd get several more men together. The sheriff and Ludwig figured they'd need to head out about noon on Friday.

Jones roused his men early. He was getting excited. They were only two days out of Bishop Creek. He really looked forward to their arrival. He figured all the help he needed to get far away from any danger was right there. Sleepy, but equally anxious to get to their destination, the others didn't put up any fuss about getting underway early. They'd traveled along about three hours just off the Aurora - Owens River Toll Road. They were near Dobey Meadows.

Mary McLaughlin had been up since long before sunrise. James had ridden out just afterwards to meet with others to round up a herd and bring it down to the winter range. She made sure her husband had a good supper packed for the long ride. She figured he'd be back just after sundown. She loved her home. Here they were about two miles up Dobey Creek from Dobey Meadows. Fall was here. The Aspens were getting ready to show off with a display of bright orange, yellow and a few red leaves.

After her daily chores, she planned to work on the quilt she was preparing for Bob and Sarah. It was to be their wedding present. She hoped the two would be as happy with married life as she was with James.

James rode down the creek and beyond to meet the others to drive the cattle down for the winter. His thoughts were on the long day ahead in the saddle. He didn't even notice the men off the trail hiding in the willows as he rode by, not 50 feet away.

"Wonder where he came from," questioned Lea?

"Don't rightly know," replied Charlie. "Why don't we find out?"

171

When James had passed some distance down the road, Jones and the others took the trail leading up along Dobey Creek. Even these hardened outlaws saw the beauty of the foliage bordering the flowing water. They had traveled about two miles when they saw the McLaughlin Ranch. Mary McLaughlin was on the

porch knocking the dirt out of her rugs. She saw some riders and two men on foot coming up the road. It wasn't all that unusual for a group of travelers to come by from time to time. Somehow she sensed these men were a bit different. Born and bred a rancher's daughter, she knew the proper way to greet visitors.

"Morning."

"Morning ma'am," responded Lea Morton. "We're powerfully hungry. Would you have some grub to spare?"

"Sure do," she replied, due in part to her upbringing. "Tie your horses up over at the barn. I'll make some fresh coffee. You can dust off over there as well if you're a mind too."

Morton, Black, Jones and Burke dismounted. They tied their horses to the rail by the barn. Each took a turn at the water trough to wash off the dust and dirt. When they were done, Russell and Cockerell got a turn.

Charlie had checked the barn and the corral. He didn't see any other mounts. He led the group to the house. Ever so politely he knocked on the door.

"Oh come on in. Coffee will be done in a minute. I've got flapjacks, eggs, potatoes and sausage. Pick a spot at the table. Just relax and make yourself to home. I won't be a minute."

Morton's dinners were not bad, but Mary McLaughlin's breakfast was something special. Her cooking was top notch. The men couldn't believe their good luck. The food was delicious. The portions were mountainous.

"You boys get enough?"

"Yes ma'am" came a chorus from the men.

"Where you boys headin?"

"We've been promised some work near Independence,"

lied Charlie. "We hope to get there in about five days. We'd have been there already, but the boys have had some bad luck with horses. We lost two this week. When part of your party's on foot the goin is slow. This bad luck has cut in on our provisions too. We're pretty much out of everything."

"Well, my husband butchered out a steer a couple days ago. I can let you have a good supply of meat. Let's see, there's some extra salt, some coffee, some flour and a few extra potatoes. Will that help?"

"Sure enough ma'am," said Burke for the group. "You're really too kind."

"No problem at all. We're blessed with plenty."

"Speaking of your husband," said Lea, "where is he?"

"Oh James is off helping to drive cattle to Adobe Meadows. Most were brought down out of the high country and are being moved down here for the winter. He'll be back tonight."

Mary had been gathering up supplies for them while she talked about James and what he was doing. She had placed what she had in a couple of large sacks.

"Well here ya go," she said pointing to the sacks. "These items will help you get along way towards Independence without starving. Is there anything else I can do for you boys?"

"Well now that you mentioned it," smiled Lea, "there is. You see I've actually been in prison for the past several months. I haven't had the company of a lady in all that time. I would really like to spend a few minutes with you alone."

The blood rushed from Mary's face. She turned and ran to her bedroom, shutting the door behind her. Charlie looked at Lea and smiled:

"Okay Lea, I guess you're first. Don't be too long and don't mess up the goods. I like my gals looking real nice."

"Don't worry Charlie, I'm a real ladies man."

"Come on boys," said Charlie, "let's leave ole Lea alone. We'll see what we might find of use around here while we wait for him. He'll let us know when it's time for the next one."

Burke, Roberts and Cockerell looked on uncomfortably. They felt very bad for the lady. She'd just done them all a good deed and now was being taken advantage of very unfairly. But none of them had the courage to speak out to Morton or Jones. Black seemed to side with Charlie and Lea. They could tell from his eyes he could hardly wait his turn with her.

While lingering outside in the living room, Roberts and Cockerell found some useful clothing, a warm coat, pants and a flannel shirt. Tilden put the coat on and gave the shirt to the boy. They couldn't help but hear the screaming from the bedroom.

Later that day, more than a 100 miles to the east, Clifford looked up at the stars. The sky was filled with them, twinkling brightly here and there. He was at a loss. They hadn't found the ranch. At this point he doubted his friend even had one. He must have lied to him. The others had depended upon him to lead them to a safe place. He didn't know what to do. He thought about ditching them. But since they all moved in the same general circles, that could come back and bite him in the future. Well, come morning, he'd level with them. After that he might not have to worry about traveling with them anymore anyway.

Willis had settled into a routine of his own. During the day he hung around just inside the entrance to their cave. He watched the activities going on outside. He delighted in seeing the various birds and animals go about their business. After dark he would venture outside. He went through folks yards stealing vegetables and anything else he could get. He figured this was his new job.

"Hey," Squires called to Willis. "I'm gonna be gone again tonight. So don't worry about me. I'll be back before dawn. Remember to douse the fire before first light. We don't need anyone to find us here."

"Okay," said Willis, curling up around his little fire.

�⋰ ⋰ङ⋰ ⋰ङ⋰

In Carson City, Lieutenant Lyman and his men were getting back from yet what seemed to be another wild goose chase. He couldn't believe it. Never in his career had he ridden so long and so far for nothing. He hadn't even see a good track of an escapee, much less an actual body.

He wondered how much longer he and his men would be subjected to this nonsense. He was ready to head back to Virginia City. Hell, he heard a couple of the convicts were parading around there. Maybe he would catch one there. This was ridiculous!

⋰ङ⋰ ⋰ङ⋰ ⋰ङ⋰

When James McLaughlin arrived home he found his wife in a corner of their room in tears. Her clothes were disheveled. He reached down for her. She pulled him to her. She just wept in his arms uncontrollably for several minutes. She couldn't talk. The words just wouldn't come out. James didn't know what to think. Finally she gathered herself enough to talk.

"Convicts, convicts," she sobbed. "They were here. They hurt me. I'm sorry. I'm so sorry."

James was speechless. He held Mary tightly and tried to comfort her. He was livid. He wanted to kill someone. He could see her tormentors had not beaten her, but they had obviously physically abused her in other ways.

"James," she said between tears. "You need to ride to Benton and get men to help you find them. Don't you try to get them yourself! I'll be all right. You need to go now. I'll be all right."

He picked her up and laid her on the bed. He covered her with warm blankets. He got her a glass of water and made her

175

drink some. He looked for their bottle of whiskey. It was gone. He kissed her gently on the forehead.

"You take care, honey. I love you, Mary. You rest now. We'll get them. I promise."

He immediately set out for Benton. His instinct was to go after them on his own. But that would be stupid. They'd have him outgunned. He rode on as fast as his mount could carry him.

Had he known that Jones and party were camped just three miles west of his ranch, James might have been riding in a different direction. With the exception of Roberts, Burke and Cockerell, the Jones Gang thought their stay at the McLaughlin Ranch was, well, stimulating. Being the lowlife characters they were, they bragged about their afternoon exploits. The more of James' whiskey the three drank, the more descriptive they got.

"Tilden," said Burke in hushed tones, "we've got to get free from Jones. No good is going to come by staying with them. I don't care who he knows. This isn't going to end well."

"I agree. But we need to leave without causing a big fuss. Such a fuss could go bad for us. We'll just find a place and time to slip away from them."

⊰⊱ ⊰⊱ ⊰⊱

Mooney finally made it to Benton Hot Springs. He inquired about the sheriff and found he'd gone home. He was directed to his residence. He found the man's home and knocked on the door. When it opened, he gave George the note.

"Well I'll be," quipped Hightower. "I'm sure we can get a posse together. Follow me back to town."

Hightower took Mooney with him back to the Benton General Store. It was long after the dinner hour. Henry and Bob were sorting through a shipment that arrived during the afternoon. George walked right in.

"Listen up, there're six convicts over near Adobe Meadows. Sheriff Palmer needs our help in tracking them down. Bob, see who you can round up. Henry, I'm going to send you ahead as soon as you can go. Bob, you'll ride with me in the morning."

"Okay George," said Henry. "I'll change and saddle up."

176

"I'll close up and gather up some men," said Morrison.

Rapid hoof beats were heard coming down the grade toward Benton. James McLaughlin pulled up in front of the general store. Bob, Henry, Mooney and George were on the porch.

"James," said Bob, "what's wrong?"

"Convicts went through our place today. Mary didn't know who they were and treated them kindly. Before they left, they hurt her. I made her comfortable before riding here. She's going to be okay. But I want to catch those bastards. They can't be too far away."

"Mooney, here, is from Aurora. He just brought us word of Sheriff Palmer and others close to your place. They were following the convicts. We're getting a posse together now."

"Good," said James. "When do we leave."

"I'm sending Henry right now. Do you want to go, too?"

"Yeah, yeah I do."

"Okay Henry, I want you to ride all the way to the sawmill tonight. If you see them, just watch em. Don't confront em. We'll join you in the morning. Don't get yourselves in trouble."

Henry and James started immediately for Hightower's sawmill. They arrived a little past 11. They didn't see anything or anybody on the way or when they got there. As much as James wanted to continue, Henry kept him in check. James decided he would wait till morning to take out his frustrations on the men he despised so much. They bedded down for the night. Henry quickly fell asleep. Not James - his mind was preoccupied.

As Morrison went through town trying to find others willing to go after the outlaws, Hightower walked back to his house. He wanted Martha to go out and help try to comfort Mary. But he didn't want her going alone. Along the way he saw Clancy Wardlow. Clancy was a former lawman from Kansas.

"Clancy, there's been some trouble out at the McLaughlin place. Those escaped convicts went through there today. Mary could use some comforting. I'd appreciate it if you'd take Martha out and stay with them. I don't expect any further trouble, but I'd feel much better if you're with them."

"I'll be happy to oblige, George."

"Thanks Clancy. Take the buggy at the blacksmith shop. That big bay will get you there in no time. I'll go tell Martha she's takin a little trip."

Bob couldn't believe so few of the men in town were willing to get involved. Some said they didn't have suitable weapons. Others just didn't seem too interested.

"How can these people expect to have a decent, law abiding community," Bob though to himself, "when people like these are on the loose. It only makes sense to catch them and put them away where they belong. I want a lawful community in which to raise my children with Sarah."

Ah, he smiled, "Sarah. I sure do miss you, little girl."

He heard a buggy, looked up and waved as he saw Clancy and Martha ride by.

� ⋍ ⋍

Back in Virginia City, Hurley was having a great time. What started as a joke between him and his friends turned into a lucrative venture. The past few days he spent his nights as a dance hall gal. He waited to make his entrance at the finest saloons in Virginia City until most of the patrons were rather tipsy.

Then he, or he as a she, moved right in. He made more money rolling drunks than he did at anything else he ever tried. Hurley thought this was funny as hell.

His friends loved to watch him in action. They also enjoyed helping him spend it later. And spend it they did. Almost every cent, every day. So it was back to work for Pat, every night.

⋍ ⋍ ⋍

Russell, nestled in the tall timber near Lake Tahoe, watched the same stars as Clifford. They probably appeared closer to him. He was at a much higher elevation. He had forgotten which trail he needed to get over to Truckee. He figured he'd get his bearings in the morning. Now he just laid back and stared off into the universe. A shooting star blazed across the heavens.

Chapter Twenty
Hightower's Posse Hits the Trail

Russell was up early. He started out to find the trail he missed that led to Truckee. He would have been very interested to know that two fellow escapees, Blair and Forrest, were but 10 miles ahead of him. They were hell bent for Placerville. The men figured they'd get themselves lost in the bustling mining center.

About a mile into his journey, he found a cabin in the woods. It looked unoccupied. He knocked. There was no answer. He went inside. To his surprise it contained a very useful item, an old revolver. He checked its workings and was delighted. It had four loads in it. He left the useless musket he had found earlier and went on his way. He wished there had been some old clothes in the place. He wanted out of these prison duds.

Try as he might, Tom Ryan couldn't get the Horton's off his mind. The short time he spent at their place made him long for a spread of his own. The peace and quiet he found there had overwhelmed him. It was now his quest to find something like that for himself. He was moving along toward Truckee with plans to get to Placerville in the next few days. From there, he figured he had several options. Now that it was daylight again, he would find a place to lay low during the day. He only moved on in the evening under the cover of darkness. So far this plan had worked well for him. Tonight he planned to walk the 15 miles to Vansickle's and hide in a hay stack until tomorrow night.

In the early morning light, James saw some movement at the sawmill. He walked over to see about a cup of coffee. Henry was still asleep.

"Morning," said James to the man in the cook house.

"You'll probably have a hungry posse here shortly."

"I figured someone would be coming pretty soon, he replied. "I saw Charlie Jones late Wednesday at the sawmill. He appeared to be alone. He rode right up, stepped off his horse, came on in and asked if I had some provisions. I gave him a few things and he rode off. I heard Charlie was one of those wanted back in Carson City. I knew him from his days working with Ben Clark. He was a nice kid. I guess prison life changed him"

"Well, I'm gonna kill him," said James angrily. "He and some others were at my place yesterday and took advantage of Mary. They' re gonna pay for that."

❦ ❦ ❦

The Benton Hot Springs posse assembled at the sheriff's office around 8 am. As the men came in one by one, George sent them over to the local dining hall for a hearty breakfast. The sheriff knew these men would be on the trail for some time.

Bob had only been able to round up eight other men to join with him and Hightower. They included Calhoun, Alonson, Moore, the Dougherty brothers, Nubors, Nesbitt and Peregrine.

He had asked Mono Jim, an Indian tracker to accompany them. Morrison and Hightower conferred as they ate their meal. It was nearly 9 am when the men mounted up and left town.

❦ ❦ ❦

Henry and James had an early breakfast at the cook house. Naturally, James was ready to start the hunt at first light. It was nearly 11. Henry used good judgment to keep James in check until the sheriff got there. They'd been anticipating the posse soon after breakfast. Finally a cloud of dust was seen in the distance.

"That must be them," Henry said.

"Finally," replied James.

Hightower led the posse into the sawmill yard. He saw James and Henry walking up.

"Good morning James. I had Clancy drive Martha out to your place last night to look after Mary."

"Thanks. She'll be glad to have Martha with her."

180

Hightower's posse coming from Benton Hot Springs

Hightower had the men dismount. The group then waited for the arrival of the Aurora party. About two in the afternoon two riders appeared. It was Sheriff Palmer and Horace Pool. The men dismounted and tied up their horses.

"Afternoon George," said Palmer to Hightower. "Sorry we're so late. By the time I knew who was going to come, it was late this morning. Most of the men are sick and had to return."

"No problem, we're glad you made it."

"Oh, excuse my manners, this is Horace Poor. His brother is the mail rider that the convicts are holding hostage."

"Howdy Horace," said Hightower. "We'll get him."

Horace smiled in return. When James heard the comment about the mail rider hostage, he knew he needed to speak out.

"George, when Mary told me about these bastards, she never mentioned anyone being held hostage. I'm sure he's not with them. She would have noticed something like that."

This wasn't information Horace wantedto hear. For the past two days he held hope these outlaws had his brother. Now it seemed his journey had been in vain. He looked over to Palmer.

"Sheriff, in light of this news, I need to return to Aurora. It's possible there's news at home about Billy."

"I think I'll ride back home with ya. George and the boys can take up the chase from here. Good luck, boys."

With that, the weary duo swung around their mounts and headed down the trail towards Aurora.

"Gather up, men," said Hightower. "We're gonna ride back toward James' place to see if we can find their track."

They went up the canyon for about two miles where Mono

Jim found the convicts' trail. They followed it for about 18 miles across the Owen's River, near Benton Crossing and down into Long Valley. Mono Jim could tell they weren't too far in front of them. Hightower had his posse move ahead cautiously.

John Wheeler was glad to be close to home. His ride to the Armagosa Mines was long and hard. He looked forward to seeing Ludwig. He knew his partner would hold up his end of their plan. He figured he'd skirt the White Mountains until he found track of

The Armagosa Mining Region

Ludwig and whoever else he had gathered together. He hoped that John had already found the trail of the escapees. It would brighten both their days to put some cash in the bank.

Chapman, Parsons and Roth took Clifford's news fairly well. For the past couple days none of them figured they were going to find this ranch anyway. They were reasonable men. Frank had leveled with them. He wasn't the first to be taken in by someone he trusted or considered a friend. The guy obviously lied about his ranch. There was none. Now they had to figure out what to do from here. It was decided they would move toward the Carson Sink region. They figured they could find some folks to feed and clothe them as they worked their way towards Utah.

In Virginia City, Squires had left a second note. He figured he'd soon have the provisions he needed. He spent another cold night outside in an alley awaiting a return message. To his total

dismay, he was turned down again. This source also wanted more than he thought was fair. John walked back to his hole trying to figure out who might be left to help him out. He was offering a lot of money. What was wrong with these people?

A dispatch was sent from the Wellington station that stated the remains of William Poor had been brought in by a group trailing the convicts. He was killed about 15 miles in a southeasterly direction from Wellington. The kid was found about a half mile below Sulphur Springs, 200 yards west of the road. He had been shot in the head and his body had been burnt. Naturally an outcry for the capture and hanging of the men responsible came forth.

At the Carson City command post the decision to disband the facility and send all the resources home was made. General Batterman was completely at a loss to explain why his troops hadn't been able to track down any escapees. It did seem they had been given some bogus information concerning the convicts. Perhaps there was something to the newspaper reports that those on the loose had help. Whatever. He knew there was no good reason to continue to commit his resources in the fight to catch them. He had given the order for his troops and the Emmet Guard to return to Virginia City on the afternoon train.

Though they didn't catch anyone, it wasn't for a lack of trying. He was proud of his men in carrying through with the various directions given. He realized how frustrated they must be. The good thing was that he too could go home and be with his wife. He looked forward to the afternoon train. Tonight he'd have dinner with his wife and a good night sleep in his own bed.

Mono Jim, Hightower and Morrison led the group following the trail. The signs were very fresh. Then, there they were, just ahead, at the base of the Sierra. Morrison immediately held up his arm. The posse stopped and saw dust rising a short distance away.

It was late afternoon and nearly dark.

"Look, those guys are following that stream heading into Monte Diablo Canyon," said Bob. "There's a lake back over that rise. They're gonna box themselves in. There's no outlet."

"Bob, I think it's better we wait until morning before we go in after them. Trying this in the dark isn't a good idea."

"I agree. I'll bet we can get fed and bed down at the McGee cattle camp just over that hill. Alney's bound to be there."

"Good idea," replied Morrison.

Turning to his men Hightower said, "We'll get them in the morning. Tonight we'll stay at McGee's cattle camp. Follow me"

He turned his horse and led his posse toward Alney McGee's place. Alney was a Owens Valley cattleman. In the summer, he took his herd to Long Valley where lush grass grew. It took about 30 minutes for the group to arrive. They saw smoke coming from the line shack and could tell it wasn't big enough for them all to settle in for the night. A man was standing on the porch.

"Howdy George, boys, what's all this," said Alney? "I'm sure you're not here to help me gather in the cows."

"Hi Alney," said Hightower. "There's six convicts over the rise there back in Monte Diablo Canyon. We're going in after them in the morning. We figure to bed down here tonight."

"You know George, I did hear something about a breakout at Carson City. Are these guys part of that bunch?"

"Yep, I reckon it's a small bunch of em. We think they killed a mail rider named Billy Poor, back near Sweetwater."

"Well, we don't have much, but we always like company,

no matter what the reason. You must be tired. Step down off your mounts. Turn your horses loose in the corral. The boys will throw in some feed for them. I'll have the little woman put another pot of coffee on. She'll have some grub ready for your men, too."

"Thanks, Alney."

"No problem. Oh, this is Han Gunter and that's Inman," said Alney, pointing to his ranch hands.

"Pleased to met ya, fellas."

Inman nodded and Han waved at George. The posse dismounted. Saddles, blankets and bridles were removed. Horses were turned out. Alney's wranglers threw hay into the corral for the weary animals. Firewood was gathered. It was going to get chilly outside overnight. Alney himself cooked thick, juicy steaks. His wife served beans and bread. They made sure the men got enough to eat. Before long bedrolls were laid about. The men wondered what tomorrow would bring. One by one they settled back on their bedrolls. Morning would come soon enough.

Mrs. McGee was busy with her biscuits long before sun up, knowing a good breakfast would be appreciated. With the scent of bacon in the air, it wasn't long before she had company. She was soon joined around the camp stove by the posse members and her crew. Steaming cups of hot black coffee helped warm them up.

The sun's rays, slowly made an appearance over the White Mountains, tooking the edge off the morning chill. Savoring full stomachs, the posse set about their chores. Pistols and rifles were checked. Horses were saddled. Hightower's men were ready.

"Thanks for everything Alney," he said. "And you Mrs. McGee, you sure know how to make a man wanna get outta bed in the morning. Ole Alney there, is a lucky man!"

She smiled and waved. Alney and Han watched as the sheriff turned and led his posse back down the trail. Hightower figured they had a 30 minute ride to Monte Diablo Canyon.

"I sure would like to ride with them this morning," said Alney, "but we've got work to do."

"Well boss," Han commented, " I'm glad we have our regular chores to attend to. I never much cared for gunplay myself."

"I'm with Han," said Inman.

Chapter Twenty One
The Gun Battle at Monte Diablo

Ambling down the trail toward Truckee, Russell was surprised to find a hotel smack dab in the middle of nowhere. The timing was perfect though. He was really hungry. Still in prison garb and with a pistol hanging out his pants, he walked right in.

He found a table in the corner. A quick look around told him there were 10 others besides him and the lady waiting on tables. She came over and he demanded breakfast. The others sized him up. Evidently no one wanted any trouble. She brought him biscuits, eggs, bacon and hot coffee. He ate while facing the door with his back to the wall. He was ready if someone came for him. He enjoyed his meal. The lady didn't bother to bring him a bill.

❧ ❧ ❧

John Wheeler decided to rest his horses before trying to locate Ludwig in the White Mountains. He was riding along looking for signs of his partner. He'd been moving up the trail since just after sunrise. A familiar sight brought a smile to his face. There was a small formation of rocks along the trail. Here was one of the markings they used to alert each other. It told him to head up the trail directly into the Whites. John knew he couldn't be more than a couple hours behind his partner. He noticed Ludwig had company. At least four other horsemen were in his group.

❧ ❧ ❧

The Devine family had taken up residence at the Pico House on North Main Street in Los Angeles. It had been built by Pio Pico, the former Mexican Governor of California. It was considered to be the finest hotel in the entire Southwest.

Sarah thought the place was wonderful. It was ornately decorated. The rooms were spacious and very tastefully furnished. Her bed was very comfortable. She slept peacefully.

Pico House in Los Angeles

The dining room was charming. The food was varied and delicious. Most of all she enjoyed spending time with her family. She missed Bob ever so much and was thinking of him constantly. She wondered what he was up to now.

Parsons was a gambler by nature. His gamble on the train robbery landed him in jail. The gamble on Clifford got him lost. During his stagecoach robber days, he was the brains behind the planning. He needed that skill now to get him out of his mess.

He knew Chapman had a good mind. Clifford had his chance. Someone else needed to come up with an idea. They were lost with no clue as to where they were.

No matter which way they went, a group of curious Indians would watch them from afar. He felt he was part of some grand experiment. He didn't like it. The men hadn't eaten anything except a coyote. They were in a real mess and he hated to admit it, he wasn't sure how he was going to get out of it. Perhaps Chapman would come up with something.

A quiet 30 minute ride brought Hightower's group back to the mouth of Monte Diablo Canyon. Each man knew this was dangerous business. They'd heard the convicts had Henry rifles. Everyone knew about that weapon. It was said the average man could fire 15 shots with the Henry rifle in about 12 seconds. During the Civil War, one Confederate General called the Henry:

"That damned Yankee rifle that they load on Sunday and shoot all week!"

They had to be cautious. Hightower had taken the lead since leaving McGee's place. He raised his arm to stop the men.

"Okay boys, from here on in we have to be very careful. I don't want anyone yelling out or doing anything foolish. We've got them outnumbered. If we keep our heads together, we'll get in, surround them and get out of here without any of us getting hurt. Any questions?"

There were none. Bob and Henry had been riding together. Naturally they were looking out for one another. The men had formed a close bond. It had developed long before Sarah had come to Benton and changed Morrison's entire life. Soon the two men would be brothers.

"Hold up Henry, I got to share something with ya," said Morrison, "I have a real funny feeling about all this."

"What's that."

"Well, I just feel if I ride in that canyon, I'm not gonna be coming out. That's a terrible feeling."

"Geeze Bob, if you're having those thoughts, it's better you stay here and watch for anyone trying to get by."

"I can't do that. I feel it's my duty to help apprehend these bastards. I just have an uneasy feeling. I'm sure I'll be okay. It's just a really bad feeling."

"Hell, we're all a bit anxious. We'll be all right."

⭋ ⭋ ⭋

A quarter mile up Monte Diablo Canyon it was a calm, peaceful morning. The sun was out. Pristine Monte Diablo Lake

Monte Diablo Lake - Renamed Convict Lake After the Battle

reflected the huge granite mountain overlooking it. Fish jumped at the flies skimming the water's surface.

Morton was sitting peacefully by the stream, day dreaming. Roberts was asleep in a clear spot among the willows. Black had gone up the hill for an early morning constitutional.

Charlie Jones had looked forward to his day with great anticipation. He had saddled up and was raring to go. He tucked a pistol in his belt. He didn't need one of the rifles today. He was so close to his destination that he just couldn't wait any longer. Today was the day he was going to find the help he knew was awaiting him. The other fools didn't need to get involved. The hell with them. It would be a lot easier to get provisions and an outfit for one than for six. He had gotten them this far. From now on, they'd be on their own. He swung aboard his saddle.

"Hey, listen up," he said to no one in particular. "I'll see you fellas late tonight or tomorrow. It's time I get over to Bishop Creek and see what kind of help I can get us. Stay out of trouble until I get back. Tell Burke and Tilden to stay put too. Hey, where are they anyway?"

"Roberts said they left about an hour ago to look for wild berries," replied Morton. "What do you care?"

"I don't. See ya later Lea."

With that he moved back up the trail along the stream they came in on the previous afternoon. No reason they needed to know they'd never see him again. He was happier right now than he'd been for over two years. Nothing could wipe the huge smile off his face. But then something did! Ahead, not a 100 yards away, were horsemen in a circle. They appeared to be listening to someone in the center. Jones immediately dismounted and placed his hand over the animal's nose to keep it calm. Quietly, he led the horse across the creek into a heavily wooded willow grove.

෴ ෴ ෴

Burke and Cockerell weren't out picking berries. They had decided this was the place they needed to make their break from Jones and Morton. Acting as though they hadn't a care in the world, with the exception of hunger, the two walked out of the willow camp, never to return. They had carefully worked their way up the steep hill south of the lake. Aside from the tin cup they were supposedly going to use for berry collecting, they each had a pistol and some cooked meat. The men figured Charlie would just get them killed if they stayed with his bunch.

As they climbed over some rocks high above the lake, the view was breathtaking. As they looked around, taking in the beauty of it all, the two men saw a group of mounted men at the head of the canyon. They immediately slunk down so no one could see them. As they watched, the body of men slowly moved up the trail toward the lake ahead. Burke and Cockerell were glad they weren't back down in that canyon, resting in the willows.

Surveying the scene they saw a figure working his way

down the mountain above where they had made camp in the willows. As he moved through the loose shale, rocks were dislodged, rolled down the hill, raised a dust cloud and a made a loud noise.

After giving his men their orders, Hightower had Mono Jim hold the horses of the men he sent to prevent anyone from trying to get out along the creek. The rest headed up the trail toward the lake. Nerves were on edge. Hearts beat rapidly.

About a 100 yards up the canyon a noise was heard and a man was seen running down the hillside. Before Hightower could remind his men to be careful, one stupid fool hollered out:

"There they are boys, right on that hill. There they are!"

The posse immediately spurred their horses. They didn't know the outlaw's camp was just 40 feet away. They also didn't notice the figure in the willows calming his horse and moving slowly in the opposite direction. While all the commotion was going on behind him, Jones managed to slip by Mono Jim and led his horse down the canyon and away from danger. Once clear, he mounted up and rode as far and as fast as he could.

The Doughterty brothers fired at the man moving down the shale covered hillside, but missed him. Morton snapped out of his dream when he heard the posse member's yell, followed by gunfire. He sat up for a second and then kicked at Roberts to wake the boy up. Together they retreated and hid behind a large

Moses Black

tree. To his dismay Morton realized neither of them had grabbed a weapon. Black, the figure running down the hill, hit the ground just a short distance above them.

"Go back there and grab those rifles kid," yelled Morton.

"Are you crazy, they'll shoot me for sure."

"Get those rifles boy or they're gonna kill us all anyway."

Fearing Morton more than bullets, he moved towards the weapons. McLaughlin saw movement in the willows and fired. In the open, Roberts was hit by the shotgun blast. Buckshot were embedded in his lower leg and foot. He winced and fell, but somehow managed to crawl to the rifles. He retrieved the saddle bag with the cartridges and the two rifles. Devine observed a figure moving in the brush and fired. Making his way back to the tree Robert's caught Devine's slug in process. It tore a hole in the fleshy part of his back. Morton and Black watched in amazement as the boy struggled to get back to them with the weapons. Roberts made it to the large pine tree Morton was hiding behind. Grabbing a Henry, he yelled to the kid.

"Get back in the willows, they'll get behind us. I'll get shot. Go on now, get down in those willows. Help cover me."

Obediently the wounded boy retreated to the willows. He lay there in pain from his injuries. Roberts was armed with a revolver, but was in no condition to fight. Morton tossed the second Henry up to Black. With a smile, Lea checked to see if a cartridge was in the chamber. There was. Black did likewise. As soon as Black and Morton opened fire on the posse, the fight was virtually over. In a matter of seconds a hail of gunfire ripped through the willows surrounding the posse. Sheriff Hightower's horse was shot out from under him.

"Oh my God," he thought as gunfire echoed off the canyon walls. Seeing it was futile to continue he yelled at his men.

"Stop. Fall back. Retreat."

His voice was barely audible over the roar of the gunfire. Morrison heard him. As he turned, his horse was shot and they fell together to the ground. The terrible gun battle continued. It lasted for more than 20 minutes. Morton and Black's intense fire power killed the horses of Nabors and Calhoun. Calhoun himself was hit in the hand. Nesbith and Albertson's horses were wounded. While Morrison tried to work his way to cover, a hail of lead was directed his way. He felt a deep burning sensation in his side. He winced. He thought about what he had said to Henry not long ago. It hurt, but he had a mission. These men had to be stopped.

No one in the posse saw Bob get shot. They didn't need Hightower's command to realize this was senseless. Knowing they were completely outgunned they retreated down the trail to a safe haven. George was there.

"Damn," exclaimed Nabors. "I've never seen anything like that. It's murder back in that canyon"

"Where's Bob," asked Henry. "Did any of you see where Bob is?"

"I saw him and his horse go down. It looked like he crawled to some cover," said Hightower. "Is anybody hurt?"

Calhoun raised his hand which was wrapped in a bloody bandanna. Nesbith stuck his finger in the hole shot through his jacket that barely missed his stomach. The sounds of gunfire had subsided. Hightower suddenly realized he was a great blacksmith, but didn't really know much about being the sheriff in this situation. Five of the horses were down. He really didn't have any idea what they should do now. Perhaps the best thing was to try and block the canyon so nobody could get through. He just didn't want to get any of his friends and neighbors killed.

"Okay men, here's what we're gonna do. I want Nesbith and Albertson to take the high ground on either side of the canyon. I want to know what these bastards plan to do. If we can't get em now, we sure can watch their movements and follow them."

Meanwhile, Morrison was intent upon getting closer to

those firing at him. He wanted a good shot at the convicts. Morton and Black watched his movements. They fired so many rounds that the barrel of their rifles were too hot to handle. Morton had a bandanna wrapped around his hand so he could hold the rifle barrel. They waited for the man working his way toward them to offer them a better target.

"There's a brave chap, I don't like to kill him," said Black.

"That's the kind to kill," remarked Morton. "Then you won't have any trouble with the cowards."

Black, armed with his six shooter, left his cover. He moved quietly while working to get around behind Morrison. He lost sight of the man for a moment. Morrison, hiding in the brush, saw someone coming toward him. The man walked right by him. Bob had a perfect shot. He cocked his pistol and pulled the trigger. To his dismay, the weapon misfired. Black, startled by the noise, blindly turned and fired a shot at Morrison. Bob was struck again.

Brave Robert Morrison - Killed by Black

Black saw Morrison jump when the bullet hit him. He thought it a fatal shot. He moved toward the figure on the ground, to retrieve the dead man's weapon. But, wounded and weak, Bob Morrison feebly attempted to raise his gun and fire at Black.

Unfortunately, he lacked the strength and fell back. Black looked down at him. Bob saw the man standing over him. At point blank range, Black shot Morrison in the head. His premonition proved to be true. He should have never ridden into Monte Diablo Canyon. Black reached down and took the dead man's gun.

During the gun battle, Burke and Cockerell fled over the mountain they were climbing. It made no difference there was no trail to follow. They knew their lives depended upon getting as far away as possible. They didn't stay to watch anything. But they did hear the roar of continuous gunfire echoing through the canyon. It was like a nightmare. The two men found some rocks in which to hide. From their vantage point they could see the trail out of the canyon. They waited to see what happened next.

Charlie Jones heard the gunfire as well. He figured Morton and Black were pleased he didn't take one of those Henrys with him. It sounded to him like they were making good use of them back there in the canyon. His timing couldn't have been more perfect. A few minutes either way and he would have been

in deep trouble. He could have ridden right into the midst of the posse. Or he could have been there next to Morton trying to blaze his way out of trouble. He remembered from his Civil War days that wasn't much fun. No matter, he had narrowly avoided all this unpleasantness. He figured Bishop Creek was but three hours away. Soon he would be among real friends. He would turn on his charm. Everything would be fine now.

≪ ≪ ≪

Black and Morton knew they had the posse on the run. For the time being they were safe. Lea figured it was time to get the hell out of this canyon. It was just a matter of time until more men came in after them. Roberts had been hiding in the willows during the battle. He managed to get to his feet. He hobbled over to Black, handed the man his gun and laid down on the ground.

Black checks Roberts

"Moses, we've got to get outta here. Help me. I can hardly stand up."

"Leave him," said Morton, "he's gonna die anyway. The kid's no good to us, never has been. Somebody will be along shortly to deal with em."

Black looked kinda sideways at Morton, but said nothing. The two started working their way out of the canyon. They were well shielded by the willows. They moved about 300 yards, then stopped. Roberts tried his best to follow them. He made a cane out of a willow branch to assist him in moving along.

Three horses were grazing in a meadow just ahead of Morton and Black. Lea watched as Moses easily walked up and caught them. He figured these animals came belonged to the posse. As they continued walking ahead leading the horses, they saw a figure standing in the willows several yards up the trail.

Mono Jim was standing on a nearby hillside. He was holding the horses as instructed. He saw two men approaching and mistook Black and Morton for posse members. As the two came near, Mono Jim shouted to them:

"There're three convicts down in the canyon without any weapons, go in and shoot them!"

Almost immediately, the Indian realized these two were not posse members. He turned and ran into the willows to find shelter. He didn't make it very far, before he was shot by Black. As he fell he fired back at the men. He missed them, but hit one of the horses. Morton raised his Henry, took aim and shot Mono Jim in the left eye. The Indian fell dead on the spot.

Morton walks away

Morton walked over and took the reins of the Indian's horse. He swung aboard. It was rodeo time. The horse bucked, turned and dodged all at once. Morton was soon airborne. He hit the ground with a thud.

Black couldn't help but let out a belly laugh. Morton stood up cussing loudly and dusted himself off. He walked toward the horse. It held its ground. Standing right in front of the animal, Lea pulled his pistol from his belt and shot it between the eyes. The poor horse buckled at the knees and went down.

ᵍᵍᵍ

Meanwhile, two posse members were able to capture a couple horses. They mounted up and cautiously followed the outlaws. As they watched from a distance, they saw the exchange with Mono Jim. It sickened them. The men returned to the mouth of the canyon to give Hightower a report.

"George, they've killed Mono Jim. There's two of them passing up and out of the canyon on that southern ridge. Anyone following them will be killed for sure. We're no match for them as long as they've got those rifles."

"You're right," replied Hightower. "We need to go back in the canyon and find Bob. I'm pretty sure the outlaws have all cleared out by now."

Walking or on horseback, the posse followed Hightower and Devine along the stream through the willows. They moved very carefully. There was a chance a wounded outlaw remained and posed a threat. They crossed the creek and saw a body lying in the willows. Henry jumped off his horse and ran ahead. He saw his friend in a pool of blood. He fell to his knees. The others crowded around the horrible scene.

"Oh no. No. No. Oh Bob, what did you do," cried Henry? "Why didn't you just stay back with us? Oh my Gawd, what am I gonna tell Sarah?"

Henry completely broke down. He sobbed uncontrollably. Hightower tried to console him. It didn't help. The other men wiped tears from their eyes. Morrison was a friend to one and all. James McLaughlin quietly took a bedroll off his saddle and laid the blanket over his friend's body. Tears rolled down his face.

❧ ❧ ❧

At the McGee cattle camp, Gunter and Alney were busy as usual. There was always something to do. Han had stopped a moment to wipe his brow. He saw dust along the ridge and realized that horsemen were coming down the hill at a run.

"Hey look there boss, there's a couple riders makin good time. Let's get up there and see what's up."

"All right."

Off they started on foot at a trot. McGee was a true frontiersman. He'd fought in the Indian wars and was no fool. He saw the riders stop and dismount. Suddenly, he became suspicious.

"Hold up there, Han. I think we'd better stay here. If they're bad news, we're stuck here unarmed."

Up on the ridge, Morton and Black saw two figures running up towards them. They dismounted. Lea had a great shot at the two from his current position. No doubt Alney's action saved his life as well as that of Han. Seeing the men stop, Morton and Black just mounted up and continued on their way.

"I'm not sure what that was all about," Alney said to Han, "but since the posse was here last night, I want to ride over to Monte Diablo Canyon and see if they're okay."

He and Han saddled up. Alney and his wrangler buckled on their gun belts and took their rifles with them. It took them about 40 minutes to find Hightower and his men.

"George."

"Alney."

198

"What's up here?"

"We got routed. Their Henrys took the fight away from us. We were just plain outgunned. They killed Morrison and our guide. I'm pretty sure they went up and over that rise."

"I'm sure they did. Han and I saw two riders moving along quickly. We started out to see who they were. When we did, they stopped and dismounted. When Han and I stopped, they just rode off. I'm sure that was two of them. How many were there?"

"I was told there were six. But we can only account for three. You said you saw two. Maybe one's lying in there dead. I sure hope so. I have no idea where the other three might be."

Owen's Valley Rancher Alney McGee

Alney was an old hand at dealing with tragedy. He asked a couple of the boys to bury Mono Jim. Morrison was wrapped up in the bedroll. His body was tied across a saddle. Alney led the horse back to his place. Most of the posse headed to McGee's place to recoup. McGee could tell these men were in shock.

The good men that agreed to go after these hardened criminals weren't killers. They weren't used to being involved in such a terrible ordeal. The loss of Morrison and the killing of Mono Jim angered them immensely.

199

Chapter Twenty Two
Lawmen Finally Get A Break

William Russell finally found his way to Truckee. It had been a long walk from the Nevada State Prison. He was parched. Wandering into the first barroom he could find, he asked for a glass of water. The bartender looked him over and gave him a shot glass filled with lukewarm water. It tasted good anyway.

It was fairly dark inside. The only other occupants in the establishment were the man behind the bar and two obviously drunk miners propped up at the counter. The bartender watched him very carefully. Russell knew he stood out, but didn't give a damn. The others were either too far gone or didn't care he was dressed in prison clothes with a pistol in his belt. One old fella actually seemed asleep at the bar.

"Hey there mister. Wanna snort," asked the drunk?

"I'd love a whiskey."

The old miner filled Russell's tumbler. He lifted it to his lips and felt the burn as it trickled down his throat. It was the first real drink he had in a long time. The bartender looked on uneasily.

"Here, have another," said the old timer.

Russell extended his glass. It was promptly filled again. This time he sipped it. The man set the bottle on the bar.

"Excuse me a minute. I need to water my horse," laughed the old drunk. "I'll be right back."

As he staggered to the door with his suspenders hanging down and with his pants at half mast, he stopped and said:

"Hey mister, I dropped a $5 coin on the floor somewheres. I can't see too good in here. I'll buy ya another shot if ya find it."

The man staggered out the door. Russell looked around on the floor. He moved the sawdust aside with his foot. He spotted the coin. The bartender watched him pick it up. He also saw three more gold coins on the bar. He took them too. Still under the watchful eye of the bar keep, he struck a match and lit a candle. He extinguished the match. He looked at the bartender.

"Thanks for your hospitality."

He turned and walked out the door. Seeing the drunk stumbling back into the bar, he stopped a moment.

"Here, I lit a candle so you can look for your lost coin. Thanks for the whiskey. I sure do hope you find it old fella!"

To avoid contact with others, he went down a back street. Halfway down the alley Russell spotted an old carpetbag on the ground. Among other things therein, he found a coat, long johns, socks, two shirts and a pair of pants. Quickly, he found a place to change. This was a great relief. He felt unexposed and less conspicuous. He walked over to the railroad station. Extending a $3 gold piece, he paid a dollar and a half for a train ride to Colfax.

෯ ෯ ෯

Back at Vansickle's, Tom Ryan was feeling cozy in a pile of straw high up in a hay barn. He'd walked nearly 15 miles through the darkness to get here. It took him nearly 10 hours to do so. His legs were so sore when he bedded down, it took quite awhile for him to fall asleep. Now he was so comfortable, he planned to stay right there as long as he could. Thoughts of the Horton's ran through his head again. "Why didn't I stay?"

Ryan's resting place

While he was thinking about them, it dawned on him it was very quiet outside in the yard. It must nearly be midday. It seemed that no one was around. He leaned over to peer out of the loft. He saw the main house. Usually there would be light smoke coming from the chimney this time of year. There wasn't any. He figured no one was home.

Jumping down from the loft he looked around the barn. He saw a horse in the stall and tack on the wall. He walked over to the house and peeked in the window. It was apparent no one was there. He tried the door. It was unlocked. Ryan entered and made himself to home. He found two shooters, cartridges, a belt, lots of provisions and saddlebags. He strapped on the belt, put the shooters in his pants and quickly stuffed everything else in the bags.

Returning to the barn, he set the bags down. Then he reached for the bridle and put it on the horse. Next he saddled the animal and tied on the saddlebags. Leading the horse out the back door of the barn, he climbed aboard. He looked right smart now. Feeling quite confident, he headed to Placerville and figured he'd arrive around midnight. That was just too easy.

"Maybe I'm just set out to be a thief like my old man!"

⋘ ⋘ ⋘

The lone black escapee, Pruitt, had been content to hold up in Genoa for a few days. He'd settled in with the feisty woman he longed for soon after escaping. She didn't disappoint him!

Life was good. It was easy for to get around in the predominately colored section of town. He would have stayed longer if not for the fact he got caught wooing another enticing gal by the very lady with whom he was given a place to stay.

To say that he was handed his hat was no exaggeration. So Marion left Genoa for parts west. He came upon a sheepherder's camp in Hope Valley. Since no one was there to offer him anything, he took everything. When the men returned, they were furious. They immediately set out after him and he was captured shortly thereafter. Since they'd recovered all their property, they let him go.

Pruitt heads to Copperopolis

They had no idea he was a wanted man. Seeing this as an omen, Pruitt found a canoe and began to work his way down the western side of the Sierra toward Copperopolis.

In Virginia City, two bits of news were noted. Warden Frank Denver was allowed to return to his home in the city to further recuperate.

Meanwhile, Chief Downey had received several reports of vegetables gardens being pilfered near the Flowery District over the past several days. Detective Ben Lackey was sent out with Sheriff Atkinson to look into the matter. The lawmen figured it had to be the work of some escaped prisoners. The timing almost perfectly coincided with the prison break. But try as they might, the men couldn't find any evidence of where these convicts might be hiding. But they remained steadfast in their resolve to locate these criminals and return them to prison.

Willis was the culprit stealing the vegetables. Squires was pleased with his associate's efforts in keeping them in food. But to his further dismay, now when he asked someone to provide him with provisions and horses, they typically answered him with meat and bread. Imagine that. In addition to notes saying he wasn't offering them enough money, they'd leave a few provisions to keep him alive. They even left a coat, blankets and a bottle of whiskey. He figured this was their way to keep him close until he met their demands. He seriously considered his other plan. Maybe it was best to steal a gun and a horse, ride into Six Mile Canyon for some of his loot and slip away in the night towards Salt Lake City.

The men with Clifford were becoming more distraught. They seemed to be traveling in circles. They were constantly being watched by Indians, day and night. None of them had eaten anything since the coyote several days ago. They were armed, but didn't even see anything they could shoot at, much less hit. They would have froze to death if not for the flint that Parsons had with him. It had become much too cold to try and move at night. They laid low in the warmth of a campfire. During the day they moved about openly trying to find a ranch, line camp or mine. They just didn't have any luck whatsoever.

In Carson City, prison guard Isaacs was proving to be a challenge as a patient. His doctors were baffled to a degree. For a period he would seem to be responding to their treatment. Then he would take a turn for the worse. They feared they'd have to remove his leg if he didn't make better progress. They didn't feel he could last much longer in this up and down state.

East of Belmont, Watson, Baker and Jacks were traveling towards Utah. They sought the $2,500 that Baker buried in Skull, not far from Tecoma by the Utah border. They hadn't experienced any fear of being caught since finding the dead miners and their mule. They'd completely blended into the Nevada landscape. Nary a day went by without Watson rehashing how he'd dump the other two once he got his hands on Baker's gold.

After their near encounter with McGee and his ranch hand, Morton and Black moved as far away from the scene of their murderous adventure as possible. Along the way they'd gathered up some potatoes and other vegetables. They stayed up high on the rim of the valley so they could see if they were being followed. So far as Morton could tell, no one was following them. He stopped his horse and dismounted.

"Moses, this is a good place to stop for the night. We've got a good view in all directions. If anyone's coming after us, we'll see them first."

"Suits me. Man that was something back there."

"That it was. I'm sure glad that Charlie didn't take a Henry with him. Our firepower kept us alive."

"Yeah, that plus that poor guy's gun misfired back there. Otherwise I'd be dead."

"Well Black, it just wasn't your time, that's all. I wonder if they found that whiney kid yet?"

❧ ❧ ❧

Roberts had watched in horror as Morton and Black deserted him. He tried to follow them but was in too much pain. He lay quietly in the willows and watched as the posse members gathered up the dead man that Black shot. He feared these men would fan out in the willows and find him. For whatever reason, they didn't. He heard the sounds of a shovel at work. He figured someone was burying the man that Morton killed. Before long it was silent, save for the birds and the wind blowing through the leaves. If not for the circumstances, it would have been the perfect place to be. He wanted some warmth, but had no matches. The embers from their fire were dead. He knew he couldn't stay here. Unarmed and crippled, he had to find a way out of this canyon. He decided to follow the trail left by Morton and Black. Using the cane he'd made, the boy was able to make 50 yards or so at a time. The pain was intense, but he knew he had to keep going to survive. After several hours of moving and resting, he reached the summit over which the two had passed. He started down the other side. He looked for a spot to rest that afforded a break from the wind. He found one in a rock formation. There was tall grass nearby. He grabbed as much as he could to make himself a bed. The rest he used to cover himself to stave away the cold. He had nothing to eat and no water. The boy was miserable.

❧ ❧ ❧

At the McGee camp, it was somber. Mrs. McGee had hot coffee for everyone. Alney helped cook supper for the despondent men. No one wanted to talk about the ordeal, except Henry Devine. Alney's brother Bart had ridden into the McGee camp earlier in the day. Henry took him aside and told him that as the posse left the canyon, he saw tracks of two men on foot that headed toward the valley. Henry asked Bart if he would help him and others from Benton find the men that left that trail. Henry wanted justice as well as revenge for the killing of his friend.

The following morning, the posse returned to Benton Hot Springs with Morrison's body. Six-year-old Ben Edwards had joined his father Thomas, a teamster, on a trip from Partzwick that day. It was a gruesome scene as young Ben stood next to his dad as they watched Morrison's blood spattered horse carry Bob's body along Main Street.

Robert Morrison's Burial Plot in Benton Hot Springs Graveyard

It was unfortunate that Morrison's joking remark to Henry about being "buried in this suit" came to pass. Thus the love of Sarah Devine's life was laid to rest in the Benton Hot Springs cemetery with full Masonic honors. A large and grief stricken circle of friends attended the solemn ceremony. Word of Morrision's passing was sent to the Devine family in Los Angeles.

A leading newspaper reported that "a gent at Benton thought the death of Mr. Morrison was a good lesson and that he would give one Burke with the best horse he ever straddled to get away with. me are charged with lending actual assistance, while others were so selfish as to refuse to lend guns for use by their pursuers."

In summation the report stated "We would gently advise these parties to haul in their horns or this climate may not prove altogether agreeable to their health."

⋙ ⋙ ⋙

When he arrived in Benton, Hightower sent a letter by messenger to Bishop Creek. It told of the shoot out and requested help in locating the outlaws. Unfortunately, the letter didn't arrive in a timely manner. Thus it was nearly 24 hours before local lawmen John Clark and John Clough learned their help was needed. They quickly assembled a posse and started toward Long Valley. Hightower's note warned them about the Henry rifles. Few long range weapons were available to the posse, much less a repeating rifle. But they were resolved. They picked up the outlaws' tracks below McGee's camp. The men had circled around the place and headed south. They tracked the two up into Pine Canyon, a rough, rugged terrain that they knew gave no exit to the convicts.

They pressed them so hard the convicts had to shoot one tired horse and lost another over a precipice. The posse went on without food and sent faithful Indians to Round Valley for supplies. But none came. The lawmen talked the matter over. It was crazy to go against these men armed as they were. So they sent a courier, a man named Yancy, to ride to Camp Independence to

Fort Independence sends help

request arms and men to help capture the convicts. When he arrived, Yancy reported seeing two men on the trail ahead of him most of the night. Everyone figured these must be two of the convicts. Major Egbert and five men were detached to help. Arms and equipment for any man who

207

wanted to come along were offered by the major. Six joined with him. They all set out for Pine Canyon.

Monday night, Roberts saw a light on the mountain side some distance away. He didn't care who this was. It looked warm. After much suffering, he succeeded in crawling to it. Imagine his surprise when he found Morton and Black around the fire.

"Well I'll be damned," said Morton, "look what just crawled in. How's things, boy? Some fellas down the hill there want us to surrender. Do you want to surrender?"

Roberts shook his head. He was happy to be near a warm fire. He was disappointed to see the two didn't have anything to eat. He'd not eaten in two days. He figured anyone rushing them would be at the mercy of Morton and Black's superior fire power. Exhausted and in pain, he fell into a comforting sleep. He was startled awake by the crack of a rifle just above his head. He looked up to see Morton leaning against a rock, rifle in hand.

"I just wanted them to remember I'm thinking of em," he said, eyeing the boy. "They'll think twice about coming in after us. Hey Black, let's have Roberts work his way up that draw to see if we can retreat up there and get out of this mess."

"Send him on."

So Roberts was forced out. He kept his head low as he maneuvered his crutch and body out of the fortification. He was blocked from view by the boulders behind which the others were hiding. He made better time this morning than he made the previous evening. During his trek, he heard sporadic gun fire. Some from Black and Morton's location and some from below. It took him about an hour to make a half mile. He kept going. He really didn't want to be around Morton. He knew the man hated him. Why Lea hadn't killed him already was a mystery to him. He decided he could travel no further. He estimated he was about a mile and a half away. The gun fire had stopped. It was eerily silent.

During Robert's trip, Morton and Black were able to sneak out of their position and move back down toward Round Valley. The posse planned to wait until Yancy got back with help before trying to apprehend the men. Imagine their surprise when the wind picked up and they could see dust swirling as two figures were running down the hill below them. It amazed them that the two could have gotten so far away without them realizing it.

Black and Morton ran for their lives. They managed to get around the posse unnoticed. When they thought it was prudent, they began running for the river. They had traveled quite a distance, all the while looking behind them. As expected the lawmen finally saw they'd out foxed them and were now in pursuit.

"We've got to find a spot to make a stand," yelled Morton. "If we can hold them off till dark, we can sneak away again."

They found a rise offering a good view of the surrounding terrain. While watching the dust of the riders behind them, they rolled rocks together to offer them better protection. Down the hill, the posse fanned out and kept an eye open for a head to pop up. When one did, it was fired upon. The range was over 300 yards. This was a good shot for anyone. One of the Indians with the posse had been watching a figure rise and fire from the right of the rock formation. He carefully aimed his rifle about a foot above his expected target. There it was again. He fired. His timing was perfect. As Black peered around the rock fortress, a slug tore through his head, taking a huge hunk of bone with it. Morton saw his companion go down. He looked over and saw that nearly an eighth of the scull was missing from the back of Black's head.

"Moses," he yelled. "Moses, are you okay?"

To his amazement, he saw the man look up at him and nod.

"How can he do that with half his head gone," thought Morton. He grabbed his kerchief and handed it to Black.

"Tie that around your head and lie still," he told him.

For the first time, Lea was scared. He never expected someone to put a slug in one of them from that distance. Although still alive, he figured Black was no longer any use in this battle. He traded shots for nearly half an hour. Finally he had enough.

"Hey," Morton yelled, "we surrender. We won't shoot anymore. Just promise us you'll take us back to Carson City."

"Throw out you guns," came the reply. "You're wanted in Carson City, so that's were you'll go. Toss out your weapons."

"Black's been shot. I'll have to help him out. It's no trick. Don't shoot."

With that said, he helped Black up, they stepped out into the open. Several men scrambled up the mountain side to them. Morton had his arms raised. Black stood there as if in a trance. The capturers were horrified upon seeing Black's wound. None of them had ever seen an exposed brain. They helped carry him down to a waiting wagon. They were taken to jail in Bishop Creek.

The men were interrogated concerning Billy Poor, Morrison and Mono Jim. Black wasn't in any condition to be much help. He said he shot the Indian and didn't know who killed the mail rider. Morton named Jones as the shooter in the mail rider's death. He tried his best to lay guilt on Roberts for other murderous deeds. Remembering how bad the boy looked the last time he saw him, Morton figured Roberts would be dead by now. When asked where they might find him, Morton gave them a good lead concerning Pine Canyon. Two local lawmen, Hubbard and Nesmith, decided they would wait until morning to find Roberts.

⊰⊱ ⊰⊱ ⊰⊱

It was a good day for law enforcement. Chief Downey, Detective Ben Lackey, Sheriff Atkinson, Constable Comstock and Marshall Harkin of Gold Hill captured Squires and Willis. Confident two escapees were hidden in the hills north of the Flowery district, the officers had watched the area for some days.

On Tuesday night they found fresh tracks. In the morning, they took to the field to search about three miles north of the mouth of Six Mile Canyon. They had worked the area for a couple of hours with no luck. They stopped to rest.

"Hey, look at that," said Lackey pointing at a wisp of smoke rising up over the yellow dirt some distance behind them.

The others looked back at the smoke. It seemed to be coming from about a mile back. Again and again they saw a wisp come up from a little dirt mound.

"That's got to be them," Ben said. "We got em holed up."

The group mounted up and wheeled about. They cautiously made their way back to the south. They kept the little speck of a mound in sight. They circled about and found the head of a small tunnel. Training their weapons on the hole, they waited as Marshall Harkin wrote a note for those inside. It read:

"You're surrounded. Come out and surrender."

Harkin tied the note to a rock and crept close to the mouth of the tunnel. He tossed it in. Excited muffled voices were heard from near the entrance to the hole. But there was no answer.

Harkin crawled close to the opening again and yelled, "Come out with your hands up. Unless you give up quietly and threw out your arms, we'll smother ya in your tunnel."

Shortly thereafter Squires climbed out of the little opening. He was quickly followed by Willis. They were well covered while handcuffs and irons were applied. Squires was very bitter about being so closely hounded by the law for the past few days. He promised to give them all the money he would make the next three years if they would let him go. He said he didn't know anything about the planned prison break until it started.

The tunnel in which the two hid was a very insignificant one, a mere coyote hole, not more than six or eight feet deep.

So small was the pile of dirt at the mouth of the little drift that the scouting party passed by it without giving it a second glance.

Squires had been right about warning Willis to keep the fire out during the day.

Home for Squires and Willis

❧ ❧ ❧

Meanwhile, Russell was enjoying his stay in Colfax until he saw a familiar face. It belonged to 26-year-old prison guard Frank Rockwell.

A chill ran down his spine as he made sure to avoid the man. That had been a very close call. He quietly walked out of Colfax and on to Sacramento. He would have to be more careful in the future.

Chapter Twenty Three
Clifford's Gang and Roberts Get Caught

Early Thursday morning Henry Hubbard and Hal Nesmith set out after Roberts. The men rode up Pine Canyon, past the rock fortification where the others had been. They found his track. He was easy to follow. They stopped for lunch, seating themselves by a spring to eat. They didn't have much food with them.

"Maybe we should keep some of this for the kid, he's bound to be starved."

"Yeah, we'll keep a couple of biscuits for the boy."

While discussing the matter, they heard twigs snapping in the willows a short distance away. The noise was repeated. Heading cautiously toward the spot with guns drawn, they found Roberts. He was in considerable pain from the wounds in his shoulder and leg. They were badly infected. He looked half starved. When helping him up he felt to them as though he was nearly frozen.

"Kill me if you must, but let me eat before you do."

The two biscuits they had left became but two mouthfuls for Roberts. The trio had a 10 mile ride to the nearest house. Over and over on the way in, Roberts asked if there was anything else to eat. He was convinced there would be nothing at the house, but he was told there was plenty of grub where he was being taken.

Morton had spent the morning going over his account of their activities since the prison break. When Roberts was brought in, he turned pale. He knew the boy's story would be vastly different from his. Lea hadn't figured the boy would be found alive.

⊰ ⊰ ⊰

Clifford, Parsons, Roth and Chapman finally found a ranch. It was the Burgess spread, about 10 miles below Campbell's Station and 27 miles east of Carson City. They decided to send Roth in to see about getting some supplies.

Burgess and Edward Healy, his hired man, were in the barn

at work when George Roth walked in.

"Morning sir," said Roth.

"Morning," replied Burgess.

"I'm starving and would like to get some food."

"Where ya from?"

"We're from Dayton"

"We, who's with you"

"There's three other men down at the river."

"Where are you going?"

"To Aurora".

"To Aurora, then what are you doing down here?"

George Roth

"We got lost. Now we need food so we can move on."

"Go to the house and tell my wife to give you a meal."

Roth moved off toward the house. Soon Burgess followed him, wanting to know more about his story. Roth was in no mood to talk, but in a hurry to get out with his food.

He showed Burgess a fine Meerschaum pipe worth $30 or $40. He said they were short of money and offered the pipe to pay for provisions. He said he'd appreciate any extra money Burgess thought would be right. Burgess told his wife to give Roth adequate provisions.

Burgess plans to out fox convicts

After he returned to his barn, Burgess figured the man was wanted. He'd heard about the escape. He shared his thoughts with Healy. The man agreed with him and they decided to capture the man and his companions. They came up with a plan. Burgess went to the

213

house looking for Roth. He found he'd left. When he returned to the barn a Paiute friend was there and said:

"Who are white men in brush by the river?"

"They're men on their way to Aurora."

"No. One told me he was going to Belmont. He told me he wants to trade my clothes with him. What kind of man do you think he is?"

Burgess now knew the men were wanted. The Indian said there were four men. He noticed they had a shotgun and two pistols. Burgess suggested the Indian and his companions go in and start a trade with them and seize their weapons. Then Burgess, Healy and Alex, who was his Indian son, would come and take them prisoner. The Indian didn't like this plan.

Finally, he persuaded five Indians to help them capture the men. The Indians still didn't like the idea, but wanted to keep his friendship. Burgess grabbed his Spencer rifle. The other two men had shotguns. Burgess, Healy and Alex rode horses. The Indians were on foot.

They reached the ridge over which the convicts had disappeared. They saw them trudging along about a mile and a half away. Roth and the others saw they were being chased. They changed their course, heading toward the nearest hills. The Indians hung back as soon as the convicts were sighted. The ranchers put their horses into an easy gallop. When they were about 20 yards from the escapees, the four turned about.

"Throw down your arms," yelled Burgess.

Roth dropped his pistol and began running around in a circle, frightened half out of his wits. The order was repeated. Chapman dropped the shotgun. But Clifford stood there steadfast, holding his six shooter.

"If you have anything further to say, you better just come along and say it," said Clifford.

"Drop the pistol and move along with the others."

Instead he began to rant about authority and the like. Tired of this game, Burgess drew a bead on Clifford with the Spencer.

"You're a dead man soon if you don't drop that gun."

Clifford saw the man met business and dropped it. All the

while Chapman was laughing his ass off as Roth continued his exercise. Parsons was getting a kick out of Roth's antics as well. The convicts were ordered forward 50 paces. Alex dismounted and secured their arms with rope. Burgess rode up.

"I'll treat you as well as you deserve on the way to jail. Alex, go home and have the wife cook dinner for 10 men. I want them to have a good square meal."

He then marched them back to the ranch some four miles away. It was about 11 am. Parsons and Chapman tried to bribe Burgess to let them go. They first offered $2,000 and then Parsons offered $250 more. They said they would have the cash there in five days. They said a masked man would come and pay him.

Burgess chatted with them for some time concerning the ransom. He was trying to lead them to believe he planned to go along with their suggestion.

But all the time he was resolving in his head on how to get the drop on the man in the mask. However, he decided that since he only had two men with him and didn't know exactly whom might be with the masked man, that it was not prudent to try it. So he told the four he wasn't for sale and that was the end of the discussion.

On the way to Carson City, the four rode in a wagon driven by Healy. Alex and Burgess rode along side with shotguns. A man named Shultz, who was lame and had been staying at the ranch, rode in the wagon too. At Sam Buckland's Station, a mile below Fort Churchill, Burgess halted.

He took the men inside, bought them a bottle of whiskey and a good supper. They traveled on all night. The next day they reached Dayton. At Buckland's Station Clifford found a newspaper in which there was some hard talk against him.

"I'm afraid there's bunch that might due me in before we reach the prison," he told Burgess.

"Well, we can't have any of that, now can we," replied the rancher. "I'll see if I can round up some help."

Therefore Burgess asked Sheriff Shaw and others to accompany the party to the prison. Burgess was paid a reward of $900 for the men. He immediately went to Carson City and spent

$20 on tobacco. He rode back to the prison and asked it be given to the men he had returned earlier. They were most surprised.

Early Sunday evening, September 30, a light spring wagon rolled up front of the Bishop Creek jail. Morton, Black and Roberts were brought out and put aboard. A strong guard of horsemen was assigned to accompany the prisoners back to Carson City. The prisoners had mixed emotions about heading back. Morton and Roberts wondered what would happen once they returned. Black, with his head wound, didn't seem long for this world. He really didn't seem to understand anything going on around him.

The group started out for Carson City. It was a pleasant evening. The stars were out and the sunset had left a faint red glow over the Sierra. The men, both the captured and their guard, expected the trip to be uneventful. About two miles out, the party was suddenly surrounded by several well-armed men.

Morton, Black and Roberts with the armed guard

"Who's the captain of the guard," said the group's leader, later identified as a Mr. Malory.

"I am," replied James Sherwin.

"Turn to the left and go on."

"I refuse to do so."

A moment of suspense hung in the air. Morton looked up at those guarding him. He sensed it was useless to argue.

"Give me the reins and I'll follow you fellas, as I'm a pretty good driver myself."

He was offered the reins, took them and drove away rapidly to his own funeral. Roberts, who was lying in the wagon, loudly protested. He had absolutely no choice in the matter. One of the armed men led the wagon. It wound its way across the valley. They ended up at a vacant house a mile or so away.

Vacant house outside Bishop

"You boys with the wagon, put your weapons over there in a stack. You'll get em back in a little while."

The order was carried out. Black and Roberts, were carried into the house. Morton looked around at the armed men. After a moment he stepped down off the wagon. He entered the house. Oil lamps were lit. A fire was built. A jury was organized. It consisted of all those present except for members of the guard. Roberts was taken into an adjoining room. They asked him to make a statement concerning the prison break and events that followed up until the present time.

After nearly two hours of questioning, Roberts' statement along with those of Black and Morton were used by the jury to help decide their verdict.

Information given by Morton and Roberts differed. During the trial, jury members were allowed to ask questions. Morton tried to put as much blame on Roberts as he could. It didn't work.

217

The jury found Morton and Black guilty of the murders of Poor, Morrison and Mono Jim. The jurors were unanimous in their decision to have Black and Morton hung immediately. The decision on what to do with Roberts was not unanimous, so they gave Roberts back to the men assigned to guard him.

No tree was available for the hanging, so supplies to build a gallows were sought. An old beam was found lying near the cabin. Some poles were located too. A scaffold was built. It was erected by placing one end of a long beam on the chimney. The other end was held up by quickly assembling a tripod from the three poles. Two ropes were thrown over the beam and secured tightly. A noose was fashioned on each. The wagon was driven under the beam. It would serve as the platform.

"Are you ready to die?" Morton asked Black as he watched the preparations.

"No, this isn't the crowd that will hang us."

"Yes it is. Don't you hear them building the scaffold?"

Black didn't respond. Asked if he would like to stand nearer to the fire, Morton looked over to Roberts and said:

"It isn't worthwhile to warm myself now. We're to swing and I mean to have you hang with me if I can. I want company."

Black was the first carried out and lifted to his fate in the wagon. Due to his head wound, he had to be raised to his feet, but once up, stood stoically still without being assisted.

Morton walked out by himself and calmly surveyed the scene. Paying close attention to the cross beam and ropes he needed but little help to get into the wagon. As the noose was placed over his neck, he said:

"Take my coat, you don't want to put a rope outside a feller's collar. Please tie my hands more tightly, as I might try to grab the rope by instinct if they were loose."

"I would like some water," Black said.

"What do you want with water now," laughed Morton?

Black was given a drink.

"Do you boys have anything to say," asked the hangmen.

"No," said Morton.

Black remained silent. They were asked if they wished

to speak with a clergyman or have prayers offered.

"I told the minister everything I wanted to yesterday," replied Morton. "He said it wasn't well for a man to be taken off without some religious ceremony. If a minister would come I would like a prayer offered."

The minister took him by the hand, a few words were spoken and Morton who was facing the crowd said:

"I'm prepared to meet my God. But I don't really know if there is any God."

Another short prayer was said which was only broken by a sigh once or twice by Black. As the word Amen was pronounced, the wagon was driven away from underneath the men. Black, being a large heavy man, died without a struggle, as he reached the end of his rope.

Morton, evidently to avoid prolonged suffering, sprung high off the wagon as it pulled away. He most likely broke his neck when the rope set. He seemed to die without a single movement of his muscles.

The armed citizens mounted up and left. Many were friends of Robert Morrison. The Bishop Creek men picked up their weapons. They put Roberts back into the wagon and drove around the house. The kid could see Morton and Black hanging from the beam. They took him to Bishop Creek. For now it looked as if only his wounds threatened his return to Carson City.

In all, the Jones Gang had traveled over 200 miles from the Carson Valley, Nevada to Round Valley, California. The impact on this beautiful region would never be forgotten.

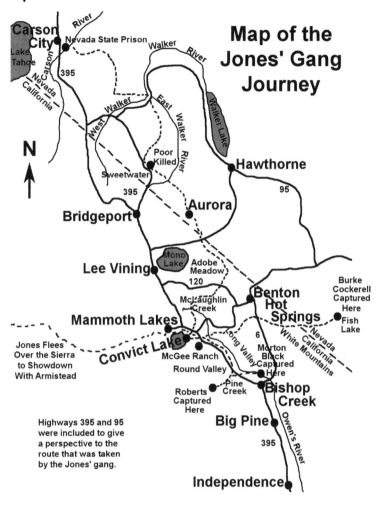

Map of the Jones' Gang Journey

Carson City
Lake Tahoe
Nevada State Prison
River
Walker
River
395
Nevada
California
West Walker
East Walker River
Walker Lake
Poor Killed
Sweetwater
Hawthorne
N
395
Aurora
95
Bridgeport
Mono Lake
Adobe Meadow
Lee Vining
120
Burke Cockerell Captured Here
McLaughlin Creek
Benton Hot Springs
Fish Lake
Mammoth Lakes
6
Nevada California White Mountains
Jones Flees Over the Sierra to Showdown With Armistead
Convict Lake
McGee Ranch
Round Valley
Long Valley
Morton Black Captured Here
Roberts Captured Here
Pine Creek
Bishop Creek
Highways 395 and 95 were included to give a perspective to the route that was taken by the Jones' gang.
Big Pine
395
Owen's River
Independence

❧ ❧ ❧

Wheeler had finally joined up with Ludwig and Sheriff Helm. Their party started into the White Mountains where they spent nearly a week looking for the convicts' trail. The lawmen went to Fish Lake Valley and found tracks. The two men left the White Mountains and went across to the Red Mountains near Silver Peak. The trackers guessed that Burke might be one of the two going toward Silver Peak. They knew that he was familiar with that region. It was near here that Burke murdered someone for which he was sent to prison. Burke had been fortunate at the time that he wasn't hung for his crime right there. He was turned over to Ludwig. Ludwig took Burke over this same route to Aurora back then. Therefore Burke became familiar with where water might be. The men figured Burke was definitely in the area.

Leaving Fish Lake Valley, Ludwig took the party up a canyon to an old ice house. At the canyon's mouth, they found fresh tracks. Nearby was a camp which appeared to have been quickly abandoned. This was close to a spot where a high red peak rises.

It was in that direction that the fresh tracks pointed. Here the lawmen divided. Helm and another went up one side of the red peak. Ludwig and Wheeler took the other side. Some distance from the top of the peak Ludwig saw someone peeking over the rocky ledge. It was Cockerell. Ludwig pointed his Spencer rifle at the man's head. Cockerell threw up one hand, Ludwig kept a keen eye on the man and told Wheeler to demand that the convicts surrender, which he did.

But suddenly, Cockerell disappeared. Ludwig dashed around the point, called out to Helm to look out for the convicts because they were headed towards him. Then Cockerell reappeared, threw up both hands and walked toward his captors. Burke followed close behind. Neither of them were armed and the officers never looked to see if they had any weapons.

Both denied being with the Jones party or having anything to do with the mail rider's death. They were taken to Aurora on their way to Carson City. Two or three efforts were made to take the prisoners from the jail. The lawmen stood at the ready all night to prevent a lawless action. Ludwig was offered $500 in gold coin to leave the jail unattended for 10 minutes or so.

❧❧❧

After Black and Morton were hung, Roberts was taken back to Bishop Creek. His wounds were so severe that the decision was made to transport him to Camp Independence so the U.S. Army Surgeon could properly treat him. He'd been wounded in the shoot out at Monte Diablo Canyon in the left shoulder and left thigh, a little above the knee. Gangrene had set in before medical aid could be obtained. But the military surgeon felt he could save the leg and have Roberts traveling in about a month. Major Egbert agreed to keep the prisoner safely under lock and key. Finally, Roberts was nursed back to good health.

Hubbard and Neismith were dispatched from Bishop Creek to get Roberts and return him to Carson City. The three had an interesting trip back to the prison. Near Benton Hot Springs, both lawmen had to draw their weapons in response to a crowd of 40 or more citizens that came out to hang Roberts. By sheer force and courage the men drove the citizens away from the door of their room. Sheriff Hightower arrived with a few men and helped the trio get out of town.

When they got close to Aurora, the men were more careful. Expecting trouble, Hubbard went ahead to check out the climate of the town. He found it very inhospitable. Upon returning to Roberts and Neismith, it was decided they'd ride around Aurora. Hubbard said Roberts prayed to be back in the Nevada State Prison. He was in constant fear of being hung along the trail.

Hubbard was quoted as saying:

"If Roberts was given a horse he would have rode like the devil to the prison himself, just to find safety from hangmen."

Epilogue
Tying Up the Loose Ends

In the final analysis, 18 of the original 29 escaped inmates were either killed or returned to jail within two months of the breakout. But that doesn't really end their story.

What happened to those that were caught and returned to the Nevada State Prison? Was there any speculation as to where those escapees that were not caught might have ended up? What was the news on the men and women impacted by those on the run in the months afterwards?

Well, the following paragraphs highlight the bits and pieces of information that became available in the months and years after the infamous 1871 Nevada State Prison escape.

In regard to those that were caught, we know about **Black** and **Morton**. They were left hanging around not far from Bishop Creek, most likely by some friends of Robert Morrison. We also know **Carter, Roberts, Burke, Cockerell, Clifford, Parsons, Roth, Chapman, Willis and Squires** were captured and returned to prison. But who else ended up back in jail at Carson City?

Well, **Marion Priutt**, the lone black man that escaped, was apprehended in Stockton, California. After the sheepherders, he robbed in Hope Valley, let him go, he worked his way down the western slope of the Sierra Nevada using a stolen canoe. Stockton Chief of Police Fletcher made the arrest. He reported Marion had taken up with a woman just outside town. Unfortunately for Pruitt, this coquette forgot to mention she had another lover, a very jealous man. Imagine the man's surprise when he returned after a few days away and found Pruitt fairly well wrapped around his woman! Pruitt ran from the scene, but wasn't out of trouble. His willing lover, looking to prevent harm to herself, told the man of Pruitt's circumstance and whereabouts. This knowledge led to his capture. Fletcher arrived in Carson City with his prisoner on October 28. The local newspaper quoted him as saying, ". . . he would not have been caught had it not been for a woman in Stockton of the fille de joie class, or a prostitute for those that don't speak French, with whom he was making his home."

Thomas Heffron was the subject of several sightings over the next few months. However, his fate seemed to be found in reports from many of the escapees upon their return. It was the consensus that Heffron died in the desert not far from the prison, due to a bullet wound sustained as the convicts rushed Warden Denver. It was rumored he was shot in the chest during the first few minutes of the melee at the prison. Many felt his body had been buried within two miles of the prison soon after the breakout. If true, he had to be one very unlucky guy, having also been shot during the 1870 prison break attempt.

Thomas Ryan, who spent such a glorious two day period with the Horton family, was arrested in San Francisco in late October. City detectives Stone and Sellinger brought the Irishman back to Nevada. Ryan had made good on his escape to Placerville and decided to continue to Sacramento. He stayed there for about a week. Needing cash, he sold the horse and bridle he had stolen for $20. He borrowed $50 from a friend, telling him that was going to San Francisco. He had been at the City by the Bay for about a month. During his stay the local police arrested him for being drunk on two separate occasions. Obviously, they didn't know who he really was. He took up residence at the Empire Lodging House. Based on a tip, the detectives went to the boarding house and arrested him. It appeared he had just gone to bed when they roused him and reported Ryan was very upset as they disturbed him from his sleep. He adamantly denied he was the man they sought. However, the officers thought his description fit very nicely with the one given to them. When questioned later, he said he went to San Francisco because he didn't know anyone there. It was his misfortune someone there recognized him and told the lawmen. He remarked to the officers, "I don't know what they'll do with me when I'm taken back to Carson, nor do I care; for I would just as soon leave die now as to serve my 16 years."

William Russell was arrested at a Vallejo coffee house by San Francisco Police Captain Lees. He was returned to Nevada late in November. Russell successfully made his way out of the Sierra Nevada to the ocean. He planned to go down the coast and then inland to Arizona. But he was broke, so he couldn't. He decided instead to sign onto a man of war and sail a year or two. Unfortunately, he got sick. While recuperating, he was captured. Russell was a convict the Warden dearly wanted back. Denver had reports that this man fired at Mrs. Denver where she was watching the fighting. The ball passed within four inches of her head and nearly missed one of the Warden's gentleman guests as well.

Pat McCue and Edward Bigelow, along with **McNamara and Ingram** were seen at Moore's Station, 20 miles from Placerville, on Saturday, September 30. An eyewitness account has an old Placerville pioneer, Dick Yarroid, suspecting the men's character. All alone, he rushed in and caught one by the neck. Single-handedly he took him to Sheriff Hume at Placerville. The other three men fled as they saw their companion carried away. The name of the man was not known at the time. However a second unlucky escapee was caught the next day. It turned out the two men in question were McCue and Bigelow. Sheriff Hume returned them to Carson City. Upon arriving, it was discovered Bigelow had nearly sawed off one of his shackles. When questioned back at the prison, the men said they had been very worried that they would be hung by the local citizens while the sheriff was out looking for a wagon to transport them back to jail. Meanwhile,

Tim McNamara and Elijah Ingram, the other men were traveling with McCue and Bigelow, were said to still be in Placerville. Based on the details of the period, these men were never caught.

    Thomas Flynn's capture, given by Rocklyn Constable Harris, was reported in the *Auburn Stars and Stripes*. On Sunday, October 1, Flynn had arrived in Rocklyn on the last morning freight train, having climbed aboard at Auburn. He stowed himself away to remain undetected and jumped off the train on the outskirts of town. He found a vacant house and rested until evening. Local resident Charlie Sprague observed Flynn after dark. Sprague found Harris and told him someone was in the vacant building. Harris and his associate, Walker, went to the house. They found Flynn and interviewed him. Not having any description of the Carson City escapees, the constable didn't know who the man really was. Since he hadn't done anything wrong he was let go. Flynn counted his blessings, quickly leaving Rocklyn about midnight. He walked the road toward Auburn. The next night at Newcastle, he broke into John Holder's cellar and took provisions. On Tuesday morning, Harris met and spoke with Sheriff Hume who was returning McCue and Bigelow back to Nevada, Harris then surmised the man he had spoken with was an escapee and set out to find him. The next evening, Harris received a tip the man he wanted was seen coming toward town along the tracks. Harris alerted Walker. Together they located Flynn at a woodshed not far from the depot at Rocklyn and arrested him. Harris telegraphed Governor Bradley and verified the man was an escapee based on the man's description, including tattoos and scars. Upon his return, Flynn was questioned. He stated that he didn't fire a shot during the prison break. He said he remained inside until the firing stopped as did many others. He told prison officials that he only obtained a pistol during the last moments of the breakout. The pistol that Flynn had when he was captured was closely checked. It was found to be fully loaded. It was determined it had not been fired in a very long time. When asked if he knew who shot Pixley, Flynn was hesitant to say that Jones was the man. But did say that Jones did most of the effective shooting during the breakout. Charlie's most effective assistant was Lea Morton.

Chris Blair and William Forrest were caught in Donnieville, California. The arrest was reported to Warden Denver. The two asked for a writ of habeas corpus. Nevada had to send someone to identify them before they could be turned over to state authorities. The Warden selected Ed Langlois, the brave prison guard to identify the pair. Due to a stroke of good luck for them and bad luck for Langlois, a December storm caused him to miss stage connections. Thus he arrived in Donnieville after the men had their examination by the local judge and were released. They quickly left for parts unknown and were not heard from again.

John Watson, John Jacks and Daniel Baker must have made it around Belmont and on to Tecoma. None of these men were reported as having been captured. Whether Watson was successful in his desire to take Baker's hidden loot also is unknown.

Pat Hurley was last reported parading around at night as a saloon gal in Virginia City, rolling drunks and then spending the money with his pals. The information was passed on to law enforcement officials. No further word was found on Hurley.

David Lynch seems to have completely disappeared. No further mention of the man was found.

Charlie Jones was reported by Morton to have ridden out the morning of the shoot out to find friends in Bishop Creek. What ever happened to the man? This was perhaps the most discussed subject surrounding the escape. Several possibilities were reported. That Jones' death was proved false on more than one occasion led to such newspaper remarks as "Like the wildcat at Piper's Opera House, he won't stay killed."

One story from a gentleman arriving at Aurora in October 1871, stated officers on the track of Cockerell and Burke found Charlie's body in an old cabin in Fish Lake Valley. It was thought Jones joined Burke and Cockerell somewhere near Round Valley after the fight with the posse. They slipped away and headed to Fish Lake Valley. There they must have quarreled and Jones was killed. His body was not returned and no reward was ever paid for Jones. Logically, if this were true, Burke and Cockerell would have taken credit for killing Jones, the man held responsible for killing Pixley, Isaacs and the mail rider. They never did.

A much more titillating account of Charlie Jones' demise was published in several newspapers, including the **Nevada State Journal**, December 30, 1871 and the **Coshocton Democrat** in Coshocton, Ohio, January 23, 1872. Accordingly, Francis Armistead, who helped capture, Morton and Black, followed Jones's trail. He followed Charlie's tracks about 50 miles from the head of Long Valley along the San Joaquin River and over the Sierra. The escape route was used by Jones after his fight with Mathews. Armistead trailed him to George Slawson's sheep camp in Visalia. Jones had stopped there for a couple days. Armistead introduced himself as a horse trader to Jones and Slawson. He said he needed to hire a crew to help drive a herd of horses on to Arizona. Jones was excited about the job opportunity and hired on. The three men got along famously while Slawson cooked a wonderful meal. After dinner they smoked, talked and finally headed off to bed. In the morning Armistead checked his rifle. He took Slawson aside to tell him who Jones really was and said he planned to take him into custody for transport back to Carson City. Jones either overhead the conversation or suspected Armistead wanted him. He went into the Slawson ranch house and loaded a Henry rifle.

"I know what you're about," yelled Charlie stepping out of the house, " you want to take me back to Nevada. I'll die first."

With these words he leveled the rifle at Armistead and fired. The first round hit Armistead, who had a Henry as well. Armistead fired back and hit Jones in the chest. A flurry of gun fire erupted. Both men fired round after round in the fight. According to Slawson, the men were but 30 steps apart. The hail of lead took its effect. From his eyewitness account, Slawson said Jones kept giving way with Armistead following him until Armistead fell to the ground. Jones rushed the fallen man. Armistead, though weak, was able to fire his rifle and shoot Jones in the head. This bullet killed him instantly. In all, Armistead reportedly fired 15 shots. Jones was hit 12 times. The last shot was the fatal one. Jones was reported to have fired 11 shots and that nine hit Armistead. Any one would most likely have proved fatal after a time. Slawson said Armistead hung on for about two hours after the battle and was the coolest man he every saw. He was perfectly calm. Armistead said that if he'd killed Jones, he was willing to die. His last words were "Tell her I love …" Slawson understood he was speaking of his Aunt Sally. George Slawson promised to write the account of this event and have it published. Evidently he did.

The men involved in the gun battle above Long Valley left a lasting impression on the geography of the landscape. The lake at the site of the fight had been called Wit so nap ah by the Paiutes and Monte Diablo Lake by early settlers. Inyo and Mono County residents alike felt compelled to rename the location after the violent and historic incident. The beautiful waterway in the deep canyon was renamed **Convict Lake.** In honor of the sacrifice made by the brave Robert Morrison, the Benton Hot Springs merchant and Wells Fargo agent, folks began referring to the towering 12,286 foot peak overlooking **Convict Lake** as **Mount Morrison**. Nearby stands, **Mono Jim**, a peak that rises 10,896 feet, named in honor of George Hightower's Indian guide that was killed by Morton.

Smiling Jack Davis reportedly never second guessed himself in regard to staying put during the escape. His sentence was cut by prison officials based on his help with the wounded at the time of the event. In 1875, Davis earned his parole and returned to Virginia City. No one forgot how he used to spend his "spare" time, robbing men and wagons of gold and bullion from any source he could find. Davis had built a small bullion mill in Six Mile Canyon. It was used to melt down the stolen gold. He then sold some as legitimate gold bars and buried much of his proceeds so people wouldn't notice how wealthy he was. Now back in Virginia City he seemed to lead a law abiding life. After a couple years, he relocated to Eureka. Evidently he enjoyed his "hobby". He was shot in the back and killed during a Wells Fargo stagecoach robbery near Warm Springs, Nevada. Many believe his cache was still hidden in Six-Mile Canyon or near the Truckee River. Over the years treasure hunters searched these locations without success. Legend abounds that the ghost of Jack Davis protects his treasure. Many who looked for the cache were frightened away. They reported seeing a white screaming phantom that was said to be capable of sprouting wings and rising into the air.

Robert Dedman, the model prisoner that helped Warden Denver run his household, was pardoned October 4. His actions in fighting so bravely against the escapees was cited by the Board of Pardon Commissioners. The members duly pointed out that the Warden would have surely been killed if not for Dedman's valiant efforts. He was restored to full citizenship. Unfortunately, just two weeks later, it was reported in *The Carson City Daily Register* that Dedman was shot and killed in San Francisco. The shooting was attributed to a Mr. Springer, purported to be the brother of the man Dedman killed. It seems that Dedman had left Carson City about two weeks after his pardon to visit his sister at Knight's Landing in Yolo County, California. It was believed that Springer lived nearby. He had taken an oath to kill Dedman.

The fate of prison guard **Isaacs** was tragic. On October 2 three doctors, Lee, Webber and Collins were in attendance when the poor man's damaged right leg was removed. It was necessary to cut it off four inches above his right knee. This was done to make sure the gangrene, which had set in, was completely removed. It was Dr. Lee's opinion that the man would survive as long as he was able to make it through the night. Unfortunately on October 12, the brave Isaacs succumbed to his massive wounds. It was believed up until the previous morning that his recovery was imminent. According to reports it was then that he began to sing. Several hours later he took his last breath. Two days later, Isaacs was laid to rest in Virginia City's Masonic Cemetery. His funeral was attended by a number of Masons from Carson City as well as his fellow Masons from Virginia City. His grief stricken wife was comforted by his friends and fellow guardsmen.

Edward Goyette, the prisoner that pulled Jennie Denver to safety during the breakout was granted a full pardon by the Board of Pardon Commissioners. They cited his bravery and general assistance at the prison during the fight for the reason they had come to this decision. Where Goyette went or what he did after this event are not known.

Jonathan Bedford Roberts was described by his captors as incapable of making decisions on his own. His story sounded believable, coming from this poor wounded boy to his stern, but big hearted captors. They felt sorry for the unfortunate lad that had been tormented by his fellow escapees. However, those who really knew the kid considered him a most heartless and hardened villain. With this information those that felt sorry for him might have acted differently. For instance, on the night he robbed the Susanville stage with Charles Beaver, he abandoned the badly wounded boy whom he had persuaded to help him. He left him in the sagebrush to die of his wound or be captured. Roberts simply turned tail and ran. He even took his partner's horse. Some who truly knew Roberts character said that they felt Leandor Morton was an angel, when compared with Roberts.

It was reported in the ***Nevada State Journal*** July, 1874, that Roberts had been acquitted of his stage robbery conviction.

The verdict from the State Supreme Court came after several years of adjudication. Roberts had filed a writ of habeas corpus, appealing that his conviction was wrongly obtained. Not even Roberts said he was innocent. The appeal was over a technicality. Roberts' original trial was evidently heard during a time when judge of the court did not convene the district court in a timely manner as was prescribed by law. Therefore the trial, in fact, never happened. His lawyer then argued successfully that if he should never have been put in prison in the first place, then he couldn't be convicted for escaping from the prison in which he shouldn't have been in.

Upon his release, Roberts returned to work with his father Chat in Long Valley, California, near Susanville in the family business. Although he threatened the life of Ferdinand Ratz, the Nevada-California-Oregon Railroad agent in their territory, the man had no further serious run ins with law.

⋘ ⋘ ⋘

Doctor Simone Lee, one of the physicians that attended to the wounded Frank Denver, the guards and prisoners, had a fascinating hobby. Dr. Lee was a collector. He has been actually referred to as a "hoarder". But this was a good thing. As a boy he had collected arrowheads. This lead to a love of collecting almost anything. During his lifetime, the good doctor spent his spare time gathering ore samples, semi-precious stones, rare ceramics, fossils, guns, stamps, coins, Native American baskets, water jugs and much more until his death at the age of 82. Lee's wife donated his entire collection to the State of Nevada just prior to her death in 1934. These pieces were displayed at the Nevada State Capital before being transferred in 1941 to the Nevada State Museum shortly after it opened. Many of the pieces may be individually worth more than half a million dollars.

⋘ ⋘ ⋘

Mason Valley rancher, Burgess, that captured Clifford, Roth, Parsons and Chapman experienced a very unfortunate incident. He was beaten and robbed by highwaymen. The scoundrels took the $550 that Burgess had left from his reward for turning in the escaped convicts. After he was down, one man jumped on him, causing three ribs to break off his spinal column. The report says that it was lucky for Burgess that Dr. Geiger was in the Walker Valley and was able to render his professional services to the injured man. The last news of this event put Burgess in a very precarious condition due to the severity of his wounds. Burgess was able to talk, but couldn't give any accurate descriptions of the villains. They men rode unshod horses. They were tracked from the Mason Valley to the vicinity of Fort Churchill, but no one was apprehended. No further news as to his injuries was found.

Playful prisoners. While 18 prisoners where on trial for the murder of Isaacs, they had a little fun. Each day they were returned from Carson City to the prison. On one such trip they decided to raise some eyebrows. It was typical to put nine in a wagon. They were chained and handcuffed. In one wagon the guard placed Burke, Clifford, Flynn, Ryan, McCue, Bigelow, Parsons, Roth and Chapman. When that wagon arrived at the prison, the guards were absolutely amazed that now only Burke was wearing hand cuffs. As a matter of fact he had on all nine sets of cuffs. The other eight men were free, except for the leg irons.

Mrs. Luna Hutchinson, was overwhelmed by those suggesting she assisted Charlie Jones in his escape. So much, in fact, that she felt it necessary to explain herself in a very public way.

Therefore, she told her story in the **Inyo Independent** in November 1871 It was her way to show she was innocent of any activities surrounding the escape. It said in part:

"As my name as been given in connection with the statement of the prisoner Morton, I wish to say a few words in relation to the matter as some may think that I had promised to aid Jones with the expectation that he was going to break prison when nothing was further from the fact or my intention. I herewith enclose two letter received from Jones, one is the last I ever got from him, the other was not written by him but someone else of the